"*Let's call a truce.*"

Watching her, Michael spoke quietly, choosing his words. "Come have dinner with me."

Lindsey gave him a dark look. "Must you turn up everywhere I go?" Lindsey accused in a raspy whisper. "I would hardly be surprised to find you in my bathroom when I stepped from the shower."

"It would be interesting, you must admit." He allowed a low chuckle.

"I am not in the mood for jokes or verbal sparring. I'm tired. Tired of getting up before the chickens, tired of drinking that detestable coffee in the office, tired of trying to read squiggly figures that don't make any sense—but most of all, tired of seeing your face every time I turn around! You can persist in this campaign of harassment, but it's not going to earn you my company."

He raised an eyebrow. "But will it earn me *you*?" he asked warily.

Dear Reader,

Spellbinders! That's what we're striving for. The editors at Silhouette are determined to capture your imagination and win your heart with every single book we publish. Each month, six Special Editions are chosen with *you* in mind.

Our authors are our inspiration. Writers such as Nora Roberts, Tracy Sinclair, Kathleen Eagle, Carole Halston and Linda Howard—to name but a few—are masters at creating endearing characters and heart-rending love stories. Their characters are everyday people—just like you and me—whose lives have been touched by love, whose dream and desire suddenly comes true!

So find a cozy, quiet place to read, and create your own special moment with a Silhouette Special Edition.

Sincerely,

Rosalind Noonan
Senior Editor
SILHOUETTE BOOKS

CURTISS ANN MATLOCK
Lindsey's Rainbow

Silhouette Special Edition

Published by Silhouette Books New York

America's Publisher of Contemporary Romance

SILHOUETTE BOOKS
300 East 42nd St., New York, N.Y. 10017

Copyright © 1986 by Curtiss Ann Matlock

ISBN: 0-373-09333-0

First Silhouette Books printing September 1986

America's Publisher of Contemporary Romance

Books by Curtiss Ann Matlock

Silhouette Special Edition

A Time and a Season #275
Lindsey's Rainbow #333

Silhouette Romance

Crosswinds #422

CURTISS ANN MATLOCK

loves to travel and has lived in eight different states, from Alaska to Florida. Sixteen years ago she married her high-school sweetheart and inspiration, James. The Matlocks are now settled in Oklahoma, where Curtiss is concentrating on being a homemaker and writer. Other time is taken up with gardening, canning, crocheting, and of course, reading. "I was probably born with a book in hand."

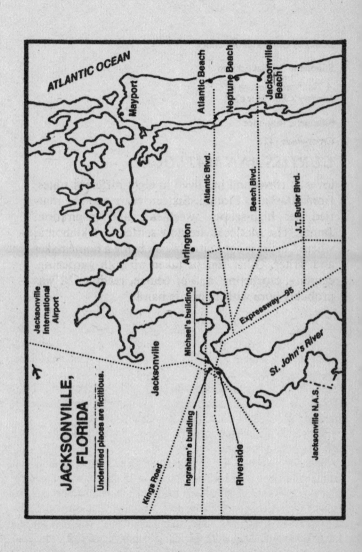

Prologue

A sultry Florida breeze drifted through the window. Beatrice preferred it to a house shut up with air-conditioning, though Selda often scolded her about it, insisting that at her age and with her heart condition, Beatrice should keep the house cooler. There were a lot of things she should do, Beatrice told herself saucily, adjusting the silver-rimmed glasses upon her nose.

She finished addressing the letter, sealed the envelope, fixing the flap with the stamp of her initials, then turned it faceup again and looked at it for a long time.

Six years and three months ago her granddaughter had left the house in anger.

Beatrice reached for the brass filigree frame that held a small snapshot of Lindsey upon the desk. It was the only photograph she'd had of her in those six years. She sighed, thinking of the way she'd failed Lindsey. The business had taken too much of her time, her energy, and she just hadn't known how to deal with Lindsey—any more than she had with her own daughter, Lindsey's mother, Mona. No, she'd never been the mothering type.

More from memory than from the small picture, she saw Lindsey's silky blond hair and sensuous blue eyes, features so like Beatrice's in her younger years. Lindsey was beautiful, sparkling as a rare jewel, and equally as uncommon in personality. She was all the things Beatrice recognized in herself.

Beatrice gave a small snort, murmuring, "We're a capricious pair, Lindsey and I."

Ah, but Lindsey had done well, Beatrice thought with a twinge of pride. Through infrequent letters and telephone conversations with Lindsey herself and various rumors, she'd learned that Lindsey had grown into a handsome woman, inside and out.

The only thing that troubled Beatrice was Lindsey's apparent aimlessness. She hadn't married—not even a fiancé—she had no job, and there was absolutely no responsibility or focus in her life. She moved through life fluttering this way and that, like a butterfly on the vagaries of the wind.

With this in mind and her own deteriorating health, Beatrice had decided it was time she took a hand in things. She'd failed in mothering Lindsey, but perhaps she wouldn't fail now. At least she had to try—to give Lindsey a challenge, some way to learn responsibility. But in such a way, Beatrice added to herself with a twitch of her lips, so as to employ Lindsey's impulsive and capricious nature, to harness it, not destroy it.

Beatrice's heart gave a tightening tremor, as if signaling for attention. Pressing a hand to her chest, she emphatically thought, not now. I've a lot to do before you give out.

The letter was a start, one she should have written long ago, but no matter, she was doing it now. She was asking Lindsey to come home. She could have telephoned but felt she could more have the effect she wished for by writing. Lindsey would come; she was sure of it.

Vital energy flowed through her old veins. A long-hidden spark of the old Beatrice Ingraham remained, and she'd decided to blow on it, force it into a flame and take charge of her life again. Too long she'd lain in the clutches of regrets, of memories of a husband many years gone, of a beloved granddaughter whom she'd failed.

They said her heart was bad. Perhaps it was, but she wasn't ready to leave this world yet. In fact, she thought with great satisfaction, she was ready to begin again.

A car drove up below. It would be Michael Garrity.

Rising from the small desk, Beatrice moved to the window, proud of the fact that she still walked gracefully and was still a slim figure of a woman who could wear ageless clothes with style.

Yes, it was Michael. The rear of his Mercedes-Benz showed beneath the front portico. He was a handsome young man who put her much in mind of her husband, Thomas. Not in looks, no, Thomas had been darker. But Michael was a young man, afire with business acumen like Thomas, sharp, perceptive, and he knew almost more by instinct than facts, what a good deal was.

She had much to thank him for. It was by getting to know Michael that she'd come to see herself in her true light.

Briefly Beatrice again surveyed the snapshot of Lindsey. She was so lovely. Lindsey and Michael would make a nice couple, Beatrice thought, not for the first time. Perhaps.... She allowed the thought to pass.

A tightening swept across her chest again, and Beatrice reached for a small vial of pills and took one. She wasn't overly concerned any longer. She now had a purpose.

She swept the letter from the desk, carrying it with her downstairs, her spirits rising at Michael's arrival. He was a charming young man. He probably wouldn't be too happy to hear she'd changed her mind, though. She wasn't sure she wanted to sell Ingraham Corporation, after all.

Chapter One

The spacious bedroom sparkled like pale champagne as midmorning sunshine spilled through the open blinds, casting a misty-white ethereal quality. Beams of summer sunlight glanced off the ivory-colored lampshade, palely illuminated the Charles Reid watercolor on the wall and slipped to form patterns on the plush ivory-tone carpet. The lustrous cherry wood of the dresser and the elegant posts of the bed, as well as the cream satin sheets, picked up the glow.

By some strange quirk of nature, for a few brief seconds, one lone beam stole through the blinds and focused directly on the letter.

Lindsey's white silk dressing gown shimmered as she turned from the suitcases on the bed and her gaze fell on the letter at about the same moment as the stray beam of sunlight. Something within her quaked. She swept the curls from her face with one hand, reaching for the letter with the other. She stopped. She didn't need to read it again.

Her gaze traced the strong bold writing of her own name and address, handwriting so characteristic of her grandmother, Beatrice Ingraham. The letter had arrived yesterday, but Lindsey had been out until after eleven last night at a party at Jay's and hadn't bothered with the mail when she came in. She'd opened it this morning.

The letter was a summons; no other description would fit. Beatrice had that way about her in person, as well.

Yes, the handwriting was the same, but the contents of the letter didn't ring true. After six years, Beatrice was suddenly requesting that Lindsey come home. And she was considering selling Ingraham's. Selling. Lindsey couldn't believe it. To a man named Michael Garrity. Was Beatrice Ingraham's mind wandering? Had the rock of Gibraltar sunk?

Perhaps the most unbelievable surprise of the letter was the four short words: I need your advice. Beatrice never needed anyone. And as for advice—Beatrice rarely asked another human's advice, and never, never, Lindsey's.

Something was wrong and it worried Lindsey. The letter set off a war within her spirit. She'd been toying with the idea of going home quite a bit of late. It was something natural, she supposed, tugging her back—didn't it happen to everyone? This order from Beatrice was a perfect excuse. Yet at the same time she was fearful of facing her grandmother, of past memories surfacing to stab her heart.

The apartment door slammed.

"Lindsey?"

It was Jay Fordham's voice. Muffled footsteps approached, and a moment later Jay stood in the doorway.

"Do you have any coffee? You know, there are still a few nuts hanging around down in my apartment." His gaze went to the suitcases. "What are you doing?"

"There's coffee made." Lindsey folded a pair of slacks. "Why don't you tell people to go home when the party is over? And I'm packing. What does it look like?"

Jay's gaze followed Lindsey as she moved from the bed to the closet then back again. "So where to?" His tone held a wounded note.

Lindsey, smiling gently, laid a sundress across the bed. "I'm going to Jacksonville for a few days. I didn't decide until this morning, so I couldn't tell you sooner."

Jay's eyebrows shot up. "Oh?"

What a word, Lindsey thought, continuing to pack. How much and how little it could convey. Lindsey couldn't explain to Jay. Not only were the circumstances too crazily involved, but so were her emotions. She desperately wanted to see Beatrice, find out if she was all right, and yet she was so afraid of facing her grandmother's stern countenance, of facing all she'd left behind six years ago. Or had tried to leave behind. One couldn't leave oneself behind, no matter how gallant the try.

"Yes," she said. "I've had a letter from my grandmother. She's asked me to come home—just a visit. You're welcome to use the apartment while I'm gone."

"For how long, do you think? What about the race? Think you'll still make it?"

Lindsey had forgotten. Jay was racing his windjammer down in the Chesapeake in two weeks. Lindsey had promised to go, to cheer him on and celebrate his victory—Jay was a very positive person.

"Of course I'll be back. I wouldn't miss it. Besides, I seriously doubt my grandmother and I can stand more than one week of togetherness. She'll kick me out about then."

She said it with a laugh, but her heart twinged. The words were true. She and Beatrice were rather like oil and vinegar. But I've changed, she thought, glancing in the mirror. *I'm not that same rebellious young girl I was six years ago. Will things be different for us now?*

"Oh," Jay said again. He watched for a brief moment then wandered from the room.

Lindsey searched impatiently through a drawer for belts, thinking that she really would like to share with Jay the conflicting emotions plaguing her. Always more at ease with men than women, Jay was the best friend she'd ever had, sharing a friendship with no demands on either side. His apartment was one flight down and directly under Lindsey's. It generally resembled Grand Central, and he often retreated to Lindsey's, seeking a few hours of peace and quiet.

Yes, he was as good a friend as one could have, but Lindsey kept even Jay at a distance. It was not her nature to do otherwise.

Pausing in her packing, she peered through the blinds to the narrow New York street below. It was a pleasant place, an old, quaintly elegant place. Her gaze touched the familiar spots: the small green square park across the street where Mr. Liebman always sat at this time of day, feeding birds; the purple-striped awning at the door of the Hawthorne apartments; the blue cap of Kirby, the doorman there, the cap way too big in a valiant effort to hide his baldness.

Beatrice's image floated before her mind, her face as it had looked six years ago. Proud, unforgiving yet sadly accepting. *I love you, Grandmother,* Lindsey thought. *I've never told you. I want to now. It's time.*

There came a rustle of movement from the hallway, and Jay appeared, holding two steaming mugs, one of which he placed for Lindsey on the dresser. He cast her a brilliant smile, yet concern was written in his deep blue eyes. That was unusual. Jay Fordham's thoughts usually ran no deeper than deciding what tie to wear with what shirt and what woman for what party.

Leaning against the doorjamb, Jay drank deeply from his cup and gave a contented sigh. "You make the best coffee in the world, Lindsey."

"Is that why you're always bumming around my place?" Lindsey asked, tucking nylons into a corner of the suitcase. It was true; Lindsey made scrumptious coffee. It had been Barry, one of her mother's many men friends, and Lindsey's favorite, who'd taught her the art of brewing fine coffee at the early age of ten. Brewing excellent coffees and teas had become sort of a hobby.

"Of course. I'm hoping I can discover your secret, patent it and make a million."

"You already have a million, Jay."

He nodded. "But I want my own million, made with my own sweat."

"It would be my sweat," Lindsey countered.

Jay shrugged then fell quiet. Lindsey felt his gaze. "You all right, Lindsey? This letter from your grandmother..." He broke off, studying her face.

To give herself a moment Lindsey lowered her eyelids, hiding her watering eyes as she reached for her coffee cup. Jay Fordham, of the Fordhams of Philadelphia, was scathingly handsome, scathingly rich and lots of fun. It was good to have such a friend. She blinked and looked at him.

"Yes, Jay. I'm fine—truly."

"If there's anything I can do..." He smiled wanly. "You're the best female friend I've ever had. Most women see this terrific old bod, hear my name, see dollar signs and want something from me. You know?"

"Yes, Jay, I know." She attempted to give him one of her sweet, ultrafeminine smiles, but it rather waned instead. Yes, how well she knew. "You might want to study the word 'humility,'" she teased. "And there's a fine woman out there for you, Jay. Just be patient."

Jay gave his characteristic easy-going grin. "Oh, I'm still looking—hard and patiently."

Lindsey looked away. "I'm sure you are." Setting her cup aside, she resumed her packing. At first she felt Jay's gaze upon her; then she drifted off into her world of thought.

She was an expert packer, she reflected. She'd been packing her own suitcases since the age of six. It was perhaps her one true skill. She'd learned the hard way, by practicing repeatedly as she'd been shuffled here and there between her mother and numerous schools. Well, she thought dryly, at least there is one thing I can do, though

Beatrice would hardly be impressed. Idly she wondered if there were a job out there—wanted: expert packer. Where was that black belt to the red sundress? She really needed to get some panty hose. What would grandmother look like? Still the same: Beatrice would never change. Mother Nature wouldn't dare mess with her. Or would she? The thought struck her uneasily.

Jay's call brought her back. "Lindsey..." He smiled. "You do that a lot, you know. Where do you go?"

She smiled back and shrugged.

"I asked if you could lend me some money." He looked sheepish. "I'm down to my last, and it's two days before my check." It was generally about this time that Jay ran out of money.

Lindsey nodded toward the dresser. "Take what you need."

"Won't you need some of this for traveling?"

"I've credit cards."

"Ah, plastic, wonderful plastic...my accounts are full up everywhere... Lindsey, you shouldn't be so free with your money. Did you really lend a wad to Ross Embury? He must have had the loan announced in the paper, along with innuendos. The guy's a louse. He'll never pay you back."

"The man is pitiful in his stubborn know-it-all existence. And if you feel I shouldn't, then give it back."

"For me it's different." He waved the bills in the air. "Pay you back in a couple of weeks—right before the race," he said pointedly, coming over and sitting on the bed after he'd pushed aside a gown.

The telephone rang, and Jay reached for it.

"Yes?" he said. Then after a moment he added, "Tell me. She's busy." He paused. "All right, smart a—" He broke off as he passed the receiver to Lindsey. "It's Stanley."

Stanley Jennings was Jay's accountant, as well as Lindsey's.

"Good morning, Stanley."

"What's wrong with Jay?"

"Nothing more than usual."

"What about selling your Norton stock, Lindsey? It's dropping like a rock." Stanley always exaggerated.

"No, hold on to it. I heard the other evening that Rick Norton is going to take over from his father. It'll go back up."

"Whom did you hear it from?"

Lindsey wasn't about to tell. "A very reliable source."

It had been Rick Norton himself who had told her at a party two nights ago, and he had wanted it kept hush-hush so he could quietly buy up the controlling stock while the price was cheap. It was sickening to see what some people would do to their own family, to anyone, in the fervent pursuit of money and success. Lindsey had stood by while her date, his arm thrown casually across her shoulder, had discussed serious investment with Norton. Her presence didn't seem to bother them; it rarely did. Lindsey was blond and beautiful and not supposed to have a business brain in her head. And she went along with that impression of herself. She picked up numerous bits of stock information along the social road this way. It was helpful in supplementing her modest trust fund—but a game to her, no more.

"Okay... what have you heard about NCNB?"

"Nothing, but I'd keep that, too. They're going to get better and better."

"Is this a hunch of inside information?"

Lindsey laughed. "Just a hunch."

"What do you need me for, Lindsey? You're a natural at this."

"I don't want to be bothered with the details, and you know I overspend. What would I do without you to slow me down?"

"You don't overspend. You overlend," Stanley countered dryly. "I believe all of New York now knows what a soft touch you are. Who in the world is Milly Sacks? You wrote on her check 'cat food.' What's that supposed to mean?''

"Oh, she's this old woman who keeps cats.''

"Cats? Now cats know you're a soft touch!''

"Enough, Stanley. By the way, I'm going out of town—Jacksonville, Florida.'' She gave Stanley her grandmother's address and phone number and hung up after promising not to provide food for the entire cat population of Florida.

Jay was prowling the room, coffee cup in hand. He paused near the oversize bed. "You know, Lindsey, a lot of our friends—and other people—think we sleep together.''

"Stanley Jennings included?'' Lindsey's lips twitched.

Jay smiled openly. "Stanley Jennings included.''

"Does it bother you?''

He gave a sideways grin. "I'm the envy of not a few men—Stanley Jennings included.''

"You've never told anyone any different?'' '

"What? And let it be known I'm not the Romeo people think? What about my image?'' He eyed her curiously. "You've never told?''

"Not a soul.'' They laughed together.

Lindsey herself was glad for the impression others had of her and Jay and took advantage of it. It seemed to keep the amorous advances of men at a minimum. Of course, she did receive her share of jealous spite from women intent on Jay, but she let it roll off her back. It didn't seem to have hurt his love life any.

"Since neither of us knows how to turn on the stove,'' Jay said, "how about me running out for breakfast? You shouldn't pack on an empty stomach.''

"Speak for yourself, Jay Fordham. I can boil an egg, soft or hard.''

Jay made a face. "Don't speak of that first thing in the morning. Which would you prefer, bagels or muffins?''

"I'm really not hungry.'' Lindsey spoke softly. "What I do need, Jay, is a nice hot bath and some time alone.''

He studied her a moment, his eyes warm. "Sure, kitten." Very gently he bent to brush his lips against her forehead. "I guess I've never really told you, but I like you, Lindsey Ryland. For what that's worth."

"That's worth an awfully lot at his moment, Jay." Her voice cracked. "I like you, too."

Jay turned at the door. "I'll drive you to the airport. What time?"

"Noon's good."

He nodded, quietly pulling the door shut behind him.

While Lindsey showered, her thoughts repeatedly returned to Beatrice and Jacksonville. She'd debated all morning whether to telephone and finally decided that perhaps it was best to let Beatrice know she was coming. She dialed, chewing her bottom lip while she waited for an answer. Thank God, Selda, the housekeeper, answered. Lindsey told her not to bother Beatrice and simply to relay the message that she would arrive that afternoon and would catch a taxi from the airport.

She hung up, breathing a sigh of relief, then scolded herself for juvenile behavior. Beatrice was not an ogre.

When he saw the amount of luggage Lindsey had packed, Jay decided he'd call Orson downstairs from the lobby for help. "You need all this—" he pointed to the two large suitcases, the suit bag, a medium suitcase and the small travel bag "—for one week?"

"Jay," Lindsey explained patiently, "I never want to need something I don't have. And I'd need all this whether I was to stay a week or a month."

The telephone rang. It was Orson in the lobby. "There's a man down here wanting to see you, Miss Lindsey—a Michael Garrity."

Lindsey blinked. Michael Garrity. Immediately in her mind's eye she saw the name written in Beatrice's handwriting, bold flowing black ink upon white linen bond. "For goodness . . . *Michael Garrity*?"

"Yes, ma'am. I told him you were leaving soon, but he won't take no for an answer."

"Well...send him up." Michael Garrity. *What in the world could he want? And wasn't he supposed to be in Jacksonville?*

The door opened immediately to Michael's knock. But it wasn't a woman standing there, but a tall handsome blond man, a UCLA graduate majoring in beach, Michael guessed.

"Lindsey Ryland? Somehow I pictured you much shorter," Michael quipped.

The blond man gave a half smile. "Come on in." The guy's eyes followed him curiously, and Michael wondered about the inborn instinct that immediately liked, or as in this case, didn't like a person.

Michael stepped into the small foyer of the apartment then to the living room beyond. It was an elegant room but comfortable, too. It was decorated with pale cream colors and had curtainless windows with blinds, and lots of hanging plants.

For a full five seconds he and Lindsey Ryland stared at each other. Michael's inborn instincts again took over, this time vibrating with definite approval—warm approval.

His mind reacted quickly, as a computer scanning a file. The information he had on Lindsey Ryland said blue eyes—no mention of how large and round, how china blue, how curious. No mention of the womanly sensuality that radiated from her, no mention of the extremely feminine tilt of her head, nor of the enticing, sweetly warm fragrance she wore.

"Miss Ryland, I'm Michael Garrity." Extending his arm, he continued to take full inventory as his hand closed around hers for a firm shake.

Her face was silky smooth, with an apricot glow. Pale blond hair, natural soft waves of silk, brushed her shoulders. Parted on one side, it fell close to her right eye. His gaze moved down to the loose-fitting pale pink silk blouse, parted widely at the neck to reveal several thin gold chains against smooth skin. He noted slim hips beneath a cream-colored linen skirt. Cream had to be her favorite color, and it suited her delicate coloring. His gaze moved back up.

There was a richness about her, like that of an exquisite diamond. A quiet, understated elegance. And an unexpected vulnerability, Michael thought as he looked again into those china-blue eyes. Her hand was warm but firm within his own. She tugged it away.

In a smooth graceful gesture, she swept her hair back, her gaze never wavering from his. "Can I help you in some way, Mr. Garrity? Hopefully...quickly..." Her voice was surprisingly deep for a woman so small. She waved a hand to her luggage. "I was just leaving—actually, for Jacksonville."

"If I'd have known you were coming, I would have stayed," Michael said, allowing his gaze to make his point and conscious of the blond Adonis scowling at him. If Michael were in his shoes, he'd do the same. "Has your grandmother spoken to you of me?"

"I've had a letter— She mentioned you briefly. What in the world can any business you have with her have to do with me?"

"I'm interested in buying her controlling stock in Ingraham Corporation." He studied her eyes, puzzled at the change he saw there. "Beatrice had decided to sell—then wavered. She feels uncertain and has suggested that she'd like your advice. Since I had to be in New York, anyway, I thought I'd look you up and talk the deal over with you. If you liked it, perhaps your approval would make Beatrice feel more secure."

Lindsey blinked. He couldn't read her face, but her eyes turned cold. She thought he was an opportunist.

"You just 'happen' to have my name and address? From Beatrice?"

"No...actually, I had someone find you for me. It wasn't a secret, was it?"

She looked at him. "I've nothing to do with Beatrice's business," she said. "I never have." Her voice dropped. "Perhaps she truly doesn't want to sell. Now, I really have to catch a plane." She reached for a jacket from the sofa, her manner definitely arctic.

"Miss Ryland—" Michael touched her arm "—Ingraham's is failing, and so is your grandmother." His words were calculated to stop her.

It worked. She looked at him, her eyes revealing surprise, bewilderment. He faced her honestly, though suddenly he realized that it was not the time to talk of this. Yet he didn't want to let her go so fast.

A knock drew all three pairs of eyes to the doorway, and the doorman from the lobby entered, rolling a luggage cart before him.

"I—I really have to go...." Lindsey said uncertainly, turning those troubled blue eyes to Michael again. "I'll miss my flight. Are you returning to Jax soon?"

"This afternoon, as a matter of fact. I've a private jet waiting at the airport. Why not join me for the flight down, and we can talk this over?" Michael seized the idea, his mind quickly calculating the changes he'd have to make in his schedule. He'd not really intended to leave until the next morning. But the key to his business deal had turned out to be a gorgeous plus, and he wasn't about to let either slip away.

"She already has a reservation," the blond Adonis said pointedly. "We were just leaving."

But Lindsey was looking at Michael. He read her interest. She glanced gently to the handsome blonde. "I'd like to take Mr. Garrity up on his kind offer, Jay. Would you still drive us to the airport?"

Adonis scowled but nodded. "Sure, Lindsey."

"Great," Michael said smoothly. "If you'll allow me to use your phone, I'll call and tell my crew to expect one more." He raised an eyebrow.

Lindsey nodded, indicating a telephone near the hall. Michael stepped over easily, turned his back and dialed. With a few terse words, too low to be overheard, he alerted his pilot to the change in plans.

Suavely, pretending not to notice the Adonis's deepening scowl and secretly pleased by the smile that touched Lindsey's lips, he added her small travel bag to the pile atop the luggage cart. "It'll be no trouble to cancel that reservation," he said jauntily. "And I think you'll find my plane a lot more comfortable." Giving a friendly grin, he ushered them all out into the hallway then extended his hand to the blond Adonis. "Michael Garrity, Mr—?"

With a wry twist of his lips, the young man shook Michael's hand. "Jay Fordham." Michael had heard the name. Rich kid, living off his father.

Again Lindsey smiled. Before she could lower her eyes, Michael caught her glance. She blushed quickly and looked away, but he'd seen the interest there—and the grudging admiration. There was more to this woman than met the eye, much more. And Michael intended to discover just what.

Fordham's car was one of those small, expensive, sporty models, so Michael was forced to sit in the back seat, though he leaned forward, putting his head, and therefore his presence, between Fordham and Lindsey, and comfortably rested his forearms on the seats' backs.

"No luggage, Mr. Garrity?" Fordham asked dryly.

"Already at the plane," Michael lied cheerfully. Actually it was at the hotel, but he traveled light and could have his bag sent on after him.

They chatted casually during the drive. Lindsey questioned him about the jet, its size and how long they would be in flight. They talked of the traffic, the fair weather and what Jacksonville was like this time of year.

"I haven't been to Jacksonville in six years," Lindsey told him. "It must have grown."

"It has exploded," Michael told her. "It's the largest city in Florida now." He tried to remember what had been in the few paragraphs concerning Lindsey Ryland that were included in the information file on Beatrice Ingraham. He seemed to recall that the sketchy profile read: wild and irresponsible, some sort of tiff, something like that.

Jay Fordham grew morose. Michael supposed that he would, too, if he were taking his woman, a woman as beautiful as Lindsey Ryland, to the airport. Michael doubted he would allow Lindsey to go without him.

Once Fordham interjected thoughtfully, "Garrity... didn't you just buy up the Superway chain?"

"My corporation did." Michael raised his opinion of the young man a notch. He read the papers.

Michael directed Fordham to the private hangars. The plane was ready. In minutes Lindsey's luggage was stowed, and they were ready to board.

Standing at the foot of the boarding stairs, Lindsey looked uncertainly at the sleek white jet. "It looks awfully small."

Michael chuckled. "It's not a 747, but there's plenty of room for two." He detected a nervousness in Lindsey. She repeatedly raked the hair from her face, while the other hand clenched her purse tightly. "All ready?" he asked, touching her elbow lightly.

"I..." She shot Jay an anxious look. Fordham took her hand, and watching, Michael had a moment of remorse. He'd butted in between her and Adonis. Momentarily he felt guilty of intrusion, but not guilty enough to back off.

Lindsey wrapped her arms around Fordham's neck and kissed his cheek. Not the kiss of a woman for her lover, Michael noticed with some puzzlement. Perhaps he'd jumped to the wrong conclusion. "I'll be back in a week—ten days at the most," she said. "Water my plants, especially Herman. He's sick." Fordham did seem to hold her awfully long, though.

"Will do, kitten." Fordham gave her a long look. "Goodbye." He released her with an easy smile. Lindsey turned and mounted the stairs.

Michael held out his hand. "Goodbye, Jay. I'll take good care of her."

A slow, thoroughly wicked grin spread across Adonis's face. "You," he said pointedly in a low tone, "can go to hell." Jamming his hands into his pockets, he stepped back.

Surprised, momentarily dumbfounded, Michael stared at him as a look of total understanding passed between them. Then he chuckled. Good for you, Adonis. Good for you. Smiling good-naturedly, he shot Fordham a smart salute then turned to follow Lindsey up the stairs.

She stopped in the doorway, turned and peered around Michael to cast Jay a final wave. Michael caught her gaze; her blue eyes were clouded with something he couldn't quite put his finger on. Taking her arm to guide her into the plane, he found she was shaking.

Lindsey caught the scent of Michael's cologne. His hand was warm upon her back as he guided her into the plane. Extremely aware of his close scrutiny, Lindsey strove to relax and to keep her stomach from rebelling. She couldn't bear to be sick right there in front of him. She couldn't bear to have him know her weakness.

The plush interior of the jet was familiar, like several she'd flown in before. Why, she wailed inwardly, had she consented to fly in this itty-bitty plane? She knew her reaction. But then, her reaction to a commercial airliner was scarcely better.

She slipped, quite gracefully, she thought, into a large cushioned chair that swiveled, and willed her hands to lie relaxed upon the chair's arms.

Michael Garrity was still watching her in that open way of his that made no apology for staring. Then he stepped through a doorway and spoke to someone, the pilot, Lindsey supposed. Her chair vibrated gently as the small jet's engines revved. It was hot and stuffy. And Lindsey Ryland, a sophisticated, much-traveled woman of twenty-seven, was terrified of flying.

Watching the movement of Michael Garrity's shoulders answered her question as to why she was here. She'd not been able to resist.

Michael Garrity. She allowed the name to roll over her tongue.

Lindsey had seen the world, traveled half of it and had met all the types of men there were in existence. Or so she'd thought, until today. There was something about Michael Garrity, something distinctly different, something within herself that recognized the same within him.

He was a tall man, broad-shouldered. His brown hair was kissed golden by the sun, and squint lines fanned from eyes the color of hard, polished steel. Eyes that missed nothing.

Returning to the cabin, he shrugged off his suit jacket, unbuttoned his vest and loosened his tie and collar button. Though she pretended to look out the window, Lindsey felt his gaze.

The plane moved and began taxiing to the runway. Michael settled into another seat near hers. "You'd better buckle up," he said. "Here, I'll help."

Lindsey was already clasping the seat-belt buckles, but was all thumbs with shaking hands. His hands brushed hers, and his gaze shot up. One look, and she returned her attention to the buckle. She didn't want him to know; in all these years, no one had ever guessed her terror. But now she feared that he'd guessed.

"Your hands are like ice," he said as he pushed her hands away and finished adjusting her seat belt. A tingling began where his knuckles brushed against her abdomen. "As soon as we take off, I'll get you a drink."

Leaning back into the folds of his chair, Michael casually took one of her hands and rubbed her fingers roughly with his own. The strokes were warming, reassuring—though Lindsey wouldn't let on.

"This plane is very safe, has an excellent record," he said, speaking almost absently, going on to explain its design and workings. The jet picked up speed; Michael's hand tightened around Lindsey's, and his tone continued on evenly, soothingly, as he talked about the plane. Gallantly he said nothing about her fear.

As the plane took off, Lindsey thought she might stop breathing, but once they were in the air, her heartbeat settled down to a relatively normal rate. Suddenly self-conscious, she tugged her hand from Michael's. He smiled slightly, his eyes holding a sensuous twinkle. Lindsey didn't look away, though. Mr. Garrity found her attractive; it wasn't something new. Yet—there was a difference. She felt his caress, though he didn't touch her at all.

He rose, stepped to a compact cabinet and pulled out glasses and a large bottle of liquour. "I'm a north Georgia hill boy, Miss Ryland. We find Jack Daniels is a great potion for our health," he said in an exaggerated Southern drawl, splashing the amber whiskey into two glasses. Handing Lindsey a glass, he slipped again into his seat.

She sipped the liquid, and it burned going down. "Do you live in Jacksonville now, Mr. Garrity?"

"Michael," he said.

Lindsey found herself smiling into his cajoling gaze. "Michael."

"Yes, I call Jacksonville home, though sometimes I'm away for weeks and begin to forget what it looks like."

His eyes told her plainly that he wasn't thinking of Jacksonville at the moment. He made Lindsey very aware of her femininity.

"What is it exactly that you do? Business, I mean," she asked slowly.

"Oh, some people refer to me as an entrepreneur. It's a good definition, I suppose."

"And you're successful." It was a statement, not a question. Michael Garrity looked every inch of it.

"Yes." He grinned.

The few sips she'd taken of the whiskey had succeeded in relaxing her, and she set the glass aside. "Just how does an entrepreneur make money?"

"A thousand and one ways."

"Name one."

"We buy and sell things." His steel-gray eyes spoke of other things on his mind, causing Lindsey's blood to warm. The man had a way of leering in a positively complimentary way.

"Like companies?"

Michael inclined his head. "Sometimes."

"Like Ingraham's?"

"Yes." He pointed to her half-finished drink. "Would you prefer something a little less strong?"

"Ice water, please."

He went to a small refrigerator, picked ice cubes from it and filled a glass with water, saying, "Only I don't plan to sell Ingraham's. I intend to use it to build my own company." Handing Lindsey the water, he fell back into the chair and stretched out his long legs.

"A chain of grocery stores?" she asked.

Michael nodded, and beams of the bright sun outside highlighted his hair.

Lindsey looked down and swirled the ice cubes in her glass. "Beatrice and I have not been on the closest of terms these past years," she admitted and looked up. "You said Ingraham's is failing, which obviously must make it a good buy for you. What about my grandmother?" Her flirtatious manner ebbed as she faced him. It embarrassed her to hear these things from a stranger, but her worry pressed her to learn more about Beatrice.

Michael rubbed the planes of his face with his hand. "Beatrice is old; her heart is weakening. She forgets things, confuses things. She's tired and needs a rest. I think you'll need to see for yourself," he added gently.

Lindsey nodded, saying quietly, "I've never thought of her as getting old. And the business—I've never thought of her without it."

"There comes a time."

"Yes," Lindsey agreed with a sigh. "I suppose there does." She looked at Michael, catching a glimpse in that moment of the kindness beneath the driving-businessman exterior.

The time flew by as Lindsey questioned Michael about his plans for Ingraham's. Plans that sounded quite exciting and extremely practical, from Beatrice's point of view. The deal would be a good one for her. Michael made them a light meal, and he teased and charmed her, leaving no question in her mind as to his sensual intentions, though he remained an utter gentleman. Lindsey enjoyed their banter, her ego boosted by his attentions.

Watching him speak and smile, she began to wonder what his lips would feel like upon her own. His fingers were long, his hands wide and strong. What would they feel like upon her body? Realizing the direction of her thoughts, she pushed them away—chagrined to find she had to do so repeatedly.

Then Michael told her to prepare to land. Again her heart rose to her throat. But Michael was there, holding her hand, soothing her with his words. And it wasn't so bad.

Lindsey even ventured a glance out the window, seeing the city approach through the clouds. She looked closer. Something didn't look right. Apprehension tickled her spine.

"Michael..." She glanced at him with a puzzled frown.

He smiled. "Nothing to fear, Lindsey. Just a detour to Atlanta."

"Atlanta!"

Chapter Two

Indignation rose in Lindsey. Looking at Michael, she opened her mouth to speak then closed it again, unable to form coherent words. The plane continued its descent, but for once Lindsey was too preoccupied to be afraid.

Michael regarded her calmly, a hint of a smile playing at his lips, making Lindsey all the more furious. "We're supposed to buckle up." He reached over to do her seat belt.

Slapping his hands away, she did it herself. "All right, Mr. Garrity, how am I supposed to get to Jacksonville?" Her eyes narrowed. "And just what are you hoping to get out of this bit of trickery?"

"You have a suspicious nature," he countered easily, and had the gall to chuckle. "Don't worry about this little detour. You're still heading for Jacksonville, but I'm afraid I have to be getting off here."

"Here?" she parroted in a small voice, her heart sinking at the thought. Then she recovered enough to still her expression. "Then why did you ask me—" She broke off with a puzzled frown.

"If I'd have told you, you wouldn't have come. Right?" his eyes regarded her knowingly. "I wanted the pleasure of your company."

Lindsey arched an eyebrow. "By fair means or foul?"

"I plead guilty," Michael said, holding up his palms. "But not sorry."

Lindsey looked at him, and he looked back. For the first time, Lindsey allowed the attraction she felt to show plainly. There was no denying it.

Slowly she smiled, her gaze not wavering from his, catching the heated message he was sending. "Thank you. I enjoyed it too."

They fell quiet, regarding each other thoughtfully, promisingly. It was an old flirtatious game for Lindsey, one she played often though never fulfilled. But this time was different—totally. This time she felt her bluff was being called. The prospect both excited and terrified her. Michael Garrity was a man to be reckoned with, a man who got what he went after. And it appeared he was after her.

When Michael began adjusting his tie and buttoning his vest, Lindsey realized she'd be in the plane all alone, and the old fear raised its head. Striving to hide it, she looked out the window, not daring to meet Michael's perceptive gaze.

Stepping to the front of the plane, he spoke to the hidden entities who were piloting the aircraft. Lindsey's stomach tightened, she glanced at her watch then back out the window, squinting in the bright afternoon sunlight. She heard Michael's approaching footsteps.

Placing his hands on the arms of the chair, he turned it, forcing Lindsey to face him as he leaned close. "You'll be fine. Pretend I'm sitting right here, holding your hand." His voice grew husky and seductive. "Remember what it felt like."

Looking into the depth of his eyes, Lindsey felt mesmerized. The heat of his gaze touched her, drew her. She

watched his lips come closer, and seemingly of its own vo-
lition, her body reacted. Her eyelids closed, her lips parted,
and sweet anticipation sent her blood racing.

He touched her waiting lips with his own. Sweetly, lin-
geringly, his warm tongue flitted within, promising much
more. It was the most erotic sensation Lindsey had ever experienced, though their lips were the only part of their bodies touching. It left her breathless, her body longing, aching
for more, and she marveled at the wondrous sensation.

Michael drew back, and Lindsey tried to focus, to gather
herself together and still her pounding heart.

"When will you be returning to Jacksonville?" she asked,
self-conscious of the breathless lilt to her voice.

"Tomorrow. For sure. I'll call you." He touched her
cheek, drawing his eyebrows together into a frown. "I'm
sorry to leave you. But I can't get around it. I could have
Tom—" he inclined his head toward the cockpit "—come
and sit with you."

Surprised and grateful for his gentle understanding,
Lindsey shook her head, forcing confidence into her answering smile.

The dark concern in his eyes lightened. "Remember—
think of my hand."

Lindsey watched through the window as Michael walked
from the plane. His coat was thrown over his shoulder and
held easily by two fingers. Lindsey would bet he whistled as
he sauntered. Pausing at the door to the terminal, he looked
back and waved. Then he was gone, and Lindsey was left
watching even after the door closed.

The plane began to taxi. Lindsey leaned back in the chair
and closed her eyes, remembering Michael's hand in hers.
The terror subsided, but a physical longing took its place.

Michael Garrity. She was left with an impression of a self-
confident, hard-driving man, a man who also had quite an
uncommon understanding of others. Definitely a male
chauvinist. A woman's place for him would be in his bed,

she thought with a chuckle. But on him it wore well; he made a woman glad to be so.

And he wasn't a man to take no for an answer, she mused. He would be a man to get what he went after. A cold suspicion teased the edges of her mind. He wanted to buy Ingraham's, he'd said. *How much of that desire was connected with his attention to her?*

The flight was quicker than Lindsey could have imagined. As they landed, she silently congratulated herself on arriving all in one piece. She finally saw at least one of the crew when a man came back and helped Lindsey get her luggage off the plane.

She was standing beside her suitcases just outside the busy terminal doors, waiting for a taxi, when someone touched her arm. Looking up, way up, she found a sandy-haired young man smiling hesitantly at her.

"Are you Miss Lindsey Ryland?" He ran the title and her name all together in the Southern fashion.

"Why, yes."

The young man grinned widely. "I've been waiting, meeting every likely plane. Must have missed yours somehow, though," he said, extending his hand in greeting. "Name's Sandy. Miss Beatrice sent me to meet you. I'll be a minute to get the car."

He'd come in the old Rolls. It pulled up sleek and low next to the walk, drawing a good deal of attention. Lindsey admired it as Sandy loaded her luggage. Her grandfather, Thomas, had bought the long white car in forty-nine. It hadn't aged a day.

Sandy regally held the door for her. Donning a chauffeur's cap, he slipped behind the steering wheel and pressed the accelerator hard. The powerful engine responded and the car surged forward, pressing Lindsey into the soft leather seat. Ingraham style, she thought. Ingraham, an old Southern family, every inch.

She watched the scenery as the car sped smoothly along the highway, her thoughts a jumble, filled with lingering images of Michael and apprehension at the prospect of seeing Beatrice.

They exited Interstate 95, and Lindsey glimpsed the St. Johns River between houses and thick shrubbery. Within ten minutes the ivy-covered pillars at the entrance of the house came into view. Then Sandy was pulling into the brick drive.

There was a white ambulance beneath the wide front portico.

"Sandy?" Her breath caught in the back of her throat.

The young chauffeur shook his head, casting her a puzzled frown.

As the long Rolls came to a stop, Lindsey jumped out, all manner of thoughts racing through her mind. Passing Sandy, she strode quickly up the shady front steps, stepped through the heavy door and into the entrance hall.

The hallway was large and airy, with another set of double doors at the far end. They stood wide, allowing faded light and a humid breeze to filter in. All around was richly polished wood. The round mahogany table still sat in the center of a multicolored Aubusson rug, and a large bouquet of bright flowers graced its top. It always had.

"Grandmother..." Lindsey breathed the word, her eyes darting around the room, instinctively looking for Beatrice's slim but imposing figure. Where was she? Why the ambulance? Please, don't let it be for her. *Not now... now when I've come home to try to mend the fences...*

She crossed the hall and mounted the steps, her gaze traveling on before her, her ears tuned to catch voices. But the house was quiet, the old walls too thick for sound to carry.

Following the curve in the staircase, Lindsey looked first toward Beatrice's bedroom door. Two men in light blue shirts stood there. The door was closed.

"Grandmother...*Grandmother*!" Lindsey rushed to the door and opened it. In horror she took in the scene. A figure lay in Beatrice's bed, but all Lindsey could see was a lump under the sheets. Dr. Dietrich was there, his white head bending near the figure. On the other side of the bed was Selda, whose startled face turned toward the door.

"Lindsey..." Selda hurried across the room and pushed at her. "Come on. Out of here."

"Is she..." Lindsey took a breath. She didn't want to know the worst. Oh, God, she didn't think she could bear it. "What happened?"

Pushing Lindsey before her, Selda stepped into the hall and closed the door. "Oh, honey, her heart. About twenty minutes ago—maybe thirty. No more. We tried her pills, then it got worse." Selda's fleshy face was pink from strain, her eyes drawn with worry. "Dr. Dietrich came in minutes—he's doing all he can. Now, come on downstairs." Taking Lindsey's hand, Selda pulled her along, as if Lindsey were a child again.

I'm too late, Lindsey thought. Why, oh why had she let the years slip by, not trying to breach the wall that stood between her and the only family she had? Twisting her head, her gaze rested on the closed door until she could see it no more.

"Pour us a drink," Selda commanded Sandy as they stepped into the hall.

In the living room Lindsey walked to the French doors and looked through the screen to the river. A gentle breeze touched her face. The house had been built in the days before air-conditioning, in such a way as to utilize natural cooling: high ceilings, shade trees, covered verandas front and back, wide windows to catch the river air. Beatrice used artificial cooling only when she had to.

Lindsey sipped her drink; she hadn't noticed Sandy handing it to her. He was gone now. Another sip, and she set it aside.

"Her heart," she asked Selda, "how bad?"

Selda wiped her florid face with her apron. "Only Dr. Dietrich can tell us, honey."

"Was she upset, too excited about me coming?" Guilt assailed Lindsey. She should have talked to Beatrice herself this morning. Was it only this morning she'd been in New York? Was it only this afternoon she'd stepped on the plane with Michael? While she was enjoying flirting with him, Beatrice had been . . .

"No, honey, don't go thinking like that." Selda touched Lindsey's knee. "Beatrice was excited, yes, but a good healthy kind. Making plans for the first time in . . . in years, I think. She was happy, so very happy you were coming home." Selda's voice dropped. "I'd been telling her to ask you home, and she was glad she finally did."

"She shouldn't have had to ask me—order me, practically. I should have come on my own."

Selda's eyes filled with pity. "You both are so much alike and could never see it."

Heavy footsteps sounded on the stairs. Dr. Dietrich entered, his strides long and sure. He was a big man with iron-gray hair and thick bushy gray eyebrows. "Lindsey! My heavens, what a time for you to come. Did Beatrice know?"

Lindsey nodded.

His frown deepened, and he rubbed the back of his neck. A man looking for the right words. The vise tightened around Lindsey's heart.

"You both may as well prepare yourselves," he said bluntly. "She's in a bad way. We've stabilized her enough to get her to the hospital. It's only a few blocks, and that's in our favor."

Lindsey closed her eyes then opened them. "How much chance does she have?"

"Slim, Lindsey, mighty slim."

Lindsey sat by her grandmother's bed in the Intensive Care Unit. Beatrice had tubes and wires running everywhere. The sight made Lindsey's stomach flutter, her heart tighten. She covered the older woman's cool and lifeless-feeling hand with her own, inwardly hoping that Beatrice would know she was there.

Beatrice's face was so ashen, a sickening gray pallor against the white sheet upon which she lay. Every wrinkle in her face seemed magnified. Her thick white hair, always done expertly upon the top of her head, now sagged and stray wisps framed her face, wet with perspiration. Her eyes were closed, pinched closed, as if in pain.

Now, as Lindsey sat there, hearing the low hum and beep of machines, the murmur of voices, she thought back over her childhood, remembering summer days spent at Ingraham House. Purposely Lindsey searched her memory for all the good times. Doing more than forgetting, she mentally let go of painful memories of the extreme deep loneliness of a child in a strict, thoroughly adult world.

Only the good memories should count now, she thought. And if somehow she could transfer these memories through time and space to her grandmother's sleeping mind, maybe it would give Beatrice strength.

The nurse touched her shoulder. "It's time now, Miss Ryland."

Lindsey nodded. They had let her stay nearly ten minutes already.

The clock said twelve-thirty, and still Beatrice flitted in and out of consciousness. Please, Lindsey thought, I need to tell her I love her. If she couldn't, Lindsey felt it would be a regret too much to bear.

The waiting room was cold. Several other people waited there for family members, their faces tired and drawn in the low lighted room. Lindsey walked out into the hall and leaned against the wall. She was tired of sitting.

"Lindsey?"

Lindsey started at the familiar voice and opened her eyes to see Michael. His thick brown eyebrows were drawn together over those unforgettable wide-set steel-gray eyes, eyes that fairly bored into her. The man appeared at the most surprising times and places.

"How in the world... What are you doing here?"

"I called Ingraham House from Atlanta. Selda told me about Beatrice. I was able to catch an evening flight down," he explained quickly. "How's she?"

"The same," Lindsey sighed.

His gaze surveyed her frankly. "You haven't been home." A statement, not a question. "Have you eaten?"

Lindsey shook her head. "I'm not hungry."

He took her elbow. "Come have something."

"No. They'll call me if she wakes up. I want to be here."

He looked at her a moment then stepped inside the ICU waiting room. Seconds later he reappeared. "They'll call you down in the café if she wakes up." He took her elbow again, looking at her and waiting for her to agree.

Lindsey nodded. He kept his hold on her elbow, and she was glad. She wondered if he could feel her shaking. Suddenly she felt so weak.

Apparently Michael felt her tremor, because he looked down and his grip tightened on her arm. She leaned against him in the elevator, taking strength from his hard frame, not caring if the position seemed familiar. He still wore his suit coat, his tie loosened haphazardly, his collar open. His tie was silk: Mediterranean blue, her favorite color. Funny she hadn't noticed that before. Realizing her mind was drifting, Lindsey peered at the elevator numbers. They were blurry.

The café was quiet. Michael ordered club sandwiches for them both, but Lindsey stopped him. "Please..." Her eyes moved from his to the waitress'. "Just a piece of pie. Any kind. And a cup of tea." She turned to Michael. "I just can't eat much."

He nodded understandingly.

They sat looking at each other. The man apparently had no compunction against staring rudely. Only it wasn't quite staring. It was more like taking account. Brushing her hair from her eyes, Lindsey lifted her chin.

The waitress brought Lindsey's tea and a soft drink for Michael. They continued their silence as Lindsey sugared her tea heavily and took a sip. It burned going down, but she thought it the most delicious thing she'd ever tasted. Michael seemed to sense her need for a few quiet moments. Several minutes later the waitress brought their food.

Lindsey looked into Michael's eyes, their color deep, the color of the ocean on a cloudy day. His face showed a hardness, a strength, and Lindsey knew instinctively he was a man whom Beatrice would like, would respect. It was the first time she'd solidly connected the two of them.

Some of her self-directed anger shifted to him. He was a stranger who in the past few months had come to know her grandmother better than she did. He'd been the one to watch Beatrice growing weaker, knew she took medication, probably knew the very color of the pills.

"My grandmother must like you a great deal," she said. "And you must care for her. Or are you simply looking out for an investment?" She meant the words to sting and saw they did, though somehow they were a double-edged barb, for she felt them, as well.

He looked at her sharply, but any reply he may have had in mind was cut off by the reappearance of the waitress. "They just called from ICU for you—Miss Ryland, right?"

Immediately Lindsey rose and headed for the door without waiting to hear more. She didn't look back. Her thoughts raced ahead, picturing her grandmother's weak, pale face. Passing the elevator, she took the stairs. Hearing movement behind her, she knew without looking that it was Michael.

Stepping from the stairwell, she sensed a tenseness on the floor. Several nurses hurried through the double doors into ICU. Lindsey's heart pounded as she burst into the waiting area. The woman in charge, a kind matronly volunteer, rose from behind her desk.

"Miss Ryland, dear, the doctor is in with your grandmother. Her heart..."

Lindsey stared at the woman, noting the eyes filling with pity. The woman put out a hand, but as if in a dream,

Lindsey turned her head toward the ICU room. She knew only one thing: she had to see Beatrice before she died.

"You can't go in there now, dear."

Lindsey pushed at the door. A hand touched her arm, slipping away as Lindsey continued on. Voices called after her as she hurried down the short hall to the doorway of Beatrice's room.

There came the faint bitter odor of antiseptic, the hospital smell. She couldn't see Beatrice. Men and women in white uniforms were crowded around the bed, their voices and movements making a hurried low murmuring. The heart monitor droned low and steady, the sound sending a piercing chill deep into the very marrow of Lindsey's being.

Then Michael was beside her, enveloping her in his strong arms. She nestled into the comfort he offered, hardly aware of what she was doing.

"I have to tell her, Michael." She lifted her eyes to his, pleading with him for help.

Michael's jaw was taut. Silently he led her back to the waiting room.

Suddenly suffocating, Lindsey pushed herself from Michael's arms and turned to the window, leaning against the cool, smooth glass. She squeezed her eyes together, but there were no tears. Sometimes things hurt too much for tears.

Gradually Michael's voice reached into her despair. "We don't know anything yet . . . Lindsey, do you hear me? We don't know."

Slowly she turned her eyes to meet his. His look was hard, determined, as if forcing her to hear him, to agree. And he was right: there was still a chance. Lindsey grasped at the tiny ray of hope.

Taking her hand, Michael led her to one of the sofas. He held on to her hand as they sat, his fingers rubbing hers roughly, offering comfort with the action just as he had that afternoon on the plane. In one day, in a matter of hours, they were no longer strangers.

"I'm sorry about what I said downstairs." She looked full into his steel eyes, eyes dark with concern. At her words they lightened. He nodded, smiled ever so slightly and pressed her hand.

Dr. Dietrich stepped through the door. Watching him approach, Lindsey held her breath. "Beatrice is still alive, but barely," he told them solemnly. "Lindsey...she's sinking. It's only a matter of time."

"Tonight?" Lindsey managed to ask.

The doctor shrugged. "I think by morning."

Hours, she thought. Only hours.

The doctor allowed Lindsey to go to Beatrice's bedside, telling her this time she could stay as long as she wished.

Michael walked with her to the door. He still hadn't let go of her hand; Lindsey was glad. How she needed his steady strength.

He touched her cheek. "I'll be out here if you need me."

She nodded, unable to speak but knowing that he could read the gratitude in her eyes. Lindsey knew that if she tried to speak in that moment everything inside would break loose—and she couldn't let that happen now. Somehow that would be letting Beatrice down. Beatrice would expect her to face this with a maximum of decorum and strength.

She moved to go through the door, but Michael stopped her. He studied her closely. "I'll be right here," he stated again.

Sitting beside Beatrice's bed in those early hours of a new day, Lindsey thought of times past and times present. In a quiet way, without words, she tried to impart her love to Beatrice.

Fatigue jumbling her thoughts, she mused over life and love. Her mind pictured Michael, wondering about him, about him and her together. Was Michael truly what he seemed? Beatrice would know; she always knew these things.

At some point Lindsey lay her head down upon Beatrice's hand and fell asleep. When she awoke at six-ten, she saw with blurry vision that Beatrice was still alive.

And an hour later, at seven, she was still alive, and possibly growing stronger, Dr. Dietrich told her with some reluctance. "I don't want you to get your hopes up, Lindsey. Now go home and rest. We'll call if there's any change."

"No, I want to be here," she said, resisting stubbornly.

"Go home. What good will you be to Beatrice if you fall flat from sheer exhaustion? My God, with the germs around this hospital...besides, your young man in the waiting room needs rest, too."

Lindsey started. Michael was still in the waiting room. He'd said he'd stay—and he had.

There was a light stubble of beard on his chin, his tie hung from his suit jacket pocket, and his shirt looked as though he'd slept in it. He smiled.

"They...they think she may be stronger," she told him, wonder in her voice.

His arms went around her, pressing her to him. "Dr. Dietrich told me."

She fingered his lapel. "You've been here all night..."

He shrugged, letting her go. "Mrs. Lewis in the waiting room plays a mean game of rummy." He took her hand. "Now let's get you home—doctor's orders."

"I telephoned Selda," Michael said as he opened the door of a sporty silver Mercedes in the nearly vacant parking lot. "She'll have breakfast waiting."

Sighing, Lindsey leaned back against the seat. The early morning sun blazed coral from the east, promising a clear day. "I completely forgot to phone her. I did yesterday evening when we got here then once later, but..." Her thoughts drifted. Was it yesterday she'd come to the hospital with Beatrice? But only yesterday, she'd been in her own apartment, joking with Jay. Only yesterday she'd met Michael. Surely she'd known him for weeks.

She turned her head to gaze at him. He was terribly handsome, even with his brown hair ruffled and lines of fatigue deep around his eyes.

"Thank you for staying last night," she said.

"It's okay."

She was quiet, thinking. "I hope Grandmother doesn't just linger—I mean..." She was so tired, she just had to close her eyes for a minute. Beatrice, Beatrice.

"Don't think about it now," Michael said. "There's nothing more you can do but wait and see."

Wait and see. Yes, he was right. Lindsey tried to tell him so, but she couldn't get her tongue to cooperate.

She next had the feeling of floating through the air. Managing to peek through heavy eyelids, she saw she was in the hallway of Ingraham House, indeed floating toward the stairs. No—she wasn't floating; Michael carried her. His arms crushed her against his chest, and Lindsey snuggled closer. She glimpsed his strong jaw and the golden-brown hair that brushed his ears. Selda's voice came to her; Michael answered, but she didn't know or even care what they said.

When she was gently laid upon a bed, she opened her eyes. "Michael." It came out a mumble. She reached for him, longing to have him pressed to her. Were they on the plane again, laughing, carefree? No, no. It was a dream.

"Shush, Princess. Time to sleep." His lips touched hers briefly, but the sensation was warm and enjoyable.

Lindsey smiled, his image dancing before her eyes. "Michael..." she mumbled again before sleep claimed her completely.

Michael stood on his rooftop terrace, watching the sleeping giant of a city awaken in the glowing hours of the morning. Though he was exhausted, without sleep for more than twenty-four hours, his adrenaline was still pumping. A light morning breeze brought with it the mingled scents of the river, the ocean, miles away, heat blistering concrete and the smell of automobile exhaust.

The building overlooked the St. Johns River. It was small, compared to those of the many giant insurance corporations around him, only ten stories, but sleek and modern in concrete and glass. Michael owned one-fourth of it—a real-estate investment, and it housed several other companies. His few offices took up only the southeast corner of the ninth floor.

His penthouse was on top, right above the offices, a modern place where he stayed while he was doing business in the city. What he considered his true home was a beach house out on Amelia Island, but he was getting there less and less.

He marveled even now at the view and at knowing he owned a part of such a building—the first of many, he vowed. He, Michael Paul Garrity, a poor boy from north Georgia whose parents had had to scrape just to get their children coats and shoes for school, had done rather well for himself.

Golden Boy, they had called him, ten years ago. He'd begun in ocean salvage, dabbled in wheat futures and lumber. With the money he earned he'd invested in lending risks that paid off big in interest. At twenty-eight he'd made his first million. It seemed to those watching that everything he touched turned to money. And that it had been easy. It hadn't. It had been hard to push himself to take the chances. But the big risks were where the money was, and that was what he wanted: money. Or perhaps better translated, what the money would mean: success and power.

He looked south to where Ingraham House was located and thought of Beatrice Ingraham. She was the main stockholder in Ingraham Corporation, a chain of grocery stores begun by Beatrice and her husband more than forty years ago. Michael planned to merge Ingraham's with two other grocery chains he'd bought, giving him a new corporation with a huge corner of the market from Florida to

Maine and over into Louisiana. It was his biggest, most ambitious enterprise yet.

Garrity's, he'd call it. Hardly original, but his own, all his own. Getting Ingraham's dirt cheap would prove to be one of his better investments. By the time he got through, it would be worth ten times what it was now. He wanted Ingraham's, needed it, and he intended to have it.

Lindsey Ryland's image flickered across his mind, drawing him like a brilliant jewel. She had hair like strands of spun silk and eyes to make a hard man humble. And he wanted her, wanted to learn what lay behind those azure eyes that held so much promise.

But it was his policy to keep pleasure strictly separate from business. And it was beginning to look more and more as though he would be dealing with Lindsey Ryland in his bid for Ingraham Corporation. His information told him that she now held Beatrice Ingraham's power of attorney.

Michael's heart felt heavy. Not only was this business deal in a mess, but Beatrice—it had hurt to see her like that. He hadn't expected such a deep reaction. Surprising himself, he'd come to thoroughly like that peppery and irascible old woman. Her chances were slim, so the doctors said, but Michael wouldn't count the old woman out yet, and deep down, he fervently hoped she'd make it.

His thoughts returned to Lindsey and he cursed mildly. He'd have to find a way through this mess.

After a call to his secretary, with several instructions for the day, Michael prowled the apartment. Hoping to ease some tension, he retired to the work-out room to lift weights. Twisting thoughts still plagued him: Beatrice's ashen face, the stalemate of the Ingraham's bid, several stock investments he needed to make some sort of decision on, and Lindsey Ryland's lingering scent, the brief touch of her lips against his—this above all.

Quietly Elwin, his houseman, appeared at his side, bringing a disgusting concoction of warm milk and who knew what all—Elwin was from Haiti.

"You sure you're not trying to kill me?" Michael complained after he chucked the drink down as fast as possible.

"I'm looking after you," Elwin said.

"I'm thirty-four years old and left my mother behind years ago."

"Your mother calls me once a week and checks up on you."

"Uh..." Michael grunted and headed for the shower. Minutes later he felt woozy. Barely buffing dry, he flung himself to the bed and fell asleep, Lindsey Ryland's image playing on the edges of his mind.

It was late afternoon when Lindsey awoke. Disoriented, she gazed around the room, her mind seeking time and place. Where was Michael? Had he truly kissed her? She imagined she could still feel the gentle fleeting warmth of his lips.

Reality returned. She was in her bedroom, the room she'd had as a child.

It was the same: double-wide canopy bed of lustrous dark oak, matching dressing table and chest, deep burgundy carpet, white draw-back sheers at the wide windows. Walking slowly around the room, she reached out to touch memories.

A picture of her parents during their happier years, sat upon the tall chest. Her father, Kurt Ryland, smiled out at her with his David Niven mustache. Dashing, she'd always imagined, though she hadn't known him. Lindsey had been two when he died in a car crash. He'd had a young, beautiful woman with him at the time, and the crash had happened on the outskirts of New Orleans, when he was supposed to have been in Charleston on business. It was something her mother Mona had never recovered from.

Mona smiled out at her too, a real smile, not the alcoholic-dazed sort Lindsey had come to know. After her husband's death, Mona, unable to cope with her own disillusionment and pain, had left Lindsey with Beatrice and

Thomas. Later Lindsey had been sent away to schools, to be occasionally summoned by Mona and travel with her to foreign cities, usually accompanied by Mona's boyfriend of the time. Mona changed men the way a small child changed socks.

Then Mona, too, had died in a car crash. Killed herself, some said. Lindsey, fourteen then, had come to live full-time with Beatrice and Thomas. She'd traded the loneliness of school for the loneliness of Ingraham House. But by that time she would have been lonely anywhere.

Beatrice and Thomas had tried; Lindsey could see that now. But she'd been rebellious, hardheaded and confused. They'd had so many fights. When they locked her in her room, she'd sneak out the window. Once she fell and broke her ankle. She'd attended three colleges; two had asked her to leave, and the third she'd dropped out of.

Pushing the memories aside, she telephoned the hospital. Fear crept in, and her heart picked up the tempo as she waited for the connection. Surely there had been no change for the worse; Selda would have awakened her if news had come.

With the assurance that Beatrice was stable, Lindsey showered and joined Selda in the kitchen for a light meal, deciding it was time she learned all that had been going on with Beatrice and the company.

"Beatrice's heart problem started about nine months ago," Selda told her. "She may have had it before, but we didn't know. I told her to tell you, but her pride..."

Lindsey gave a wan smile, appreciative of the fact Selda didn't seem to place all the blame on her.

"The heart trouble made Beatrice feel old—which, of course, she is at seventy-two. I told her being old isn't so bad. It happens to everyone. She got more and more depressed. With the heart condition and then the problems with Ingraham's these past few months, she just went downhill."

"Just what is going on at Ingraham's?" Lindsey asked earnestly.

Selda pinched her lips disapprovingly. "For quite a few years now, Beatrice had been gradually turning the management of the company over to Lyle Cummings. She just seemed to lose interest as time went by. I told her to be careful. Never did care for that man," Selda mumbled. "But Beatrice had perfect confidence in him. Why, he was a friend of Thomas's." Selda raised a knowing eyebrow. "Then six months ago it all broke loose. Beatrice discovered Lyle Cummings had been stealing from the company—running the company into the ground, he was. It was enough to give anyone a heart attack. That's when Beatrice had the first one, a mild one."

Lindsey sat stunned. "Lyle Cummings?" She could hardly believe it.

"Yep," Selda said, obviously enjoying the telling of scandal. "And the other shocker is it was his secretary who came and told Beatrice. Woman scorned, plain and simple."

Lindsey could only sit and stare. Her mind went back over the years, picturing Beatrice and Thomas discussing the company in the evenings. It was their life. "What did Grandmother do?"

"She had it checked out by an on-the-spot audit. Then Lyle confessed. Right to her face, not batting an eye. Then he politely said he'd be in his office—then he wasn't—in his office, I mean. He went right down to the airport and left for South America—quick as a flea."

"South America?" Lindsey parroted.

"Well, no one really knows for certain," Selda conceded. "But that's where crooks go all the time."

Lindsey smiled at Selda's fancies then thought sadly of Beatrice. Her heart ached for her grandmother and condemned herself for not being there to give support.

"What about Ingraham's now?" she asked. "Who's running it?"

Selda sighed. "Beatrice has been trying to handle it mostly, like in the old days. For temporary help she's put Robert Boyle in charge. He don't want the job full-time, though he said he'd do his best. I don't think his best is all that good. It was like a gift from heaven when Michael Garrity made an offer for the whole shebang."

"Did Beatrice like the idea of selling to Michael?"

"Not totally, but she was resigned. At least for a while."

"She's changed her mind, Michael says."

Selda smiled. "She's stalling—and only she knows why. I think maybe she liked having that Michael Garrity come visiting. They had some lively conversations. He's been good for her, Lindsey, bringing her out, like she used to be. He even got her arguing again."

Lindsey could easily picture Michael charming Beatrice. They would be good together. An unpleasant thought slipped into her mind. *Had Michael simply been charming Beatrice to get what he wanted?*

Selda's voice broke into her thoughts. "I almost forgot—Robert Boyle told me to tell you Beatrice left you her power of attorney with him. Had it drawn up right after she wrote you."

For the second time, Lindsey sat stunned. Beatrice had given her the power of attorney. *The power to literally sign her life away.* She couldn't comprehend it all. What could Beatrice want from me? Lindsey thought. I know nothing about the business. It all pointed up her grandmother's failing health, her failing mind, her failing spirit.

A deep ache assailed Lindsey. Guiltily, she realized she felt trapped by it all. She didn't want this burden, this responsibility, which seemed to be growing by the minute. She wanted to be back in her apartment, laughing with Jay, back to sleeping until noon, shopping until three, dinners at Tony's or Cochran's, and parties until all hours of the night.

"Leave the dishes, Selda," she said, suddenly needing very much to see Beatrice, needing the reassurance of her presence, however precarious at this moment. "Let's get to the hospital."

Chapter Three

Sandy drove them to the hospital in the Rolls. Lindsey felt conspicuous and would have preferred to drive herself, but the long classic car was now the only one Beatrice kept, and Lindsey found the thing intimidating. She was, however, amused to see that Selda loved it. Apparently she even went grocery shopping in it.

There was some question about Selda being allowed to see Beatrice. Lindsey wasn't about to take no for an answer. Selda and Beatrice were more than employee and employer; they'd been together for twenty years. Lindsey sought and secured Dr. Dietrich's permission, and the duty-bound nurse led the way, muttering something about the dire consequences of contamination from a parade of people.

Beatrice's color was better, and she was sleeping peacefully. Selda stood at the bedside, big tears rolling down her pudgy cheeks. "You get better and come on home, Beatrice," she said, patting the other woman's hand. She turned to Lindsey, gulping out the words between tears, "I'll be outside."

When Selda had gone, Lindsey stepped closer. The next instant she was surprised to be looking straight into Beatrice's pale blue eyes. They gazed at each other for a long moment. And in those seconds, the cold wall of long ago was pierced. Or perhaps it had happened in the hours Lindsey had sat beside her grandmother, communicating mentally as she never had with words.

"Hello, Grandmother." She took Beatrice's hand.

"Hello, Granddaughter." Beatrice's voice was a hoarse whisper. She tried to grip Lindsey's fingers. "I've been awake...didn't want to be bothered...Selda would've talked my ear off." She closed her eyes for a moment then opened them again.

"I'm so glad you're better, Grandma." Lindsey could hardly get the words past the lump in her throat.

"I'm...a tough old bird." Beatrice attempted a smile. "I'm glad you've come."

"Oh, Grandma. I'm sorry I took so long." Lindsey blinked away the tears.

Beatrice's hand moved within her own, as if she were desperate to say something. "Lindsey...my power of attorney. I fixed it...you can sign anything...that needs be... Please...go to the office...Robert."

So like Beatrice; the business would be her main concern. Anxious to reassure her, Lindsey nodded. "I will, Grandma. Everything's being taken care of. Please don't worry."

Giving a small sigh, Beatrice closed her eyes. Lindsey thought she'd fallen asleep, but she spoke again. "Have you met Michael, Lindsey?"

"Yes, Grandmother."

Beatrice gave a small smile; her hand relaxed in Lindsey's. Moments later Lindsey tiptoed from the room.

She leaned against the outside of the door. Go to the office? And do what? And, yes, she'd met Michael, recognized the unique qualities Beatrice had seen. Had Beatrice also foreseen the attraction Lindsey would feel for him? More than likely. What did Beatrice have in mind?

Oh, Lord, what have I gotten myself into? Lindsey moaned inwardly. It was beginning to look more and more as though she was going to miss Jay's race on the Chesapeake.

At home once more, Lindsey shared a snack with Selda then shooed the housekeeper off to her room, promising to clean the dishes. Selda's expression hovered somewhere between shock and disbelief. Lindsey had never done the dishes before nor bossed Selda around. But Selda wasn't getting any younger, and fatigue from the night before etched her face. She allowed Lindsey to have her way.

Lindsey smiled wryly, for a split second seeing herself as she'd been when she used to live in this house: temperamental, lazy, totally introverted. No wonder Selda didn't know what to think. But time had a way of changing things.

She looked at the dishes; then her gaze slipped to the dishwasher. Actually, it felt odd, and she wasn't at all sure about her expertise in cleaning. In New York she had a morning housekeeper five days a week; rarely had she ever touched a dish, at least for washing purposes. With an amused grin she rolled up her sleeves, determined to leave the kitchen spotless.

It was dusk when she heard Michael's car pull into the drive. Lindsey had been walking along the side of the house on the wide brick drive that led to the garage and the river. She admitted she'd been waiting for him.

"Michael."

He stopped then turned toward her with his characteristic saunter. He wore faded denims, a pale T-shirt and sneakers that appeared, even in the fading light, well past their prime. Still, something about him radiated electricity. Even dressed casually, he could command a boardroom meeting.

"I've just come from the hospital," he said.

"Beatrice?" Lindsey asked in a breathless whisper, fearful he would say there'd been a change for the worse, though she herself had called the hospital only half an hour ago.

"She's okay. She even spoke to me," he hurried to assure her.

Lindsey let out her breath. "I can't seem to rid myself of the fear. She could take a turn for the worse—any minute. The knowledge hangs around me like a cloud."

"Well, rest easy for the next few minutes—she's sleeping and has the nurses shaking their heads at her constitution." Holding out a small bag, he dug into it. "Have a pretzel?"

"Is that Dr. Garrity's prescription?" Lindsey teased, taking the pretzel.

"Never-fail remedy." His arm brushed hers purposely, and Lindsey's worry faded.

Together they walked the drive to the river and leaned against the bulwark. The water lapped gently below; a round moon had just begun rising in the east.

"This is a magnificent old house. Did Thomas build it?" Michael asked. The sun had almost fully set and Michael's eyes were dark pinpoints in the low light.

"No—Thomas's father. Only two years after it was completed, they lost all their money, and it fell to Thomas to build the business up again. For a while Grandfather was afraid they'd lose the house." She bit into the pretzel.

Lindsey sensed a change within herself, her feminine side becoming stronger. She tilted her head, looking at Michael. It had been a long time since she'd welcomed the attentions of a man. "I like the doctor's prescription," she said, holding up the pretzel.

"Glad I could oblige." He spoke huskily. His gaze rested heavily on her mouth; then he made no attempt to hide a downward slide of his eyes to her breasts.

Lindsey sensed the magnetic pull; her blood flowed warmly. The force of the feeling frightened her, and she stepped back.

"Care for some coffee?" she asked lightly.

Michael looked at her, but she couldn't read his expression. And in that split second she couldn't read herself, either.

"Sounds good," he said in his low, slow drawl.

Michael turned on the lamp near the big chairs in the living room while Lindsey went for the coffee. He leaned near when she placed the tray on the low table, and she almost dropped it. What in the world was wrong with her? A breeze off the river wafted through, bringing Michael's faint scent. She felt his admiring gaze and lowered her eyes, hiding an unaccountably pleased smile.

He drank deeply of the coffee, looked at the cup, drank again and looked questioningly to Lindsey. "Did you make this? I know for sure it wasn't Selda." His tone echoed disbelief.

"Yes. I admit, I'm not too handy around the house, but I can do some things."

"You do coffee very well. What's the secret?"

"I'll never tell."

"Ah, a woman who can keep a secret," he teased.

Lindsey smiled in return. "That women can't keep secrets is a myth spread about by men. Actually we keep quite a few."

"I get your point." Michael eyed her lazily.

Lindsey averted her eyes and folded her legs beneath her in the large chair. They each sipped their coffee, and in the quiet that followed, Lindsey's thoughts returned to worrying over Beatrice.

"How soon must you know about the sale of Ingraham's?" she asked Michael, the question popping from her thoughts.

"As soon as possible," Michael replied. "I'm converting the two other chains now. I'd like to begin bringing Ingraham's in line along with them, and before Ingraham's suffers more financial setbacks."

Lindsey raked a hand through her hair. "I'm worried what selling Ingraham Corporation will do to Beatrice. You must have come to know her well enough in the last months to know it's been her life."

"It's Ingraham Corporation that has put her in the hospital," Michael stated flatly. "She's too old to try and handle it. She was a sharp cookie in her day. But that day is past. She's simply not up to salvaging what neglect and Lyle Cummings have done to it. And why should she be? She's earned some rest and relaxation."

Again Lindsey pushed at her hair. "I know that—I agree. Only—she must have something to live for."

"She has you. Or are you hightailing it back to New York in the next few days?"

She looked long into his steel-gray eyes. "No," she said sharply. "I'm not hightailing, as you put it, back to New York. But Beatrice has always needed the work. I don't think I'm going to be a very good substitute. I never was." Painfully aware that she revealed herself in those last words, Lindsey shifted her eyes, and the subject. "You're awfully intent on buying Ingraham's."

"Yes, I am. I'm a businessman."

"So you are."

"It doesn't take away from how I feel about Beatrice."

Lindsey wanted to believe him, but God help her, she couldn't be sure. She said nothing.

"You have your doubts," Michael said softly.

"Let me just say, I've come to learn that where money is concerned a person's welfare usually rates second. No matter what the good intentions."

Michael was very still, his eyes narrowing. "Aren't you in an awkward position to be so disdainful of money?"

"It's not a disdain of money—it's people's reaction to it."

"You speak with the voice of bitter experience."

"Experience, yes. But not bitter—only wiser, I believe. More cautious." She met his gaze. "Perhaps in this case, a bit overcautious," she allowed.

Michael held on to her gaze. "In this instance," he said pointedly, "what is good for me, is also the best thing for Beatrice."

Lindsey sighed. "I do believe Beatrice should sell." But she doubted if her grandmother would see it that way. That's why Beatrice had been stalling and seemed so confused. She would never want to sell Ingraham's, whether it was for the best or not.

"Beatrice will be all right," Michael said, sensing her train of thought. He took her hand; his was hot upon her own, strong and sturdy, like the man himself. Rising, he pulled her up with him. "It's late. I'd better be going."

Watching him look her over again, she smiled inwardly. She held open the front door, extremely aware of his nearness, of the electricity again springing up between them. And she knew he was going to kiss her.

Touching her cheek, he brought his lips gently to hers, once, twice, in a feathery motion. It was such a pleasant sensation. With surprise Lindsey felt the heat of passion leap within her body at the simple touches. Then his arms went around her, pulling her against him. Or was it she pressing toward him? He crushed his lips to hers, forcing her mouth to open, probing within with his tongue. He tasted faintly of rich coffee.

The muscles of his body, rock hard, burned through the fabric of their clothes. Lindsey's heart pounded, and she felt herself going breathless. Her world was spinning. It was a wondrous sensation: lighter than air, floating away into a world of color. His hair felt like silk beneath her fingers, and the fragrance of cologne mixed with his own virile warmth tantalized her nostrils.

Michael lifted his head. Lindsey didn't want him to. For a brief instant she couldn't open her eyes and found that her head still whirled. She clung to him for support. Finally she looked into eyes that were dark, steely pinpoints. Why was he looking at her that way? His arms still held her; her toes barely touched the floor.

"I'm glad you're going to be around awhile," he said in a gravel whisper. "We definitely need to get to know each other better." His eyes searched hers, questioning her, promising her. "And the next time you give me those come-hither-looks, you'd better be ready to accept the consequences, Lindsey," he said, letting her go abruptly.

"I beg your pardon?" Lindsey replied, jutting out her chin.

He gave a wide grin and mock salute. "Good night, Princess."

She almost slammed the door on that self-satisfied grinning face, but at the last minute caught it with her hand to keep it from banging and waking Selda. "Ouch!" she said in a loud whisper, shaking her pinched fingers.

Yes, Michael Garrity was a perceptive man. It both irritated and intrigued her. He read her better than she read herself. She'd often flirted with a man, subtly, like she had with Michael. It was part of her nature, as much a part of her as her rhythm of walking or her handwriting strokes. Most men enjoyed it, though not all of them realized what she was doing. But Michael had.

She gave a throaty chuckle. Michael Garrity was a most interesting gentleman.

Remembering his lips on hers, she grew warm again. Absently she touched her fingers to her lips. This was the first time in all her life she'd felt such magic.

Three mornings later, Beatrice had grown strong enough to be moved from the ICU. The tentative prognosis was good: an expected return to normal life, with several cautions; change in diet, and mild therapy. The hospital staff considered her one of their miracles of the year.

Once more in the Rolls, Lindsey arrived at the hospital early enough to bring a live plant along with a few pictures and amenities to place around the private room and make Beatrice feel more comfortable. To inject a note of gay whimsy, she also brought a bouquet of gaily colored balloons. It was an occasion, after all.

Hearing the door open, Lindsey turned from where she was fastening the balloons to the bedside table, smiling, expecting to see Beatrice being wheeled in. But instead she saw a man's trim waist. Quickly her gaze moved up, taking in a heather-tone tie, loosened at the neck, and freshly shaved tanned cheeks and at last meeting steely gray eyes.

"Michael!" She hadn't seen or talked to him since the night he'd kissed her, though she knew he'd visited Beatrice each day. At the sight of him now, and at the surprising though unmistakable glint of pleasure in his eyes, a warmth glowed within her. Quickly her inner caution rose, banking the glow.

"Mind if I join in on this big moment?" He stepped near, holding out a portable tape player. "Saw the hoard of flowers at the desk. All for Beatrice, I presume?" Lindsey nodded. "Well, I thought she might prefer some music in her quieter moments."

"Yes, I think she might." Lindsey smiled.

"Flowers are so humdrum." His voice skimmed over the words, his gaze deliberately telling her he was thinking of other things.

"Not to florists." Lindsey, caught by the magnetic energy that flowed between them, couldn't tear her gaze away.

"Okay, flowers are nice, but I wanted something original." His eyes searched hers. "I need to keep in Beatrice's good graces, after all."

Catching the subtle reminder of their last conversation, Lindsey lowered her gaze. She couldn't face him fully, for the doubts still lingered.

The door bumped open, and a nurse entered, smiling brightly. "Here she is." Careful and competent, as though they were bearing a queen on her litter, two orderlies rolled Beatrice's bed into place.

Lindsey's heart tugged at her. It did every time she saw her grandmother, so small upon the wide expanse of hospital bed, so weak and vulnerable.

The nurse checked the IV then cranked the bed into partial sitting position.

"More!" Though Beatrice's voice was weak, it was definitely a command.

The nurse gave another half-crank; Beatrice frowned but said no more. "Not too long, now," the nurse advised Lindsey and Michael, shaking a finger at Beatrice, as well. "You've had quite a morning. You need rest."

Beatrice waved her away. "I'm not about to expire in the next ten minutes," she said saltily in a near breathless voice. Holding out her hands, she motioned Lindsey and Michael to her. Lindsey sat on the edge of one side of the bed, while Michael pulled a chair close to the other side. Each held one of Beatrice's hands.

Lindsey's heart stopped its worried pounding. Though her face was still pale, Beatrice's eyes were bright and full of life.

"This is the first time I've seen you two together," she said, her gaze moving back and forth between them.

"Hello, Duchess." At the tone in Michael's voice, Lindsey glanced over quickly to see that his eyes mirrored the same warmth. Yes, Michael did care, very much.

"What do you have there, Michael?" Beatrice asked.

"Oh, thought you might enjoy some music to doze by— Mantovani." Gently he placed the recorder on the bedside table.

"Thank you. I believe I might. They won't let me have my nightly brandy in here." Her voice grew faint, though her eyes twinkled, and the hint was plain.

"I'll see what I can do," Michael returned smoothly.

Beatrice turned her face to Lindsey, her hand seeking a tighter grip. She didn't say anything for a moment; Lindsey was quiet too, each content to just look at the other.

"Need my hair done," Beatrice said at last.

Lindsey smiled, reading between the lines. With those words Beatrice was saying; I'm getting better. I must get on with things. "I'll arrange it," Lindsey said.

"There's something I need to speak of now, while you're both here." Beatrice spoke slowly, though in a surprisingly firm tone. Her eyes moved thoughtfully from Lindsey to Michael and back again. "I've decided not to sell Ingraham's."

Oh, Lord, Lindsey thought. She glanced at Michael. He was looking at Beatrice, his expression guarded though obviously curious. Now was not the time for this. Beatrice didn't need to get upset and have any strain at all and possibly end up right back in ICU—or worse.

"We don't need to talk about this now, Grandmother. There's..."

"I'm not talking about it. I'm telling you. And Michael needs to know."

Lindsey nodded, a reluctant smile touching her lips. "All right, Grandma. We're listening."

"Good." Beatrice looked pleased, knowing neither of them would dare upset her. "I want you to run it for me, Lindsey."

Lindsey sucked in a deep breath. Quickly she darted a glance at Michael. He regarded Beatrice thoughtfully then raised his eyes to Lindsey, waiting for her reaction.

"Ingraham's, Grandmother?"

Beatrice's eyes, too, watched Lindsey carefully. "Yes, Granddaughter."

"But I know nothing about Ingraham's, about running any company, even working in one, for that matter." Lindsey's voice softened. "You know that." How in the world could she contend with this foolish, insane idea? She searched for words. "It seems to me that the smartest thing now, the wisest business choice, is to sell. What do you need it for anymore, Grandma?"

"It is Ingraham's. I don't want to sell," Beatrice stated, her weakening voice pulling at Lindsey's heart.

And yes, Lindsey realized at the same time, her voice was weak, but her will, though rusty, was still solid iron. Sighing, she looked at Michael, casting him a silent appeal. A bit of a dubious grin touched his face.

"Is this a bid for more money, Duchess?" Michael joked softly. "You are a sharp trader. I'll up the bid two dollars a share."

Beatrice rewarded him with a rakish smile. "Determination...I like that, young man. But you know me better."

"That I do." Lindsey was drawn to his voice. It held laughter, respect—and fondness.

Oh, what a mess, Lindsey thought and she felt for him, knowing this was important to him, yet she was proud of Beatrice in some crazy way. It was a sign of her strength and that she wanted and intended to be among the living.

Beatrice closed her eyes a moment, obviously tiring. "You're a sharp trader yourself, Michael." She opened her eyes. "I'm sure you'll find a way around this."

"Grandma, please forget the business for now. Please put all your strength into getting well; then we'll decide."

"I have decided."

"Yes...but I haven't." Lindsey said the words softly, but they were plain. She would not be pushed nor bamboozled into a direction she had no intention of going.

Beatrice gave her a long, measuring look. "We'll let it go for now."

Lindsey returned the look. Never could she remember Beatrice sounding so meek—but then never had she dared to give what amounted to a command to Beatrice. Apparently, they had both changed quite a bit.

Lindsey found her eyes watering in the elevator. "She's just so devious, Michael. She planned that—both of us being there—telling us like that. And knowing, by God, knowing the fix we're in. We don't dare upset her." Lindsey didn't know whether she wanted to laugh or cry. Her voice softened. "She is something else, you know. There's not another like her."

"No," Michael agreed. He smiled, too.

The elevator doors opened, and Michael walked close to her as they crossed the lobby. A furrow creased his brow.

"What are you going to do now, Michael?"

He regarded her quietly, his eyes unreadable. He opened the plate-glass door. "I'll wait. Proceed with my plans as far as I can."

"I don't think she'll change her mind, Michael."

"Perhaps not. But circumstances may change it for her."

Looking up at him, she had to squint in the bright light as her eyes searched his. The white Rolls glided to a stop at the curb beside her, and Sandy waited a polite distance away. "What do you mean?" she asked at last.

"With every passing day Ingraham's grows closer to bankruptcy. Beatrice may be forced to sell in the end, anyway. And there are other ways," he added.

"Then you still intend to have Ingraham's? No matter how Beatrice feels about it?"

"I'm not a shark going after meat, Lindsey. I do care about Beatrice, no matter what you may think. If I can get what I want, fine. If not, I'll change my plans. But no matter how you or Beatrice feels, Ingraham's is going to have to go—and I intend to be the one to get it, at least as long as it remains a viable investment."

Lindsey frowned impatiently. "I do believe you care for Beatrice. But it goes back to what I said before—sometimes all feelings get lost in what happens to be best for business." She pushed the hair from her face. "What if we manage to keep Ingraham's going, even manage to turn it around, make it thrive again?"

"We?" His eyebrows rose, and his eyes were steely. "Then you intend to do as Beatrice asks?" His voice betrayed what he thought of the idea. It was foolish, and she was foolish for even considering it.

"Yes, I do." It was stubborness speaking. Her mind whirled. Of course it was a crazy idea, but she didn't appreciate him telling her.

"I don't think you can manage it, in what? Eight days? Isn't that when you intended to return to New York? What about Fordham? I'm sure he's waiting for you." His gaze was cool, mocking.

"Meaning you don't think I could handle it?"

"Meaning I know you'd have a better chance of shooting for the moon than to even make one day. Have you even ever balanced your own checkbook, Princess? Have you ever read anything besides fashion magazines?"

Lindsey gave him a scornful look. She turned to the Rolls, and Sandy moved quickly to open the door.

Michael leaned against the car, his hands on the open window. "I don't think that you're going to be able to run Ingraham's."

Lindsey looked at him, seeing his mocking grin, the challenge in his eyes. *I accept,* her steady gaze said. *I accept the challenge.*

In that moment she felt the electricity that sparked between them, the heady pull of passion and marvelous, vibrant life.

His eyes bore into her own, his expression changing swiftly as he, too, felt the chemistry come alive between them. And he, too, was shocked. Desire flickered in the smoky depths of his gray eyes, and a trace of confusion, as well. Lindsey couldn't look away as his gaze turned to red-hot heat.

"Goodbye, Princess," Michael said huskily. "For now."

Lindsey couldn't say anything.

She watched his long, sure strides as he walked away. The blood still pounded in her temples, and she became aware of an aching warmth, a pulsing from deep within, spreading throughout her body.

The force of her reaction to him amazed her. She'd wanted to reach out and pull his lips to hers, to feel again their power, their gentleness. She'd wanted . . . It frightened her. It was too much, too strong, beyond her control, and she didn't like that.

Michael Garrity was a businessman, first and foremost, no matter how handsome, how charming and beguiling. He made that clear. He wanted Ingraham's. How far would he go to get it?

"Miss Ryland . . ." Sandy's call brought her back.

"Yes?"

"I asked where to?" He peered hesitantly at her in the rearview mirror.

Lindsey raked a hand through her hair, thinking. "Down to . . . to the Ingraham's offices," she said. She may as well go, not that there was anything she could do or even wanted to do. But at least she could tell Beatrice she had gone, had talked to Robert. That the building was still there, for one thing.

Michael was right about Beatrice's whole idea of Lindsey's being in charge of the company: totally insane. He'd said bankruptcy was forthcoming. That much was true, certainly, and it would come about probably in half the time if Lindsey tried to have anything to do with the company. But what would happen to Beatrice if Ingraham's did go into bankruptcy?

All Beatrice needed was time, Lindsey thought. She would stay noncommittal, then in a few days, maybe a week, she would tell Beatrice gently, that she had no intention of going along with the crazy idea of running the company.

Responsibility. It was grabbing her around the throat. She'd had so little of it in her life, beyond that of taking care of herself. For the first time in her life, someone needed her. Beatrice did. And Lindsey would have to find a way to help her as best she could.

But, not by doing what Beatrice wanted—trying to run the company—that was impossible. Where in the world had Beatrice come up with the idea? Obviously she was grasping at what she wished could be. Lindsey would just have to find a way to get through to her and explain the impossibility of it all.

An idea dawned on her suddenly. Maybe this was Beatrice's way of seeing to it that Lindsey stayed. Of course. *I'm not going anywhere, Grandmother,* Lindsey thought, her heart tightening at the lengths to which Beatrice would go. *Oh, Grandma, I'll stay.*

She thought of her apartment, of Jay, of her carefree life in New York with regret. She would miss it all. But for now, Beatrice needed her. She turned the thought over for a moment. It was new, frightening, but very good. She wondered where Michael Garrity fit into all this. She could get hurt with him, terribly hurt—but she wasn't at all sure she could resist him.

Michael Garrity had a temper but had learned years ago to keep it under ironclad control. Perhaps too much control, because when he did need to let off a bit of steam, he found it impossible. It was all bottled up inside him. He drove through the light late-morning traffic automatically, his emotions embroiled in an internal war.

He was angry; at Beatrice, at Lindsey, at the situation, but mostly at himself. Was Lindsey Ryland right? Did business deals mean more to him than people? Lindsey's words whispered in the back of his mind, and he squirmed at the truth in them.

He had been deliberately rude, telling her that she was incapable of running the business. But he'd meant it. Lindsey Ryland could make unbelievable coffee, would excel as a diplomat, would adorn a man's arm with her beauty and warm a man's bed with her passion, but in business, it was safe to say, she probably didn't know the red ink from the black.

Her blue eyes floated before his mind, and again the throbbing started within his loins. Giving a caustic laugh, he thought of his fantastic impulse to have her right there on the plush leather seat of the Rolls. But there was something more to his desire than physical need, something that lay hidden in those beautiful eyes, something that intrigued him, drew him almost against his will as a kite pulled in against the wind.

A horn blasted long and hard from behind, alerting Michael to the fact that the light had changed; he was only two blocks from his offices, and didn't even remember the drive.

Okay, cool down, he told himself as he shifted into gear. Think.

His plans for the grocery chain could proceed, for the moment, without the Ingraham's deal. He just wouldn't be able to include the southeast region right away. But there was still time. He'd rather wait for Ingraham's than go and build his own stores. It took an awful lot of time and energy to build, establish inventory and a clientele.

And damn it, he swore softly, Beatrice meant more than any deal. She was going to lose Ingraham's no matter what. He'd find a way to make it easy on her.

And he'd find a way to Lindsey Ryland, as well. He'd find what lay behind those china-blue eyes. The thought came reluctantly. It wasn't wise—didn't fit in with his business plans. But he couldn't shake his overpowering desire.

Chapter Four

The building was a squat brick block of three stories, slate gray and covered with a film of fifty years of fine dust and pollution. It was in the older business section of Jacksonville, in what had become mostly a warehouse district. There were wide streets, large parking lots, and wide, low buildings. It still had the imposing genteel air of another era, with decorative masonry above the wide glass doorway and the name, Ingraham's, engraved there.

Lindsey almost told Sandy to drive on. It was silly to come here. What could she do? She didn't want to do anything. Stepping inside was like forging one more link in the chain of responsibility under which she was beginning to sag.

"It's too hot to wait out here," she told Sandy as she stepped slowly from the car. "Come on up with me."

From the parking lot there was a side entrance that led to the small front lobby. The building, Lindsey decided, was neglected and smelled stale. Her gaze took in scuffed floors, marked walls, filmy glass and the elevator that smelled like a Havana cigar.

"I know the way," Lindsey said, dismissing the receptionist and leaving Sandy to flirt with the young girl. Rapid and anxious glances were thrown her way as she walked slowly down the wide hall, and the low hum of whispered speculation seemed to spread throughout the floor.

When she finally took a seat across from Robert Boyle, Lindsey decided he was stale, too. Perhaps in his early forties, he had receding hair, and continually pushed his dark-rimmed glasses up onto the bridge of his nose, and he wore an ever-worried expression.

"Yes. Palmer, Beatrice's private attorney, called me last week about Beatrice drawing up the necessary papers giving you power of attorney." He pushed at his glasses. "Makes it easier for me... I have some papers I really need you to sign—some orders—let's see..." He shuffled through an array of papers. His desk looked as though it had been stirred by a blender.

Watching the shuffling, Lindsey wondered if he was nervous because of her. "Robert," she said gently, using his given name in a friendly fashion, "Grandmother is very grateful for the job you're doing here. I understand you'd rather not have taken it on."

"No, I really didn't want to. Accounting is my forte. But someone had to, and Beatrice said she'd get someone else as soon as she could." His head jerked some more, and Lindsey decided it was just plain habit.

"I think I'll go into Beatrice's office," she said. "I'd like to have a look." And watching you makes me nervous, she added silently to herself.

He gave a jerky smile. "That'll be fine. I'll... I'll bring the papers in a moment."

"Take your time..."

The office that had once been Thomas Ingraham's looked much the same: quiet elegance, dating from the early thirties, deep mahogany walls and desk, and leather chairs.

With some surprise Lindsey saw a picture of herself propped next to Thomas's upon the desk. She couldn't put her finger on why she was surprised, only that it would seem more in line with Beatrice to have a picture of the Ingraham building in that place.

She ran her fingers along the wide marble windowsill; there was a thin layer of dust. Fleetingly her mind played back pictures of years past; memories of the busy offices, the noise and excitement of the warehouse.

Beatrice really did need to sell, Lindsey thought. It was too much for her now. Michael was right. And his ideas for the company were sound and solid. Under his dynamic business expertise the stores, though no longer called Ingraham's, would flourish again.

The door opened and Ivy Reed, Beatrice's secretary, entered. "Thought you might like a cup of coffee."

"Why, Ivy, you're still here?" Lindsey said in surprise, reaching for the offered cup. Ivy looked nearly the same: flaming red hair, definitely from the bottle, madeup lips, and fingernails to match.

"Yes. Sort of like a fixture along with all this other stuff." She inclined her head toward the rest of the room. "I have a husband and a little boy now—better late than never," she added at Lindsey's look. "But I'm still here. How's Beatrice? Is she truly getting better?"

"She talked business this morning." Lindsey gave a wry grin. "Yes, she's better. They moved her to a private room today."

Ivy shook her head in admiration. "Just like Beatrice. She'll probably outlive us all." She eyed Lindsey. "You're looking real good, honey. Bet the men buzz around you like gnats on a melon."

Lindsey smiled, her mind involuntarily picturing Michael. Shaking the thought aside, her gaze moved about the room. "It's so changed from what I remember."

"Sure is." Ivy perched on the edge of the desk. "You heard about Lyle Cummings, didn't you?"

"Selda told me, perhaps with a few embellishments."

"I doubt if it was too much embellishing. The story was pretty wild as it was. I—" Ivy put her hand to her chest for emphasis "—had no idea all that was going on under my very nose."

"How could it have happened under Beatrice's nose?"

"Honey, it couldn't have—not in the old days, anyway. But for the past, oh, four or five years, Beatrice seemed to just let go, kept turning more and more over to old Lyle, like she just didn't care, ya' know. Why, she got to only coming into the office on Fridays."

Gazing down at the desk, Lindsey pictured Beatrice. Her heart felt heavy with regret. She looked back up. "How bad is it, really? The place looks so..."

"Run-down," Ivy finished for her. "Well, we've closed three stores. One in Atlanta, one in Bristow and one in Jackson. We're going to have to close more. Though some are still making a profit, overall we're losing money daily. To put it short and sweet—our stores are all hopelessly out of date, and people don't want to shop in them. Of course, that's the broad picture between you, me, and Robert."

Lindsey's gaze fell thoughtfully to the desk, wondering at the extent of it all.

"Let me get a few books—you can see some of what's been going on," Ivy said briskly.

Before Lindsey could stop her, Ivy hopped from the desk and whisked from the room. Oh, well, it couldn't hurt to look, Lindsey told herself. She sipped the coffee Ivy had brought; it was bitter—stale. She fingered the Styrofoam cup. Thomas must be rolling in his grave. Pushing her hair from her face, she gave a big sigh. Books? She hadn't come here to look at books. She probably wouldn't even understand them.

But with Ivy's help, she did understand. It wasn't so hard, much like a giant check register. Anyone could see losses were far exceeding profits. The reasons were more obscure, though with Ivy pointing a few out, Lindsey could see the shoddy mismanagement: notes on lost invoices, lost shipments, shipments costing more than agreed upon, and by heaven, even money spent that couldn't be accounted for. Two years ago, Lyle Cummings had closed the warehouse part of the building, Ivy told her, and also the satellite warehouse in north Georgia. They had to depend on various wholesalers, most with dubious reputations and practices. Lyle had screwed it up terribly, caring only about kickbacks for lining his pockets.

Lindsey was sitting in Beatrice's high-back leather chair, with Ivy at her elbow when Robert entered.

"Ah...found those papers." His eyes shifted as he passed them to Lindsey.

Ivy went for more coffee while Lindsey looked over the papers that seemed to be simple payroll sheets and stock orders. Lindsey signed them, realizing wryly that she wasn't at all sure of what she was doing.

Passing the papers back to Robert, she said, "Ivy's been explaining the state of the company. Do you think selling to Michael Garrity is a sound idea?"

Looking nonplussed, he pushed at his glasses, stammering, "I—uh, yes, I suppose so."

Lindsey sighed, giving a small nod. "Do you know the details of the deal?"

Robert nodded. "Some. I went over several of the books with Garrity."

"Is it a good offer? The best Beatrice could get?"

Robert pushed his glasses and shrugged. "There's no one else who has shown any interest. That's the main problem. Ingraham's would only be a good buy in exactly the right circumstances."

Ivy, juggling cups of coffee, caught the last of the conversation. "Michael Garrity...right?" Ivy made wide eyes. "I'll work for his thirty percent any day."

"What?" Lindsey shot her a puzzled glance.

"Didn't you know he owns about thirty percent of Ingraham's already?"

"No, I didn't." Lindsey arched an eyebrow, her heart picking up speed as the threads of anger began to weave. She glanced to Robert.

"Roughly thirty percent," he stammered.

Over one-fourth. The thought sat there heavily.

Lindsey took a deep breath and lowered her eyes. So Michael Garrity owned thirty percent of Ingraham's. And he'd never said a word. Not the night they'd discussed selling, the night they'd shared coffee in the dim closeness of the living room, the night he'd kissed her, not that very afternoon after he'd spoken so tenderly to Beatrice then scoffed at Lindsey on the sidewalk. *He hadn't said a word.*

Ivy was fishing for papers in Beatrice's desk. She plopped them in front of Lindsey and pointed. "Beatrice and Thomas once owned seventy-five percent, the rest was owned by various investors. In the last years the company had continually needed money. To get it Beatrice gradually sold off some of her stock. Though it brought her down to fifty percent, she still controlled because the remaining stock was widely scattered. Apparently Michael Garrity started buying up Ingraham's stock from its individual owners late last year at the same time he began putting his grocery chain together. He now owns roughly thirty percent of Ingraham's, the second largest chunk. The remainder is still scattered."

Lindsey closed her eyes then opened them again. Scanning the page before her, she didn't totally understand the muddling figures, but she knew all the same what it must mean to Beatrice.

There are other ways. Michael's words of the morning floated back through her thoughts. Oh, yes there are other ways; a low chill swept down her neck. If he could buy enough stock, he could force control. Poof—Ingraham's would become Garrity's.

"I care about Beatrice," he'd said. Ha! Mr. Michael Garrity cared about what was good for his money, and power plays.

Lindsey looked at the figures, her brain struggling to understand. There was something here, something clicking way in the back of her mind, pieced together from the many boring conversations she'd taken in at parties and articles she'd partially read in the business section of the newspapers. Piecemeal, she tried to sort out the pulsing thoughts.

Michael Garrity wanted to buy Ingraham's, a failing company. Why? So he could annex it to his own chain, remodel, make it pay again. When he got done, the Ingraham's stores, though no longer called that, would be worth much more. And any stock in it would also be worth much more.

Gradually Lindsey felt her adrenaline begin to pump, just like it did when she played her games in the stock market or challenged an unsuspecting gentleman to a quiet though lucrative game of poker.

"There's one more thing to consider," Ivy said. She glanced to Robert then plunged ahead. "Beatrice took a sizable loan out of the bank, right after Lyle's dealings came to light but before word got around about the state of the company."

Lindsey looked at Robert. "A loan?"

Robert coughed. "Yes. We had to have the money to keep going. Half payment was due this month. I paid some when we closed the Bristow store and managed to get an extension until October to finish that payment—Adam Hendry, the bank president, is an old friend of Beatrice. And I don't know where we'll get the money for next month, much less the final payment, which is due in six months."

Lindsey sighed. It seemed the company was about to fall into a good many people's hands.

"If Garrity is going to make such a profit out of Ingraham's, do you think he'd be willing to pay more for Grandmother's stock?" she asked Robert.

He chewed the end of his glasses while both Lindsey and Ivy looked at him. "Maybe. Anything's worth a try, but Michael Garrity is known as a tough businessman, and for buying cheap. That's why he's successful. And, like I said before, there haven't been any other offers—isn't likely to be. And Beatrice needs to sell, Miss Ryland."

"True..." Lindsey agreed, closing the ledger and straightening the papers. "It might be fun, though," she said thoughtfully, the ideas still not fully formed but there and enticing, "to see if I can get a bit more money for Beatrice's stock."

Ivy caught her eyes and grinned wickedly. "Dealing with Michael Garrity would have to be fun. Get him to take you to lunch, dinner, yachting..." She laughed. "The man is very single and very sexy."

"Shame on you, Ivy!" Lindsey laughed. But in her heart she had to agree. For this reason she'd have to be extremely careful with Mr. Garrity. He was a tough businessman and obviously intent on getting whatever he wanted.

Riding down in the elevator, Lindsey noticed again the neglected shape the building was in. Who in the world did they have cleaning the place? Oh, well, it didn't really concern her. Soon the building, the bills and everything else would belong to Michael. Let him worry about it.

Michael Garrity. Her mind pictured the steely gray eyes with the fine lines at their corners, the strong, tanned planes of his face. She'd begun to think she was wrong about him; she'd wanted to believe in him. She'd thought him different, and perhaps he was in his way, but, she thought grimly, like so many of the men who had colored her world, when it came to business, all was fair, so the saying went—no matter who got stepped on.

The Florida sun was blinding. Lindsey lingered, though, taking a deep breath. She'd missed it, she decided. Missed the faint scent of the old river in the air, the humid heat radiating from concrete and tar of the city, the palmetto trees and sweet fragrances of boxwoods and hibiscus in the old neighborhoods.

Sandy held open the rear door of the Rolls. His hair was damp where his hat sat at the hairline, and his boyish face was flushed.

"Sandy, do you like wearing that hat?"

"Well, it's sort of hot, but Miss Beatrice likes me to wear it."

"Then, since it's me you're driving around, I think you should take it off. And get rid of that tie."

Lindsey settled back in the leather seat of the Rolls, content for once to have Sandy behind the wheel. She was tired and had developed a tearing headache. Good grief, she'd had to get up before seven this morning. It was obscene.

A trickle of fear touched her spine. *Beatrice. She'd seen her only hours ago, and yes, she was fine, but . . .*

Sandy was looking at her for instructions.

"How do you use this thing?" she asked him, picking up the car phone. Sandy gave her the number, and through the operator Lindsey called the hospital. At the nurse's calm, reassuring words, Lindsey relaxed. Beatrice was resting peacefully, had even eaten quite a satisfactory lunch.

Once again Lindsey settled back against the seat. "Back home I guess, Sandy."

Her gaze drifted up the dirty brick of the Ingraham building. Okay, it looked as though Michael Garrity was going to get Ingraham's, but she'd see to it that he had to pay a bit more. She'd show him there was a brain under her blond hair.

A wonderment hit her, idle at first, then more intense. Why did she care what he thought of her? She never had cared with any man. And generally, she had to admit, purposely played the part of the brainless blond beauty. It was so much easier to hide behind. Why not now? Why did she care?

"This is one assignment I'll enjoy, Michael," Ty Connors told him with a wide grin, following Michael's rapid steps toward his car in the dimness of the parking garage. Ty was his legman and all-around expert assistant.

"I want an in-depth report on Lindsey Ryland," Michael said more sharply than he intended. "But nothing personal on your part." It was ridiculous, but Ty's ardent interest in Lindsey rankled. He understood it; she was beautiful, but he didn't like it.

Ty had been a friend for a long time. Beyond casting Michael a curious glance, he didn't let his friend's tone bother him. "Will do," Ty said. "Think I'll need to fly up to New York for a few days."

"Fine." Michael nodded. Slipping into his car, he peered up at Ty's earnest face. "And thanks." The two grinned at each other, then Michael shifted and pulled away, heading for the Ingraham building.

The white Rolls had just backed from its parking place and was preparing to leave the lot. Michael pressed the accelerator, sliding up and stopping in front of the Rolls, blocking its exit.

He'd known he'd find her here, though his reasons for wanting to were a bit jumbled. Part of it was a bit of information he'd neglected to tell Lindsey. Forgot. Only she probably wouldn't believe that. He wanted to tell her before anyone else did—though the chances of that were slim, he admitted to himself. And she was sure to take it wrong.

Another part of him hoped she'd be more cooperative now that she'd seen the mess Ingraham's was in. Another part felt responsible, wanted to help her, and still another part—well, she was a beautiful woman who drew him, nothing mysterious or unusual about that.

No, he allowed. Nothing mysterious; he'd always enjoyed a beautiful woman. But he had to admit that no other woman had ever had this effect on him, had ever been able to make him compromise his business rules.

Slowly, knowing she was watching his movements, he walked around the Mercedes and over to the back window of the Rolls. The window slid down.

He and Lindsey looked at each other for a few seconds, opponents sizing each other up. The humor showed first in her blues eyes then tugged at her lips.

"You're blocking our way," she said coolly.

Michael gave his car a deliberately lazy look. "That was the idea."

Another few seconds passed while Michael enjoyed watching Lindsey.

"Will you have lunch with me?" he said at last, rueful that he hadn't been able to get her to speak first. She'd have waited him out if it had taken all afternoon. Her stubborn pride was just like Beatrice's. "We do need to talk business—" he glanced at the building "—now that you've had a look at the company." And now that you've seen the hopeless mess, he added to himself.

Her eyes narrowed, losing their hint of humor. "Yes, we do... But I need to investigate further into the state of the company. Such as how the stock is divided. I found out just this morning that quite a bit more of the stock than I realized is owned by outsiders." She let those words hang there a moment.

Michael didn't flinch from her gaze. As he'd halfway expected, she'd found out about the stock; her reaction wasn't unexpected.

"Have lunch with me, and we'll talk about it." He wondered what kind of chance he had of getting her to believe him, to crack through this insane stubbornness.

She looked uncertain then nodded. "But not too long. I want to get back to the hospital this afternoon... We'll follow you."

"No need—I'll drive." Michael reached for the handle and opened the door. "Head on home," he told the driver. "I'll take Miss Ryland wherever she wants to go."

Lindsey started to protest then apparently changed her mind. "That'll be fine, Sandy," she said, swinging her shapely legs from the car.

She was so close that Michael could smell the sweet warmth of her. Her breasts pushed at the thin summery material of her dress. It was as if heat waves vibrated between them. She was one beautiful woman, he thought.

Her blue eyes, shiny crystals in the sunshine, met his, and Michael remembered the flickering heat that had lingered there that morning, only hours ago. He remembered wanting to ease her back against the smooth leather car seat and feel her silky skin beneath his hands. Even right now, he wanted to reach out and touch her. Instead, fearful of frightening her away, he opened the car door for her, careful not to so much as brush against her.

It was nearly one o'clock, and the lunch crowd in the restaurant had thinned. Michael noticed the firm curve of Lindsey's waist as he risked placing a guiding hand to her back as they followed the hostess to a table. He greeted several business acquaintances along the way, aware of their curious glances flickering to Lindsey, but didn't stop to make introductions.

He ordered steak, Lindsey, iced tea and chef salad. He studied her for a moment; she looked back. She was a puzzle. An exciting puzzle. One he was feeling more and more drawn to.

Her lips parted slightly, and her eyes widened in an alluring manner. The look had its effect—Michael felt a growing desire for her. Yet at the same time he sensed it was a ruse. Something didn't ring true. He studied her eyes. They told him nothing—except that she was hiding.

She glanced around the room. "You like the finer things in life, Mr. Garrity?"

Michael nodded. "I've learned to enjoy them."

"You come here often?"

He nodded. "Often enough." It was small talk, and Michael was never very good at it. "You saw Ingraham's." It was a statement.

"Yes." Something flickered in her eyes.

"And?"

"It's not what I remembered."

"No, I don't imagine it is."

"You failed to mention the other night that you owned about thirty percent of Ingraham's."

"Yes, I did," Michael answered matter-of-factly. "And failed is the word. I just didn't think of it. My owning the stock really doesn't matter at this point. Beatrice still controls."

"I suppose that's true." She ran a slim finger up and down her cool glass. "And besides, a good businessman plays it close to the chest, right?"

"Why are you so distrustful of me? What have I done, but tried to help? I just didn't think about the stock when we were talking. Period. And my owning that stock doesn't change things. Beatrice still controls," he repeated.

She inclined her head then asked bluntly, "Do you intend to buy up the remaining stock?"

"Not at the moment—though I haven't ruled it out," Michael answered.

She toyed with her glass. "What do you feel is the main problem now at Ingraham's?"

"One among the hundreds?" he asked.

"Yes."

Michael sighed. "Ingraham's strong point used to be their produce," he told her as their meal arrived. "And that's where they finally broke the last straw—when Beatrice allowed Lyle to close the warehouses that had served as a channel for some of the best produce out of Florida."

Lindsey nodded, and her voice became softer. "The family began in produce back before the turn of the century, you know." At Michael's nod, she continued thoughtfully. "Summers, when I was a little girl, Grandfather used to take me into the warehouse—the one right there in the building. It was noisy with trucks, people yelling, crates and boxes plopping. And it made you hungry just to sniff: oranges everywhere, and key limes, kumquats, muskmelon, tomatoes. It was his pride." Her manner had changed as she reminisced; she was natural, no longer hiding. "When I was older, it was the first place he started me working."

"You worked in Ingraham's?"

She gave a small laugh. "Yes—see I have worked in my life. Beatrice and Thomas insisted when I reached fifteen that I needed to learn the business. I'm afraid I never was a very good pupil, though. I used a lot of my brain power figuring out ways to sneak away and not be missed. How bad do you want Beatrice's stock?"

The question surprised Michael, and it took him a minute to answer. "Am I to suppose you are hinting at a higher price?" Could she really be trying to deal with him? It struck him as laughable, but he hid it well. "I've made my bid."

"I think her stock is worth more." Her tone was soft but firm.

"How much more?" He was fascinated by this new side to Lindsey.

"Half again as much," she said blandly, sipping her iced tea, her eyes hidden by the glass.

He raised his eyebrows and stared. "Half...I don't think so," he said, regaining his cool. There was something here, and in her. She was enjoying it.

She shrugged. "Beatrice doesn't have to sell."

"She'll go bankrupt."

"The company will—thirty percent of which belongs to you. Yes, she'd lose, but Beatrice has separate funds." She played with her salad.

"I can afford to lose, too. It becomes a tax deduction."

"Okay. Perhaps I can find another buyer."

"You?"

"I have her power of attorney at the moment." Her eyes told him it was just a reminder and that she figured he knew all along. The moisture on her lips and the sexy way she parted them didn't escape Michael's attention.

"Princess, you are one hell of a poker player." He smiled. He admired her manner: soft, but cool. Yes, there was more to Lindsey Ryland, and something told him he'd only seen perhaps a fraction of it. "But even with that power something tells me you wouldn't go against Beatrice's wishes about selling."

"But you can't know for sure."

Deep in thought, Michael cut into his steak. He was thoroughly enjoying the banter. "No, I can't."

"You're going to make plenty off Ingraham's. Therefore, it should be worth more to you," Lindsey reasoned.

Michael looked at her. She meant business. How in the hell had things got so complicated? It had started out as a nice, simple buy-out of a relatively small grocery chain. And he'd certainly not expected any of this from Lindsey Ryland. He'd thought she'd come to him all confused and needing his help and advice. And he, like the knight in shining armor, would take the burden from her shoulders. She'd be grateful, and they could get on to more interesting and passionate business. But the Princess was doing all right on her own.

He paused, considering. He could just chuck all this haggling right now. Let Ingraham's go, take his tax deduction, go on to building his own stores, which would start out modern and up-to-date. Life would immediately be a lot simpler.

Simpler, but a whole hell of a lot more costly. And definitely not as interesting.

"Instead of me buying outright," he said slowly, "how about a merger? Beatrice's stock being exchanged for stock in the chain I'm putting together. Her stock will grow in value rapidly and provide income for the rest of her life."

Lindsey's eyes widened, giving Michael the satisfaction of knowing what she was thinking this time: Why didn't I think of that? A grin tugged at his lips, and he averted his eyes.

"Evenly?" she asked.

Astonished, Michael looked up. *"Evenly?"* His voice rose a notch. "Lindsey, you're pushing it."

"Well, what then?"

"We'll work something out."

She gave him a long look. "I'll consult with Beatrice."

Michael raised his glass. "What will you do if she refuses?"

"I . . . I'm not sure. I really don't want to go against her wishes, Michael." She gave a sheepish grin. "No matter what I said before."

"Lindsey," Michael said quietly, "you may have to do it for her own good. Think what the mess of bankruptcy may do to her."

At the look of pain and confusion that slipped across her face, Michael felt his heart tighten and a tide of protectiveness rise in him. He wished he could wipe all this away for her and to hold and comfort her.

The next instant her forlorn look was gone, replaced by a cool smile, leaving him wondering if it had ever been there at all—and wondering at his own reaction.

Taking a deep breath, he cut into the steak again. Lindsey Ryland was one mighty interesting woman. He hadn't expected this, not at all. Nor had he expected his reaction to her. Looking again at the velvet smoothness of skin at her throat, he felt a knot tighten within him. His eyes flitted to hers. Was that a flicker of answering desire he saw there? Michael couldn't be sure. It was gone too fast.

Lindsey squinted in the bright light, keeping her eyes on the passing scenery. They kept wanting to stray to the man beside her. It seemed every cell in her body was singularly aware of him, of his virile presence, of his every move. Once, when he'd shifted gears, his knuckles had barely brushed her leg, and she'd felt the vibration go all the way up.

He was a quiet man, strong and confident, secure within himself, so that he didn't need to advertise the fact. And exciting. Lindsey felt it.

She wondered if he'd ever been married, and then the startling thought occurred to her that he could be, even now. How would she know? But no, she didn't think so. Immersed as he was in wheeling and dealing, he probably didn't have time for a wife. Affairs would be his style.

"Have you told Fordham you'll be staying down here longer than expected?"

His voice startled her from her thoughts. "No." What business was it of his—and why in the world had she answered him?

"I think he may be disappointed." Apparently he thought the matter amusing.

"So am I," Lindsey said.

He cast her a quick, dark look; then his attention was drawn back to the road as he pulled into the hospital drive.

He stopped in front, hopped out and came around to open the door, but Lindsey had already opened it. Slipping from the seat, she stood up, her shoulder brushing his chest, his face very near.

"I won't talk to Beatrice about the merger just yet," Lindsey said. "She has to get stronger. Maybe then she'll be able to see it clearly for herself, even decide that merging is the logical step all by herself."

Michael nodded. "I can wait, Lindsey. And no matter what you think, I do care about what's best for Beatrice."

Lindsey looked at him, searching his eyes. His gaze met hers then slipped to her lips. A warmth trickled up her spine, her pulse quickening. The fleeting moment was broken when two children burst from behind them, screaming with laughter.

Michael grinned. "I'll be in touch."

"Yes . . ."

His gaze again lingered briefly, and Lindsey could almost feel the warmth of his lips against her own, though he hadn't touched her at all.

Beatrice was dozing. Her room was dim, with the drapes drawn. Lindsey telephoned Sandy and arranged for him to come for her in about a half hour.

"You don't need to whisper." Beatrice's soft Southern voice broke the stillness. "I'm awake. Pull those blinds and give me some light. My eyes aren't as young as they once were—none of me is."

Lindsey smiled, doing as she was bid. It was good to hear Beatrice giving orders in her customary fashion. Ruefully she remembered how it used to be. Beatrice's commanding manner used to alternately cower her or make her angry.

"How are you doing, Grandmother?"

"As well as anyone who's suffered a near fatal heart attack and been given up for dead," Beatrice quipped. "Sandy didn't bring you? Who did?" She looked at Lindsey, and her eyes, despite protests to the contrary, were as sharp as ever. "Michael?"

"Yes," Lindsey said quietly, wondering what Beatrice would make of it, and not intending to get into a long discussion on the matter.

Beatrice let it go, though there was a flicker of curiosity on her face. "You've been down to the office?"

"Yes, Grandmother. Things are running smoothly. I signed the payroll sheets. The building is still there. Ivy and Robert send their best." Lindsey sat on the edge of the bed, taking Beatrice's hand. It felt fragile and small within her own.

"You've grown into a beautiful woman, Lindsey," Beatrice said after a moment.

"Thank you, Grandma."

"What have you done with yourself, besides frittering your life away?"

"Not much, Grandma."

Beatrice surveyed her. "I told Thomas to make your trust fund smaller." Lindsey said nothing. "Well, you have developed some strength; I'll grant you that. And style. How about this Jay you've written about? Are you having an affair with him?"

Lindsey laughed. "No, Grandmother. Jay's just a friend."

"Pity. You need a man, you know." Her face clouded. "I still miss Thomas—even after all these years—his quiet strength. I didn't realize how deep my love for him went until he was gone. A big regret, Lindsey." She pinched her lips, relaxing upon her pillow. "I'm tired. Hate getting old. Go on home now, Granddaughter, and quit placating me." She opened one of her eyes. "Didn't think I noticed, did you?" Her manner softened, and she squeezed Lindsey's hand. "I love you, Lindsey. Now I'll never have the regret hanging over me that I didn't tell you."

Lindsey's eyes watered. "Me too, Grandma." Gently she bent to kiss Beatrice's forehead; then impulsively she hugged her close.

Lindsey lay on the patio lounger, watching the stars twinkle above. A light, humid breeze teased her skin. If she lay real still, she could hear the gentle lapping of the St. Johns against the bulwark, and she tried to listen to the relaxing rhythm, to keep thought away. She wanted to let her mind rest; she was so tired from it all.

But slowly the problems of the moment forced their way back. How long would it take Beatrice to recover? And how long could Lindsey put off serious discussion of Ingraham's? What could she do about her apartment in New York? How long would she have to be away?

And Michael. Thoughts of him dominated all others. He attracted her, and it was wonderful and frightening at the same time. What was she going to do about it? She had an inkling that if she didn't keep a tight rein on herself, she would . . . would what? Fall in love?

She'd never been in love. Oh, she'd thought she had, but since that time when she'd made a complete and utter fool of herself, she'd kept her heart protected. Lindsey wasn't sure she believed in love everlasting and other fairy tales, but yet—she wanted to.

Selda appeared in the golden light from the hallway. "A telephone call, Lindsey. Jay Fordham." She brought the cordless phone.

"Tell him I'm not in.... No, no." She motioned for the receiver, taking a deep sigh. She might as well get it over with. "Jay?"

"Hi, sweetheart. How goes it in the South?"

"Warm, Jay." It was good to hear his voice.

"I've watered Herman faithfully. I thinks he likes me. But he's asked me every day when you're coming home."

Lindsey laughed dryly. "Ah, Jay, I'm going to be down here a bit longer than I anticipated." The line buzzed faintly. "My grandmother has had a heart attack and is in the hospital."

"I'm sorry, Lindsey." His voice was concerned.

"I'm sorry to miss your race. But you'd still better win."

"Of course I'll win. We'll all work extra hard just for you. What are your plans now?"

"It's all so complicated, Jay, what with Grandmother and the business mess with Michael Garrity. I just don't know, but it will be another few weeks before I can get back, I'm sure."

"So Garrity is still around, huh?"

"Yes..." What else could she say?

"Well, don't worry about anything up here. I'll handle Herman and the rest of the green guys."

"Thanks, Jay. You're a good friend."

"Yeah, well... Lindsey, could you make this old friend another loan?" The bantering humor seemed to slip from Jay's voice.

"Jay? What's wrong?"

"Dad's cut me off again. He's really mad this time."

"Of course, you can have some money, Jay. I'll call Stanley first thing in the morning. And your father will cool off. He always has."

"I don't know about this time, Lindsey," Jay said glumly. "He's different this time."

"Oh, Jay..." Lindsey bit her lip, thinking of his boyish face.

"Hey, smile." Lindsey could tell even at this distance that his voice had become cheery, forced. "These things do pass, so they say. I hope your grandmother gets better real fast."

"Thanks, Jay. I'll talk to you soon."

Very slowly Lindsey's thumb broke the connection. What had happened to her carefree, uncomplicated life? she wondered. And why couldn't she have met Michael Garrity in another time, another place?

Chapter Five

As the days passed, Beatrice grew stronger. Once again her silver hair shone, her smooth complexion was as radiant as that of a much younger woman, and her eyes sparkled when she talked.

Lindsey's intense fear over her grandmother's precarious health abated. She still called the hospital first thing upon waking and last thing before going to bed, but the compulsive knotting in her stomach had stopped.

Somehow she managed to steer all conversations clear of business, though she spent endless hours with Beatrice. She suspected that Beatrice, for reasons of her own, avoided the subject of Ingraham's, as well. That didn't for one minute mean she'd lost interest. Ivy had reported Beatrice had called the offices three times.

Tired of being at the mercy, as she saw it, of Sandy and the Rolls, Lindsey rented a car. She shopped for all new lingerie for Beatrice, and in doing so, quite by accident, drove past one of the local Ingraham's stores. Curious, she pulled into the parking lot, surveying the store. The lot was cracking, weedy on the edges, trash-littered. The store looked so...used.

Did they all look like that? Briefly Lindsey considered going in to take a look around but shook her head. Why in the world would she want to do that? Michael was the one who needed to be concerned, not her.

She hadn't seen or heard from Michael in all these days, though he'd called Beatrice every day. He was out of town, so Beatrice told her. At first his telephone calls to Beatrice worried Lindsey. She was afraid that they were talking business and that Michael was pushing. One afternoon she came in on one of their conversations. Beatrice was laughing then gave some terse opinions of jazz. Hearing her grandmother's side of the conversation, Lindsey gathered they were discussing the city where Michael was at the moment—Charleston, Lindsey deduced. She tried not to listen, but not too hard. After all, she was right in the room.

"Michael's coming home Thursday," Beatrice said as she hung up.

"That's nice." Lindsey smiled blandly. She asked herself why she cared. Well, she was a normal female, and Michael Garrity was a very attractive man—nothing special or earth shaking about that.

Michael called her on Thursday afternoon. "How are you doing, Princess? Sounds like a good storm is underway down there." The line buzzed.

"Yes...just a noisy afternoon shower. I'm fine. Where are you calling from, Michael?"

"Charleston. I'll be home this evening. How about having dinner with me?"

Lindsey was too surprised for a moment to say anything.

"Lindsey? Are you there?" The line crackled softly.

"Yes...I don't think I can make dinner. I like to spend the evenings at the hospital." She didn't dare have dinner with him. Did she?

"I know. Beatrice mentioned it and thinks your getting out to dinner is a fine idea."

"Oh, she does. Are you trying to please her by attending to her granddaughter?" She knew the remark was uncalled for, yet she couldn't stop herself from saying it.

Silence hung on the line, angry silence. "If you think that, then you haven't looked in a mirror lately." He let out a breath. "Look, have dinner with me. We'll talk about anything but Ingraham's. You've been cooped up in the house and the hospital, and I've been working sixteen-hour-days up here. We'll have dinner and relax. I'll pick you up at seven."

"I haven't said yes."

"I'll still pick you up at seven."

Lindsey couldn't stop the smile that touched her lips. She wanted to say yes but hesitated, for some reason skirting the word. "Can you at least tell me where we're going? A woman likes to know how to dress."

"Put on your best bib and tucker, Princess. We'll dine at the finest. Great food and a view of the lights of the city."

"We might not see much if it's still raining."

"Okay, so we'll see blurry lights of the city. Remember—seven." The line clicked and he was gone, not giving her a chance for further comment.

Lindsey told Selda she'd be dining out and found it fit perfectly into the housekeeper's plans. "It's our group's card night," Selda said. "And I'm way behind my turn at hostessing. With Beatrice so ill, I've skipped having it here the last month, but now I think I can get right back into it, if it's all the same to you."

"Why, Selda, I hope you weren't thinking of skipping tonight because of me. My being here shouldn't change your plans in any way."

"Well, fine. I'll just get Sandy to drive me to the market for cold cuts. I pressed that slinky white gown you brought. Why don't you wear it? It'll knock Mr. Garrity's socks off."

Lindsey's eyes widened. "How did you know it was Michael Garrity?" Suspicion rose. "You weren't listening on the extension..."

"No, No!" Selda protested vehemently. "I'd never do that. You were in the hallway, and the kitchen door was open..."

Lindsey smiled wryly. "Yes, and you can hear quite easily—if you step to the door and cock your ear." She walked to the door then turned back. "In case you're interested, I'm now going to call Beatrice and tell her I won't be there tonight.... And for your information, I don't care about knocking Mr. Garrity's socks off." She left the room, chuckling as a dish towel came hurtling after her.

After her call to Beatrice, Lindsey took the white gown from the closet and considered it thoughtfully. She glanced at the rest of her dresses. It would have to be this one, no other would do. And Jay had thought she got carried away with her packing. She wished she'd brought her dusty-rose dress. It wasn't quite as...well, as sexy as the white one. Oh, well, the white one would have to do—and it would do very nicely, she admitted.

An unaccountable flicker of pleasure touched her spirit.

She took a leisurely bath, relishing the large tub with its comfortable slanted back. The oversize bathroom was designed for pampering; it was a pleasure just to look at, with its brass and ceramic handles, shining tiles, dusty-blue colors, and a skylight that provided natural light for humans and plants alike.

Lindsey relaxed, deliberately letting go of her concerns for Beatrice, the problems of Ingraham's, and all the other uncertainties life had brought her recently.

Moving about the bedroom, she mentally redecorated it with new furniture, new bed linens and drapes. The room with its dark oak and shades of burgundy, didn't fit her anymore. She wanted furniture with finer lines, and peaceful pale colors of blue and green. And a car, she'd really like to have a car of her own here.

She realized she was considering staying in Jacksonville for much longer than a few weeks. Uneasy at the thought, she turned her mind away, and it promptly conjured up the handsome image of Michael Garrity. Didn't she have any discipline at all? she scolded herself.

Pattering downstairs in her robe for a glass of tea, she found Selda coming in the back door with a bag of groceries.

"Let me help you." Lindsey took a bag, noticing the store's logo on its side. "Selda, you don't shop at Ingraham's?"

"Oh, sometimes, but I like these meats better," she answered absently, taking off her plastic raincap and shaking off raindrops into the sink. "Whew—I think it's going to clear, but it's sticky out there now."

Lindsey began putting the sandwich meats in the refrigerator. "What don't you like about Ingraham's?"

Selda shrugged. "Their luncheon meat, mostly. Their cooler doesn't seem to keep it fresh . . . or something. Does it matter, me not shopping there? I just thought it important to get the most for our money."

"I suppose that is important," Lindsey said slowly. "And I don't suppose it matters now, anyway."

"Are you going to sell the stores to Michael Garrity?"

Lindsey nodded. "We'll talk to Beatrice about it when she's stronger."

"Yes . . . I guess that's best," Selda said, her voice reflective.

Lindsey heard the doorbell just as she zipped up her dress. Six-fifty. Michael was early. A bit surprised, Lindsey found that her hands shook slightly. For heaven's sake, Lindsey, she scolded herself as she took a breath and allowed her hands to go limp.

She paused for one last check in the mirror, and what she saw gave her confidence: the cowl neck of the white gown rode high, draping softly across her breast, and the back dipped low to her waist, leaving her skin bare. The soft fabric flowed to the floor and clung to her curves. Her only jewelry were fiery opals set in gold that graced her ears and the fine gold chain she always wore around her neck.

Whatever Michael Garrity wanted from tonight, she'd be his match.

What did Michael want anyway? Did he simply want an enjoyable dinner, as he'd said, or was he seeking something bigger—a way to insure his deal for Ingraham's perhaps? Maybe this dinner was simply an extension of all the attention he'd been paying Beatrice.

Lindsey felt slightly guilty at her thoughts, but still, the questions lingered. She'd learned long ago that most people wanted something from her.

Determinedly she stepped to the dressing table for her purse. She would enjoy tonight and hopefully get some answers to all of this.

With light, rapid steps and a fluttering heartbeat, Lindsey descended the stairs and crossed the hall to the living room archway. Her gaze swept the room, stopping when it came upon a familiar head.

"Jay?" Her breath caught in the back of her throat as she quickly recognized the pale head of hair. He turned and grinned broadly, holding out his arms. At first her body wouldn't respond; then she was running into his embrace, hugging him hard.

He drew back and gazed down at her. "Now, that's a special greeting..."

"Oh, I see you've come down," Selda said from the entry. "I was just coming to tell you—had to check something on the stove first."

"That's all right, Selda. Mr. Fordham's an old friend." Selda nodded, and Lindsey's gaze swung back to Jay. He looked slightly rumpled in his pale crumpled slacks and a white cotton shirt. Dark circles rimmed his eyes. "What in the world are you doing here? I thought you'd be at the bay, spiffing up the boat by now."

His smile slipped. "Doesn't look like I'm going to sail, after all."

Lindsey searched his eyes. "Not sail?"

Jay's lopsided grin didn't reach his eyes. He drew back, stuffing his hands into his pockets. "Dad means it this time. He's cut me off completely. Even access to the boat. Says I need a job, need to learn responsibility. He's not going to give me another cent until I go to work."

"Oh." Lindsey searched his eyes, feeling terribly at a loss for words.

"I'm behind on the rent. They were going to kick me out, so I sublet the place to Mark Heath. He paid up what I owe." Jay shifted. "I . . . I drove down, didn't even stop, brought Herman and all the other green guys from your apartment. I didn't trust Mark to do the watering." He paused, and his next words came slowly. "Do you think I could stay here with them for a while?"

"Of course you can stay," Lindsey said quickly. "There's plenty of room here."

"Thanks, Lindsey. It'll only be until I can figure out what to do." He raked a hand through his hair. "I just need some time to get myself together. Go to work, he says." Jay gave a caustic laugh. "And do what? A college degree looks good on paper, but I still can't do anything." He looked every inch the small boy, trapped in a grown man's body.

Lindsey nodded, smiling gently. "It's okay, Jay." In that moment, somehow Lindsey saw that her life had turned. That she could never go back to the childish, even irresponsible life she'd lived before. She had changed. She was growing.

Relief washed across Jay's face. "Thanks." Reaching out, he hugged her to him, rather like a drowning man reaching for a lifeline. She could feel his strain, his need of support.

"Well, good evening. Hope I'm not interrupting anything." Michael's deep voice sounded across the room.

Breaking from Jay's arms, Lindsey whirled, coloring as she realized what the embrace must have looked like. Her instincts regarding his conclusions were confirmed when she met Michael's mocking gaze. He leaned against the door-frame, his arms crossed in front of him, steely eyes glittering, though a genial smile lit his lips.

Selda stood beside him, nervously wiping her apron through her hands. "I...Mr. Garrity..." she mumbled, her eyes moving from Lindsey to Jay.

"Thank you, Selda," Lindsey said. Selda hesitated then stepped away. "Hello, Michael." She tossed back her hair, coloring more as she watched Michael's gaze slowly skim the length of her dress. Though she realized it was silly to be feeling like an adolescent schoolgirl caught in an amorous embrace, it didn't remove the feeling. "Jay has just this minute got in. He drove down from New York."

Michael strode forward, extending his hand. "Good to see you, Fordham," he drawled slowly. "Rough trip down? It's raining halfway up the coast."

Jay accepted the handshake, though his cordial smile was reluctant. "It was okay."

Lindsey watched the two as they eyed each other. "Michael and I...we're going to dinner." Her voice sort of faded at the last, and the glance she sent to Jay was uncertain. His gaze flickered to Michael and back again, taking in her dress, realization dawning.

"Hey...go on. I don't want to horn in...."

"Good of you to take it like that, Fordham," Michael broke in before the words were hardly out of Jay's mouth. "I won't keep her out late."

Jay glared. Lindsey felt that if she needed to light a match she could just wave it in the air between them.

"I'll tell Selda you're staying, Jay," she said, retreating to the doorway. She needed a minute to catch her breath—or let it out. Rounding the archway of the living room into the hall, Lindsey ran smack into the wide girth of Selda, who'd obviously been eavesdropping.

Selda looked sheepish. With an accepting shake of the head, Lindsey silently drew Selda into the kitchen. In a few terse sentences she told the housekeeper that Jay Fordham was an old friend, would be staying for an indefinite time and to please see he had everything he needed for the evening. She left the kitchen, and the door swung several times in her wake. In the shadow of the hall outside the door, she leaned against the wall to catch that breath she needed and to collect her thoughts.

A repressed chuckle at the ridiculous situation shook her. Why, she'd actually felt embarrassed, caught... What in the world did she care what Michael thought of her relationship to Jay? She fumed in amused irritation at herself. It was absolutely none of his business whom she chose to be involved with. Straightening her shoulders, she strode back into the living room.

"I'm ready, Michael." With a gliding motion she retrieved her purse from the couch and moved to press her cheek close to Jay's. "I won't be late. We can talk if you're still awake." The words were for Michael's benefit, as well, but as soon as they were out, she regretted them. Why was she insisting on needling him? She glanced at him from under the shelter of her lashes. His face was impassive.

"I'll probably turn in," Jay said. "Good night."

"Good night..." Lindsey felt torn to be leaving him.

Michael's hand closed around her bare arm. It was warm. "Good night, Fordham. No doubt I'll be seeing you."

Jay said nothing.

The evening air was filled with gray, misty rain. Opening the car door under the cover of the portico, Michael nodded to Jay's small sports car, which was jam-packed.

"Looks like Jay has come to stay a while." He raised a questioning eyebrow.

"Yes, he's come to visit awhile," Lindsey said. His gray eyes studied her, but she didn't volunteer more, and he didn't ask.

He pulled the Mercedes smoothly into a parking garage, and parked at the rear near an elevator. Lindsey waited while he rounded the car to open her door then concentrated on slipping from the seat as gracefully as possible in the slim-fitting dress, knowing Michael's intense gaze was on her.

"You look very beautiful tonight." He gave his charming smile and reached for her hand.

It wasn't the words; Lindsey had heard them often enough in her life. It was the way Michael had said them and the look in his eyes. Or perhaps it was her reaction. She was glad he found her attractive, glad for the strong feel of his hand closed over hers.

"Thank you," she said softly, almost shyly.

Her suspicions rose when Michael inserted a key to open the elevator doors.

"Michael? Where are we going?"

"To dine on the best cuisine in town," he replied, guiding her into the elevator. "My apartment." The doors slid closed.

"Your apartment?" His incredible nerve astounded her. Pulling away from his touch, she stood looking at him, feeling the elevator rise. She should have known, she cursed herself. Michael Garrity was not to be trusted.

"Don't go looking at me like that, Princess. I have a wonderful view of the city and the best cook, as well. It will be quiet and relaxing."

He made it sound so plausible, even quite innocent, Lindsey thought. She really should turn around and go right back down again. But at that moment the elevator opened into a small entry hall. He placed a hand at the small of her back and lifted a questioning eyebrow. The light in his eyes softened, but he said not a word, letting her decide.

Hesitantly Lindsey stepped from the elevator then beyond the hall, her gaze scanning the low-lit apartment. She wasn't sure what she had expected to see...but this was very nice. It was small, very male, but comfortably so, and rather inviting. Oriental rugs graced polished oak, and two cushioned couches faced each other across a finely carved teakwood coffee table. An enormous recliner and lots of brass fixtures made the place cozy.

One wall was of plate-glass windows that framed the gray sky of the moment. Next to the windows was a small table covered with linen. In its center two tapered candles flickered. Soft music emanated from somewhere.

A grizzle-haired dark-skinned man appeared from the kitchen, smiling broadly.

"Lindsey, I'd like you to meet Elwin, my houseman, and the finest cook in all the city." If possible, the man's smile widened.

"Hello, Elwin."

"Good evening, Miss." He inclined his head slightly. "Would you both be wanting cocktails, or should I serve dinner?"

"Serve, Elwin. I'm starved," Michael told him. His hand warm against the small of her back, he led her to the windows. "See—a chaperon. Nothing to worry about."

Lindsey hid a slightly embarrassed smile. How silly of her. She was a woman in charge of herself. She didn't need a chaperon. What was she afraid of?

The view was indeed breathtaking, though the building was far from being the highest around. The windows faced east, giving a full view of the St. Johns River. The rain had stopped, and rays from the sun sinking to the west turned the thick clouds above to hues of violet and pink. Pale, dusty blue sky showed to the south.

"Look!" Lindsey pointed. "A rainbow!" Oh, how she loved them, and the view was perfect from here. For a minute, gazing at the magical, shifting colors, she forgot where she was, even forgot Michael. Then his head came very near, and she felt his breath on her neck.

"Come out on the terrace." He took her upper arm; her gaze met his. His crystal eyes twinkled with pure unadulterated joy.

He was enjoying the rainbow as much as she was, Lindsey thought as he hurried her outside. The knowledge swept across her like a breeze of pleasure, and she smiled broadly, turning her eyes back to the sight.

They stood quietly watching. Michael stood behind her, and his breath teased her hair. The humid air was still, as if resting after the storms of the afternoon.

"Look, over there," Michael whispered. And as they both seemed to hold their breaths, another arch formed, vibrating with color.

"A double," Lindsey breathed.

"Double pots of gold," Michael murmured.

They watched, neither of them moving, as the colors slowly shimmered and shifted, fading to shades of green and blue, then disappeared into the sky as magically as they had come.

"It's over," Lindsey said quietly.

"That's the beauty of them, the magic."

She breathed deeply. "I love the scent of rain. It makes everything smell fresh and new. You were right, this is a lovely view—oh look!" She pointed to the towering concrete building several blocks away. The sun's rays had painted it coral. "Isn't it beautiful?"

"Yes, it is." Michael's tone drew Lindsey's eyes to him. His gaze flowed in a gentle caress over her hair and across her face, settling on her eyes.

She looked back frankly. "Now, Mr. Garrity," she said after a moment, tossing her hair back. "I'm sure you've known your share of beautiful women." She truly couldn't imagine herself being any different from the string of women a man like Michael had obviously enjoyed. And for once, she had no patience with pretense.

His eyes narrowed as he studied her. "I've known a lot of women, Princess. But none quite like you." He let the statement sit there, almost as a challenge. "We'd better go in. Elwin has this dinner planned."

He left the sliding glass door open, and the scent of fresh, cool evening rain followed them into the room. He held her chair then took the one across from her. As if on cue, Elwin appeared with dishes of shrimp salad. "Would the lady care for white wine?" he asked.

Lindsey shook her head. "Just ice water, please."

Michael shot her a brief, puzzled look then poured himself some of the wine, while Elwin appeared smoothly with her water, as if he'd had it waiting.

"Your apartment—your building, as well?" Lindsey asked.

"Not exactly. I'm a partner on the investment in this building. It's a company apartment, but I'm the only one to have a need for it. Occasionally it's available to a business client, and I stay at my house out on Amelia Island."

She sipped her water. "Are your offices in this building?"

Michael smiled lazily. "All three of them—directly under this apartment. There's a private stairway in the hall, and the elevator will stop there too."

"I imagine one day you will have your own building."

"Oh, I intend to," Michael said in his slow Southern drawl. "Though I doubt very much if I'll need to expand my own office space."

Looking at him, Lindsey also had no doubt he would succeed in whatever he decided to do. "Obviously humility is not one of your character traits," she observed dryly.

"As a very wise man once said, modesty is a vastly overrated virtue."

His grin was warm—and catching. Lindsey had to smile, and it was at more than his teasing. It was with the man himself, the energy she felt between them. The light was fading fast outside. The candle flames reflected in the nearby window glass. Michael held her gaze, and the flames reflected in his eyes, too. But it wasn't their flickering that caused the warmth she saw gathering there. It was the flames that seemed to ignite between them.

Many men had taken her to dinner, with candlelight and soft music, in the most exotic and romantic places in the world, but no man had ever made Lindsey feel as she did at this moment. As if the only world was right there in that room, all that she could need or could want.

It confused her, made her feel out of control. And frightened, terribly frightened. Yet she was fascinated, as she'd never been in all her life.

But did Michael feel it? Was it all on her side? Was this magic real or simply a delicate mirage Michael had contrived to help pave the way to a business deal he very much wanted to go his way?

"You know quite a bit about me," Lindsey said as she picked at her shrimp. "You know my grandmother intimately, know the house where I grew up, even know Selda who made me eat my spinach. But I know nothing about you."

"And you think the story will be interesting."

"It's something to talk about, anyway," she teased.

"Okay—I'm a north Georgia boy, left there when I was eighteen to do a bit of college—and contrary to what a lot of poor country boys say, I do go home again, as often as I can."

"You were a poor boy?"

"No we were average. In material possessions, anyway," Michael allowed. He told of his family, his father who was a lumberman, his mother who sewed all their clothes and taught him to love electrical storms and rainbows. He was one of five children, a very close-knit family.

Lindsey enjoyed watching him as he spoke. He obviously adored his mother and respected his father a great deal. Through his tales she could almost see them.

Elwin came and went quietly, bringing and clearing dishes, bringing more, refilling Lindsey's water glass. "Michael did not exaggerate," she said to him when they'd finished. "You are truly an accomplished chef."

Elwin gave his broad grin. "Thank you, Ma'am. Would you care for an after-dinner liqueur?"

Lindsey shook her head. "Coffee would be fine."

"Elwin's coffee won't be any match for your own, I'm afraid," Michael whispered, leaning close as he led the way onto the terrace. His hand slid to her back, and his thumb caressed her bare skin. Lindsey found herself involuntarily leaning toward his firm frame, and she moved away.

The light of the city twinkled like sparkling diamonds. Together they enjoyed the view, neither of them feeling the need for words.

Elwin brought a tray onto the terrace.

"You don't drink, Lindsey?" Michael asked as he handed her the cup of coffee. Elwin had brought him a Scotch and soda.

"Occasionally." She leaned against the parapet of the terrace. "Usually only when I need its relaxing effects. My mother was an alcoholic. I saw enough of the effects of liquor to make me skeptical of imbibing too freely. I'm not one for cocktails at every turn."

"And what happened in your past to make you skeptical of me?" He leaned on the parapet, watching her closely. The light from the living room illuminated one side of his handsome face, shadowing the other.

Lindsey gave a wry smile. "Some analyst would say it's a classic case: a brief affair in which I thought a man loved me deeply. But when I defied my grandmother, broke with her to run away with him, I discovered that what he had really wanted all along was to be manager of Ingraham's."

Michael didn't raise an eyebrow, didn't nod in condescending agreement, didn't say anything, just listened, his shoulders relaxed.

"That did happen," Lindsey said with a mild sigh. "But it was a long time ago. And I don't think I loved him. It was another form of rebellion." She raked at her hair. "I was born with a healthy skepticism. It's kept me asking questions. And I was born the granddaughter of an Ingraham—Beatrice and Thomas Ingraham, who were quite wealthy and influential in their day. It seems all my life people have wanted something from me: my mother always wanted me to make up for my father cheating on her and then dying, leaving her alone. Beatrice and Thomas wanted me to be a business whiz and to toe the line, schoolmates wanted friendship because of who I was, not just for me. Plenty of people want money, and men..." She smiled slightly, letting the innuendo stand.

Slowly Michael straightened. "Lindsey, I want Ingraham's. I won't lie about it. I need it. But I'm not a ruthless character stepping on people to get where I am—and I don't intend to start now. I'll do what I can to get Ingraham's, but I choose my methods. And they don't include intentionally hurting Beatrice, or using you."

With measured motion, his eyes on hers, he took the cup from her hand and set it beside his glass on the parapet. The palm of his hand stroked her cheek, and Lindsey couldn't move, didn't want to. She closed her eyes, pressing her face into the pleasurable roughness of his hand.

"This..." Michael brushed his lips to hers. Her breath caught in the back of her throat. Oh, Lord, how she wanted his kiss. He drew back and nibbled her lips seductively, as he cupped her cheeks in his hands. "This is the desire of a man for a beautiful woman. Nothing else involved."

Then his mouth closed over hers, massaging her lips apart. He stroked within with his tongue. His hands slipped downward, encircling her, burning enticingly as they kneaded her bare back. Blood pounded in her ears, and heat churned and boiled in a single instant, deep within her stomach, then flowed throughout her body. She melted into his strong frame, as if he sapped her strength, her very life.

Michael, oh Michael, her mind called. *Love me.*

He was crushing her, taking her breath, his kiss turning to a heated demand for fulfillment. The muscles of his shoulders beneath his shirt rippled as her hands stroked back and forth. Breaking his lips from hers, he kissed a trail across her cheek and down the sensitive length of her neck.

She savored it, her mind reeling, her body luxuriating in the wondrous sensations. More...how she wanted more...

No . . . No! Her brain countered as the sensations rose with such force that they frightened her. She wasn't in control any longer. Almost before she realized her actions, she struggled, pushing at his chest.

Lord, she was so confused. She buried her face below his neck, her body trembling into his. Tightly he held her, rubbing his cheek against her hair, and after a few seconds Lindsey realized his breath came as raggedly as her own.

She couldn't look at him, couldn't stand to see the desire she knew would burn in those wonderful, magical gray eyes, eyes that could be so tender one minute, so measuring the next, eyes that saw into her soul at times.

She'd never felt so overwhelmed. How could this be happening to her? She was always in control, she'd never... The thoughts whirled as Lindsey tried desperately to slow her breath, to make some sense of her thoughts.

The desire, Michael had said, of a man for a beautiful woman. Nothing else. The words stabbed her heart.

Many men had desired Lindsey; it was as natural and as inevitable as the sunrise. But it wasn't what Lindsey had always longed after, dreamed of, since she was a child. Someone to love her. Her, just as she was. Lindsey wanted that something else. She wanted love—though she wasn't sure the elusive dream even existed. And a whispering within told her she wanted Michael to love her, as she never had any other man.

Unable to face the thought that would mean a weakness she didn't feel capable of dealing with, she shied away, burying it deep within the recesses of her mind.

Slowly she broke from his embrace, still not daring to look at him. "I'm . . . I'm not ready for this, Michael," she stammered. Her body betrayed her by trembling, as every cell in her longed to press against his hard frame again. If he touched her, she'd melt into his arms, and she knew she couldn't stop—not at all.

How could he have done this to her? No other man had ever made her feel this way—so lost, so powerless. And she couldn't bear to have him know.

But when he reached out and turned her face to the light, she knew the knowledge was written plainly in her eyes: the fear, the wonder, the confusion.

Her shaking shoulders tore at his heart. He was shaking himself. Gathering a measure of control, Michael reached out and turned her face toward him. Gently he brushed the golden strands of her hair aside.

The light shifted in her diamond-studded blue eyes. Damn, he wanted her. He could read the answering desire in her eyes. All he had to do was pull her to him, but he saw the fear and powerful doubt written there, as well. The knowledge stopped him.

He took a deep breath; it came out raggedly. Her cheek was soft beneath his fingers. "I don't think either of us is ready, Princess," he said, feeling the cooling control flow over his body. Relief reflected in her delicate features.

The fact that he wasn't ready any more than she was surprised the hell out of him. But it was true. If it could have been just a casual affair, he'd have her in his bed this very moment. But it wouldn't be casual between them. Michael knew that.

And when the time was right—for them both—it would be an experience worth waiting for. And at that moment Michael had no doubt the right time would come.

Holding out his arm, he gave a coaxing grin. "Come in and tell me about this insane guy who only wanted to be manager of Ingraham's."

It took her a minute; then she laughed, a delightful sound. Taking his arm, she cast him a doubtful look. "You mean you want to talk?"

"Yes." He led her to the couch. "I think we need to get to know each other."

She regarded him thoughtfully. "You are definitely one of a kind, Michael Garrity." She settled gracefully into the corner and tucked her legs under her. "Not all men are interested in talk."

"I don't imagine they are, but then, they're the losers." He eyed her carefully. "But don't be mistaken, Princess— someday you and I will get to the other stuff." Not waiting for a reply, he moved toward the kitchen. "In case you haven't noticed, we've lost our chaperon. I'll get our coffee."

They talked leisurely, with no thought of time, going through an entire pot of coffee. Michael saw the real Lindsey, as slowly, even hesitantly, her sophisticated facade softened. She was as fresh as the first rays of sun touching the beach. Michael would have been less than honest with himself if he said he wasn't surprised. And he was further impressed to realize that beneath that beautiful blond hair was a sharp brain.

Lindsey Ryland was an extremely intelligent woman, quick of wit, possessing a down-to-earth though perhaps slightly off-beat way of looking at life. She saw herself quite clearly, talking of her early introverted nature that had turned to rebellion then to acceptance. Her life hadn't been any picnic, but she hadn't turned resentful or bitter. She'd picked out the best of it and concentrated on that.

She also had a way of getting him to talk about himself. Before he realized it, he was telling her his big dreams of the future, dreams he'd never spoken aloud before. When he realized he'd been rambling on about ideas that had to sound ridiculously out of this world, he stopped, feeling embarrassed.

"Well, that's all far into the future," he said.

"Yes, but you have to dream it now, or it will never happen," she answered practically, apparently oblivious to his discomfiture, or else ignoring it.

It was nearly two o'clock in the morning when Michael walked her up the steps of Ingraham House. He pulled her to him and kissed her, savoring her lips, the response of her body, and mentally imagining the curves of her feminine form beneath the thin gown. By feel, he knew all she wore underneath was panty hose.

Showing real restraint, he kept the kiss light and released her quickly. Her eyes were wide against her face in the pale lamplight.

"Lindsey," he said huskily. "There's something between us, something you can't deny—and it's not just sex." Once more he brushed his lips against the silkiness of hers. "Or Ingraham's." He backed down a step, looking up at her. "Don't forget that. No matter what doubts crowd in."

As he drove home through the quiet early-morning streets, Michael knew he was falling in love with Lindsey Ryland.

He began whistling. Things were looking up. Plans were rolling along with his grocery chain, Beatrice was growing stronger every day, soon he'd close the deal on Ingraham's, and there'd be no more distractions between him and Lindsey.

Chapter Six

Beatrice came home Monday. It took Lindsey somewhat by surprise and pointed clearly to the fact that she couldn't put off talking about Ingraham's much longer.

Regal as a queen, her hair brushed into its customary lustrous swirl atop her head, Beatrice once more ruled the house from her wide four-poster. Her complexion glowed, her faded blue eyes twinkled, and indeed, it was hard to believe she'd ever been near death's door at all.

Tomorrow. I'll talk to her about it tomorrow, Lindsey thought, watching her. Though she was fully aware she'd been promising herself that for the past week.

Beatrice's homecoming was a grand occasion calling for celebration. Lindsey, Michael, Jay and Selda, along with the private nurse who would attend Beatrice during the day and see to her recovery therapy, ringed the bed in the spacious, elegant bedroom.

Michael ceremoniously poured brandy for them all, a scant glass for Beatrice. She gave the amber liquid a scornful look then held it up to him, raising an eyebrow, commanding without a word. Smiling, Michael easily poured a bit more into her glass. The nurse frowned.

"To you, Duchess," Michael said, raising his glass. They all followed suit, calling a salute in unison. For a moment Michael's gaze rested on Lindsey, and his eyes held a secret warmth meant just for her.

Lindsey smiled slightly, and the sweet memories of his kisses, his hand stroking her skin flitted around her mind, as they had invariably in the past few days. Feeling her face flush, she averted her eyes.

Beatrice sipped her drink, savoring it. "You never did bring me my brandy in the hospital, Michael," she complained.

"I failed you, Duchess, and I'm heartily sorry. But those nurses had eagle eyes." He bent to kiss her cheek. "And now I have to run. I have a plane to catch. I'll call." He surprised Lindsey by reaching for her hand. "Let me steal your granddaughter to see me out."

His hand remained tight on hers. He gave her no time for protest, and as they stepped from the bedroom, Lindsey was fully conscious of Beatrice's and Selda's curiosity and Jay's scowl.

Michael leaned on the open door of his car, studying her. "I'm sorry about our dinner date, but I have to make this trip." There was a problem with several of the stores he'd recently purchased, and he'd been called to Pittsburgh just that morning.

"It's fine, Michael." A bit of her disappointment showed through, but she no longer tried to hide it. She returned his studying gaze then slowly reached up to trace his lips with her finger. Pressing toward him, she kissed him. And though the motion was swift, her lips touching his for the briefest of moments, heat gathered and flowed through her veins, sending her heart pounding.

"I'll make up that dinner when I get back, Princess," Michael said huskily, his eyes promising more, much more.

Lindsey smiled, feeling every inch a woman, and glad of it.

He touched her hair then slipped into his car. With one last wave he was gone.

Lindsey didn't stand to watch his car. She turned and walked back into the house, trying to still the betraying throb of her body. She'd awakened Friday morning with a smile—and had known it was because of Michael. She'd tried, truly she had, to erase the memories, but it seemed every cell in her body had recorded the sweet sensations and longed for fulfillment, clamoring harder every time she saw him.

Closing the front door, she leaned against it, enjoying the cooler air of the interior.

Since their dinner Thursday evening, Michael had sent her roses, taken her to lunch at the beach and called several times a day. She'd learned that he loved fishing, soccer, pretzels and beer. And the exciting challenge of high-stakes business. Failing rarely entered his mind. He put his thoughts where they would do the most good, he said, on what he wanted, on winning.

He discussed the deal for Ingraham's with her, treating her not only as a woman but as an equal—well, almost equal. He had his moments when his chauvinist side came out.

They'd worked out a deal that Lindsey felt was more than satisfactory for Beatrice, as well as for all the employees of Ingraham's.

Now all she had to do was get her grandmother to agree, Lindsey thought. But what would happen to her relationship with Michael after the takeover? she wondered.

Her doubt about Michael's motives still plagued her, but she pushed it aside for now.

Lindsey had come to the bold decision that the next time they were alone together, she would be in his arms, in his bed. How wonderful it would be to feel him touch her again as he had that night, feel his gentleness and his strength.

Involuntarily her mind pictured what his body would look like, pictured her lying next to him.

Though they'd been together often over the past days, Michael had not touched her, as if he were afraid of frightening Lindsey away.

She smiled. Yes, he'd kept his hands off, but often with a word or a look, his more carnal thoughts came through. He never let her forget that he found her attractive. And the compliments pleased her, as they would any woman.

The energy had flowed, unmistakably, between them. More than once Lindsey had felt Michael lean close as if to kiss her, but he hadn't. And she hadn't. They each wanted to give the other time. She knew very well she was opening herself up for heartbreak. Michael Garrity was a hard-driving man who meant to build an empire. Even if he did care for her, there would be scant room in his life for any sort of permanent relationship. Once he had Ingraham's, Lindsey wasn't sure how long his interest in her would last.

But this was something she'd waited half her life for. Michael Garrity made her feel as no other man ever had. Quite simply—she'd fallen in love with him, and had decided to give in to this puzzling, frightening, wonderful thing called love. She would take what she could get and worry about regrets later.

And she'd never let him know how she felt. She'd never let him know that the only man in her life had been six years ago, the man who'd wanted only Ingraham's, not her love.

The next day had come and gone, and still Lindsey skirted the matter of Ingraham's. Beatrice was doing so well. Lindsey didn't want to risk a relapse.

Coward, she scolded herself. Upsetting Beatrice wasn't her only concern. She wasn't at all sure she could be strong enough to bring her grandmother to the right decision. What in the world would she say if Beatrice simply refused?

Jay was another concern. He slept until noon and was drinking far too much. Thankfully, he and Beatrice had hit it off. They enjoyed playing chess for hours in the afternoon, and often Jay played cards with Selda at night. He rarely went anywhere. He didn't need to, Lindsey thought wryly. Everything, even the cigarettes he had taken to indulging in lately, were provided right there in Ingraham House.

"What are you going to do about Jay?" Beatrice asked over breakfast. It was early for Lindsey, eight o'clock, but she liked the quiet hours with her grandmother.

"About him?"

"Yes. He's wasting himself, drowning in self-pity." Apparently Jay had explained why he was there. "He's a fine boy, and it's time he became a man. For his own good, you may have to force him out of this nest, Granddaughter. That's all his father is trying to do." Beatrice leveled a questioning gaze at Lindsey.

Lindsey smiled slightly. "Like you did me, Grandmother?"

Beatrice nodded. "I suppose it's much the same."

"I do need to talk to him." Lindsey brushed the hair from her face. "But I thought I'd give him time."

"Umm..." Beatrice sipped her tea. "You made this, didn't you? Damned good. You'll have to teach Selda." Her gaze settled thoughtfully on Lindsey, and Lindsey sensed that something she didn't want to hear was coming. "Speaking of time...it's time we discussed Ingraham's. You've only been down there once, Granddaughter. I think..."

Beatrice's words were interrupted by Selda bustling into the room. "Mail's come." Handing several envelopes to Beatrice, she began scolding her about not eating enough.

"I've been ill, not totally senile," Beatrice broke into the housekeeper's lecture. Selda stopped. "I will decide how much I wish to eat. Now do bring more tea. I'd like to enjoy one more cup over my reading before that nurse gets here with her infernal therapy.'' Selda nodded, murmuring under her breath.

Lindsey brushed a kiss across Beatrice's cheek. "It's so good to see you being your old self again, Grandmother.'' Beatrice eyed her speculatively, and Lindsey knew she was thinking about their interrupted conversation. "We'll talk later," she promised.

She studied Beatrice carefully the rest of the day and decided the time had definitely come. Beatrice was stronger now, did her therapy amazingly well. Her mind was sharper than it had been in months.

That afternoon Lindsey sat at Beatrice's desk in the small library, meticulously putting together a presentation of all the facts. If she were to win Beatrice over, she'd have to be totally prepared with every small detail of the deal that she and Michael had worked up.

She hadn't realized how involved she'd already become in the running of the house, as well as Ingraham's. Selda consulted her each morning about menus, various maintenance jobs, bills, and Robert called daily, discussing the smallest of things that he couldn't seem to decide on. Finally Lindsey learned that Beatrice had referred him to her. Lindsey generally made the decision and prayed it was right. Good heaven's, she didn't know what she was doing, but at least it was movement.

One of the latest problems was not so small, however. Cash was extremely low, and the partial loan payment loomed as the months passed. Where was the money to come from?

The telephone rang, but she ignored it and gave a sigh, thinking that she would discuss the sale with Beatrice and get her approval. Then everything would be set for Michael to take over—and it would be all his headache.

A knock sounded at the door. Jay stood there, the fine stubble of a day-old beard upon his cheeks, his hair ruffled. "The telephone's for you," he said. "Michael Garrity." His eyes were lusterless, though a half smile crooked his lips as he turned away.

Reaching for the phone, Lindsey made a mental note: it was time she spoke to Jay, too.

"Michael?" She couldn't keep the breathless sound from her voice.

"Hello, Princess. Fordham sounded a bit tired. Has he been working too hard?"

Lindsey frowned at the dig but remained quiet. She had no answer.

"How about that dinner tomorrow night?" Michael's voice turned husky. "I'll be home by then—we'll go out to the beach house."

Lindsey's heart picked up a fast tempo. "I'd like that," she answered slowly. Even in that split second, her mind pictured his steel-gray eyes and the way they could warm her with just one look. "Michael...I'm going to speak to Beatrice about the sale of Ingraham's tomorrow."

The line was quiet for a minute. "I'm not pushing, Lindsey," Michael said. "You decide when you think she's ready."

"I know...Beatrice is doing very well. We must go ahead and do something. We're having cash problems again."

"Okay, look—" she could practically see Michael rubbing at the back of his neck "—I'll be more than glad to get on with our deal—everything's set up, can go over in a matter of days. But if anything changes, if you think Beatrice should wait, I'll lend Ingraham's the money to tide them over. After all, I'm a stockholder."

"Okay, Michael." Relief washed over her. Michael would help her handle it.

"See you tomorrow."

Lindsey's heart tugged. Did she dare risk believing that Michael could be in love with her, as well?

Replacing the receiver, Michael stared at it, lost in thought. He'd studied the report Ty had done for him on

Lindsey, and had read between the lines of facts: dates, times, incidents. He knew Lindsey still doubted him, and now he understood why. Her life had been relatively lacking in real love, the kind that offers itself and asks for nothing in return, except to be allowed the simple act of loving. He surmised that although Beatrice and Thomas had tried they'd had neither the time nor the skill to deal with Lindsey's problems by the time she came to live with them full-time.

For all her wealth, Lindsey had had a bare childhood. Thinking of his own family and childhood, Michael found it hard to comprehend.

He also found it hard to comprehend her relationship with Jay. It rankled—he was jealous, he admitted, hating what he saw as a weakness. According to the report, Jay and Lindsey had spent a lot of time together. Friends, they said. Lovers, many people intimated.

Friends? Michael had never had that sort of relationship with a woman. Indeed, most of them wanted to be in his bed or to share his name—preferably both.

He rubbed at his chin, remembering Lindsey's silken hair, her captivating eyes. Michael didn't like Jay in the house with Lindsey.

Hell, it had been hard during those days they'd spent together to have her so near, catch the scent of her perfume and not touch her. But he intended to convince her of his feelings before making any more moves. She was coming around. He could see it, feel it as instinctively as he did when a deal was going right.

He loved her, and she was beginning to believe it. And he'd keep on doing whatever it took to convince her. It would be easier, he thought with great satisfaction, when the takeover of Ingraham's was completed.

It occurred to him to wonder, honestly, how much the deal with Ingraham's was tied to his feelings for Lindsey. Irritated at the thought, Michael tossed it aside.

"Ty!" he called, walking through the suite of hotel rooms that was serving as a makeshift office. "Find us some pretzels and drinks. And where are the cost-projection reports? Let's hustle it up."

Tomorrow he intended to be at the beach house; he intended to have Lindsey Ryland in his arms.

"And out of Fordham's reach," he murmured aloud.

Lindsey sat with Jay on the patio after dinner. Beatrice was surrounded by books on her bed upstairs, books dealing with heart disease, diet and health. She was avidly reading out of several at once. A determination to aid her own recovery had sprung up strongly within her. Lindsey was greatly pleased, truly believing that Beatrice was to be with her a long time now. Selda had gone to a friend's for a game of poker. Apparently Selda had quite a gambler's streak in her; thankfully, the games were kept to nickles and dimes.

It was dusk; the crickets and cicadas began their nightly serenade. Lindsey tried to let her mind rest.

"You're pretty involved with Garrity, aren't you?" Jay said.

"Uh-mm." Lindsey wasn't sure how to answer, or even if she wanted to. "Yes, I suppose I am."

"It's serious this time, isn't it?" He didn't look at her.

Lindsey thought for a moment. "It's more serious than I've felt in many years. How serious that is, I'm not sure...Jay...it doesn't change our friendship." Jay was so quiet that Lindsey turned to study him. "Jay?"

"Did it ever occur to you, Lindsey, that I might be interested in more than friendship?"

Lindsey drew in a breath. "Yes."

"Have you ever been?"

"I've thought about it, yes." She struggled for the words. "Our relationship is special Jay, but it is friendship—a very dear friendship. We could never make it any different."

Jay let out a ragged breath. "I know it. But I'm damn jealous of you and Garrity—and the crazy part is, I'm not sure why!'' He tried for the old charming smile. ''I'm not in love with you. Crazy maybe, but I'm not. But I envy you and Garrity and what you have going at this moment.'' He laced his fingers through hers. ''And you, Lindsey. You have something now...some place...some place in life. I'm so messed up, that I don't know whether I'm coming or going.'' Leaning his head back, he looked off into the sky. ''I think I knew that morning—the morning you were packing to leave—that our lives were changing. That you'd never be coming back.''

She looked at him sharply. ''I haven't said that. My apartment is still there.''

''Is it?''

A cold shiver shook her. Something within her spoke of the truth in his words—and that she'd sensed it that morning weeks ago, as well. Yes, her life had turned. And she didn't know where she was headed. Pushing her hair from her face, she forced the thoughts aside.

Her chest constricted as she glanced to Jay. He looked so lost. What could she say to him? She certainly wasn't about to start in on him about shaping up at that moment.

''Jay, have you thought of going to your father...maybe going to work for him?''

He nodded. ''But we'd be in a fight within twenty-four hours. He wants me to have ideas, to make something of myself—but his way.''

She gripped his hand. ''It'll come out all right. Give it time—and you're more than welcome here until you figure it out. We love having you.''

''Yep,'' he said, giving a sarcastic grin. ''Everyone loves old Jay.'' His gaze moved sadly to the river.

It was afternoon. Beatrice's therapy was finished for the day. She'd napped and was reading quietly. Selda mixed a cake in the kitchen and watched television instruction on card games. Jay had gotten up early and gone somewhere, mysteriously telling no one.

Tomorrow had come. There was no getting around it. And once she started, Lindsey was glad she was getting it over with.

She laid it all on the line. She didn't need to do any exaggerating; Ingraham's was on the verge of bankruptcy. Even she, with all her inexperience, could see it. Michael's offer looked magnificent next to the alternative. It was quite a bit better than what he had first offered. Lindsey found a bit of pride in that and hoped Beatrice would, too.

Beatrice listened. She didn't say a word. She even studied with care the fact sheets Lindsey presented to her. But absolutely nothing showed on her face, no emotion whatsoever. The most Lindsey observed was a narrowing around the eyes as she listened. Lindsey could practically see a thinking process taking place, but what sort, she had no idea.

"And Grandmother," Lindsey said, her voice softening as her eyes sought some response from Beatrice. "I've decided to stay down here quite a bit longer. If you'll have me. Why, we could even take a cruise down to the islands." She waved her hand. "We could cruise around the world, if you'd like. There's time now—and with Michael's deal, you'll have the money."

Then there was nothing more to say. Lindsey waited.

Light from outside filtered through the curtains and dusted the room a bright rose. Beatrice's white hair shone like a crown and her head was erect, her chin slightly elevated, as was her habit. She looked at Lindsey for a long moment, her pale blue eyes making a critical study.

Lindsey felt a kinship with her in that moment, more than she ever had in her life. Why, I have her eyes, she thought. And I do that with my chin. I must be very close to being a carbon copy of Beatrice in her youth. How strange I've never noticed before.

She could see how hard it must be for Beatrice; her body growing older, but not the soul, not the inner person, made up of emotions, love, hates, desires, compulsions.

Beatrice's voice broke through her thoughts. "Lindsey, I don't want to sell," she said calmly.

The words sat heavy upon Lindsey's shoulders. Looking down, she placed a hand upon Beatrice's, fingering the heavy gold of her rings without even seeing them. What more could she say? Was she going to be forced into taking it all from Beatrice's hands? Oh, Lord, she didn't think she could. She simply couldn't do that to Beatrice.

"I know that, Grandma," Lindsey said, still looking down. Slowly she raised her eyes pleadingly to Beatrice. "But there is nothing else we can do. Think—think about what will happen if we don't. Then think about it if we do. It's much better. *We* not *You.* It had slipped out. It was how she felt, and she'd not even noticed.

"I am thinking, Granddaughter." Beatrice inclined her head. Her lips twitched into a smile of remembrance. "I'm thinking of when Thomas began the chain. Oh, the produce business was good to us—but not enough for him. He always wanted a new challenge—and I did, too," she admitted, her smile widening briefly. "So we went out on a thin, mighty thin, limb. Seeking capital, we mortgaged everything we owned and asked many people we knew to buy into our company. We worked, we built. And the time we had! I'm not sure I've ever felt as alive before or since those early years."

Beatrice's eyes danced with the memories. Then her gaze fell once more upon Lindsey. "I want that again. I want to share it with you."

"But I don't know anything about the grocery business!" Lindsey rose in exasperation. "I don't know anything about any business."

Beatrice turned cool. "How have you managed to live so well on the small trust Thomas left you? I've heard you've invested."

Lindsey, looking out the window, gave a wave of impatience. "I've had advice. And the investing was never serious. It never mattered. It was only my money at stake." She faced Beatrice forcefully. "We're talking here about many other people than just you and me. There are lots of people out there who need the jobs Ingraham's stores provide."

"So you've had advice in investments. There—you've learned something," Beatrice countered. "And I know those people depend on Ingraham's. If we can improve Ingraham's, they'll do better."

"And what about Michael, Grandmother? You know how much he wants and needs Ingraham's. You know what he can do with it. I thought he was your friend."

Beatrice regarded her. "How much does Michael enter into this with you?"

"Grandmother, it will hurt him. Don't you care?"

"Of course I care! Very, very much. And if this were a decision that would affect him in any way other than business, I would think again. But Michael is an extremely astute businessman. He will survive—and I venture to say quite nicely." Her eyes sharpened. "Do you think you need this deal with Ingraham's to buy him like you did Claud...or Clyde...or whatever that nincompoop's name was?" Her rings sparkled as her hand waved in the air.

Anger flashed hot in Lindsey like a poker fresh from the flames. "*No...I...do...not!* And his name was Clark...Cliff...oh, it doesn't matter!" Oh, she was angry, feeling foolish at not even remembering the man's name, and totally at a loss as to what to do about the whole impossible situation. Stalking from the window, she crossed her arms in front of her, then turned sharply to face Beatrice.

Beatrice simply looked back, her blue eyes cold with anger. Then her lips twitched, and laughter slipped into her eyes. Watching, the absurdity of it all dawned on Lindsey, and she started to grin. She threw up her hands. "I don't remember his name!"

They laughed hard, clearing the air. Again Lindsey sat on the side of the bed and took Beatrice's hand. "What do you want to do, Grandmother?"

"I want us to run Ingraham's—you and me," Beatrice said crisply. "I want to turn that company around, make it glow again." Her voice softened. "I let things go. Without Thomas to share it with, it wasn't the same. And then you left ... Now, now," she said, silencing Lindsey's attempted protest. "It wasn't your fault. I just realized then that the company wasn't enough, that I also needed those I love. But I was too damned proud to admit it."

Her voice turned businesslike again. "So you're here now. I want to share the excitement of the challenge with you. And we can do it. I know we can."

Lindsey deliberated, trying to keep an open mind but seeing all the hazards. "But what if we fail, Grandma?"

"Honey, it's not the winning or losing—it's the challenge." She waved her hand. "We won't fail, anyway."

"And what do you propose to use for money? I certainly don't have it, and you're not winning any prizes at the bank anymore."

"Details. Details. Are you game or not?" Beatrice's voice turned cajoling. "I'm old, Lindsey. I want to live again. Now. With you. It's my last chance."

Hugging her elbows, Lindsey walked to the window again. She squinted. Even though the light was filtered, it was bright. Her gaze flowed down the rough bark of the tree, across the lawn, lit on a squirrel then moved to the vivid pink crepe myrtle.

Her thoughts went in circles as she tried very hard to be practical. Perhaps practicality had never been her strong suit. She obviously wasn't getting anywhere as she desperately tried to sort it all out.

She needed to choose the lesser of all the evils in this situation. But what was that? She didn't want to tell Michael. *Oh, Lord, she didn't want to tell Michael.* He was counting on this deal.

And what would happen to their relationship? The thought stabbed her like a knife and at the same time raised

Lindsey's ire. If Ingraham's was all they had between them, she'd face it now.

She had to think of herself, though. Good grief! She didn't want to get involved. She'd have to get up early in the morning, for one thing—what a horrible thought. And so many people would be depending on her. So many decisions she wasn't in the least equipped to make. Images, the image of her apartment, leisurely brunch on the terrace, afternoon shopping sprees, dinners, going to the theater with friends, flitted across her mind. They tugged at her.

Beatrice. She couldn't get around what she felt for her.

Ingraham's. A whole company. Nothing like going to the top.

The gamble. The challenge. Her blood stirred faintly.

She decided with her heart, her feelings, her instincts. To hell with practicality. It made you feel old. Was that what Beatrice was trying to tell her?

She turned from the window. Beatrice looked quite relaxed, resplendent, in fact, waiting calmly. What style she had, Lindsey thought even at that moment. What a gambler she was.

"Okay, Grandma. We'll give it a try," she said, giving a crooked grin. Her heart soared for three wonderful seconds. What a challenge! Beatrice had made her believe they could do it.

Then she thought of Michael, and her spirits plummeted like a lead balloon. She'd have to tell him. Tonight. He was coming for her tonight.

Beatrice was digging into her nightstand, pulling out papers. Lindsey watched her, but didn't really see what she was about. Her thoughts were in turmoil. She was thinking of Michael, and her body longed for him, yet she was fearful.

Beatrice shook the papers at her, pointing. Lindsey blinked and tried to listen. "I have some ideas," Beatrice said. "I've been jotting these down. I've talked to Robert quite a bit—and Ivy. Isn't she a wonder?" Her eyes danced. "Now, take a look at these figures..."

"You've been talking to Robert...?" Lindsey's gaze flew over the papers. "You've been doing all this? You started this in the hospital, didn't you?" she accused.

"Well, I had to do something. This bed rest is boring. Now listen."

Lindsey tried to listen and did actually comprehend some of what Beatrice said, but her mind repeatedly returned to Michael. How would he react?

It was a minute before Lindsey realized that Beatrice was gathering up the papers. "We can talk about this tomorrow," she said. She looked at Lindsey thoughtfully. "How deep is this thing with Michael? Have you been intimate with him?"

Lindsey colored, but faced her. "No." She paused. "But I want to. I care for him, Grandma. He's...he's like no man I've ever met." Her eyes narrowed. "Did you plan this...set us up?"

"No, Granddaughter. The possibility did occur to me, and I even admit to wishing a bit. I'm very fond of Michael. But I feel these things are better left to the angels. I can manipulate a company, not people's lives."

You're doing pretty well at the moment, Lindsey thought, but withheld the comment. She, and only she, had made the decision to go along with Beatrice. She could have said no, and was well aware of it.

"If you care for him, and he for you, any plans for Ingraham's shouldn't make a difference," Beatrice said.

Lindsey nodded. "I know."

"But you're wondering?"

"Yes." The answer brought pain.

"I...I think you've found a man in Michael. A very rare man."

"We'll see—tonight. We have a dinner date."

"Would you like me to tell him? After all, it's my decision to change the plans."

"Not totally, Grandma," Lindsey reminded her gently. "As I remember, we're partners.... I'll tell him. I must."

Beatrice reached up and tucked a stray hair behind Lindsey's ear. "I love you, Granddaughter."

"I love you, Grandma."

At the door, Lindsey paused to look back. "Oh, the nincompoop's name was Clarence."

Beatrice looked skeptical. "Are you sure?"

Lindsey thought about it. "No," she said with a grin.

Lindsey took a long bath, liberally laced with perfume. Michael called while she was still in the tub. She spoke to him, and her voice was normal, though perhaps restrained. He'd made it home and would pick her up around six-thirty. He sounded charged, animated, and there was no missing the hint of his thoughts for the night. His trip had gone well; he'd tell her all about it tonight.

"Wear something for ocean breezes," he cautioned, then as usual, without a goodbye, the line clicked.

She dressed, moving automatically, strangely feeling very little as she erected a protective shell. She chose a pale-apricot sundress, recently purchased. It complimented her skin tone and hair color and felt smooth against her body. Almost automatically, she applied makeup and fixed her hair. The light above the mirror seemed harsh to her face. Or was it that her face was lined with strain?

When he arrived, she was in the back, leaning against the bulwark and watching the placid river.

"Hi, Princess." His voice startled her. She hadn't heard him approach.

She looked up into his gray eyes, which danced mischievously. The next instant his strong arms swept her to him, and he pressed his lips to hers.

For a fraction of a second, she stiffened. Then eagerly she kissed him in return, savoring the sensations of desire that ignited and flowed throughout her body. His kiss deepened, forceful and demanding, until Lindsey's head swam. His hands stroked downward over the bare skin of her back, forcing her close to him. His firmness pressed against her.

At the action her legs went weak, causing her to lean against him, to take his strength then give it back.

She grasped that precious moment, forgetting all the doubts, letting the problems swirl away with the river current. Michael held her and desired her. Her heart embraced the emotions, the sensations.

Michael lifted his head but continued to hold her against him, pressing against her. It was so good. She couldn't get her breath, clear her head. But she didn't want to. She wanted to hold the magic for as long as she could.

"That was a hell of a kiss, Princess." Michael's words were ragged, and his breathing uneven. "Did you actually miss me?"

She stroked his cheek in answer, looking up at him, her vision foggy. His eyes were beautiful, sparkling with life, the evening sunlight crystalizing their varying shades of gray. His gaze flowed over her face warmly, betraying his wonder. Or was it simply a reflection of her own marveling?

Abruptly he pushed her from him, slipping his hand in hers and giving a regretful sigh. "For propriety's sake, I need some room. I certainly can't do what I'm thinking about right here." He stroked the hair from her face. "You're beautiful."

Her gaze searched his face. He smiled eagerly, still on his high, a high that his business had generated, Lindsey knew. How could she tell him now?

"How's Beatrice? I probably should go up and speak to her, but, well, it can wait." He tugged at her hand. "Let's go. Elwin's made an elaborate meal; you spurred him with your compliments the other night. He went all out for this one, and it's waiting."

"Michael." Her voice came out hoarse; she couldn't seem to get her breath. In an instant she considered letting what she had to say wait until after their dinner, after she'd experienced his lovemaking. For if she told him, she may never get a chance...

She let the thought go. She had to tell him first; it was only fair. "I have to talk to you."

"Good. I have to talk to you, too. Later, at the beach house."

"Michael." Tugging her hand from his, she backed up against the bulwark.

His eyes narrowed. It was dawning on him that she had something important to say. "Okay. I'm listening." He was wary now.

"Beatrice...Beatrice and I...have decided not to sell Ingraham's." Straight-out was best. And, there, now it had been said. The words had come out almost defiantly—she hadn't meant it that way.

His eyes registered something very near shock then grew dark as pinpoints. A cool chill swept over Lindsey's shoulders, and it seemed as though the world had stilled, an eerie quiet setting in, where all Lindsey could hear was her heartbeat.

Chapter Seven

Though Michael didn't move so much as a fraction of an inch, Lindsey sensed that he recoiled. He studied her.

"Lindsey, you can't go along with Beatrice," he said. "You're going to have to buck her this once."

Lindsey closed her eyes then opened them. "I'm not just going along with her. We've decided together. We want to give it a try."

Michael's expression hardened in anger. "While you two females are trying, you'll run Ingraham's into the ground. Have you given any thought to what this caprice will cost you? Beatrice? Me?"

His words stung her heart. "Beatrice needs this challenge a lot more than the money you so highly prize."

"Damn it, Lindsey! I'm not only talking about money. This challenge, as you call it, could end up killing Beatrice—or leaving her sick and penniless. Can't you see that?"

"Yes," Lindsey said coolly. "I can see that, and a lot more."

"You're being blind as well as stubborn." Michael's voice was low, almost threatening.

"You're entitled to your opinion," she said, matching his tone. "But at this point there's nothing you can do about our decision."

Michael took a deep breath and rubbed the back of his neck. "Use a bit of common sense, Lindsey. This is an insane idea."

"Why? Because we're inexperienced?" Lindsey replied hotly.

"That's about the size of it. At least one of you is, and the other is an old woman who should know better."

"Thank you, Mr. Garrity, for your expert opinion. Pardon me if I choose to ignore it." Lindsey's eyes blazed. She should have known all along where Michael's interests lay. She had to give him credit; he didn't give up easily.

She half turned then paused and spoke icily. "I'm sorry you failed to gain control of Ingraham's. But believe me, I enjoyed your gallant efforts."

She took a step, but Michael's strong hand snaked out and clamped upon her upper arm, stopping her. He pulled her around to face him.

"I'm tired of you throwing that 'I'm after the company' routine in my face." His tone was steely, and his eyes glittered. "All right, I want Ingraham's. It makes a hell of a lot more sense than a pretty thing like you playing tycoon while a company with fine potential sinks around you. I can make something of Ingraham's. I can make Beatrice a whole lot of money. What can you do?"

"I don't know what I can do," Lindsey told him as she stiffly jerked her arm from his grasp. "But I do know I want the chance to try. The same as you did when you were my age." She flung the accusation at him. "And I also know that there are some things more valuable than money."

"Woman, you can have your precious company. Play your silly games. Run it into the ground. Yourself, too, for that matter. I'm tired of trying to get through to you. I think you like hiding behind your wall of distrust, and you can just damn well stay there."

Michael pivoted angrily and strode quickly away.

Lindsey refused to watch him go. It would be like giving him the last word. She turned her back, and her hands clutched the rough stone of the bulwark. The cold silence was broken only by the gently lapping river. It was a long moment, one in which Lindsey had to use all her restraint to keep from turning and running after Michael and flinging herself into his arms, arms that every cell of her body remembered heatedly. How could she even think of such a thing? an inner voice mocked. He didn't care for her, never had. It was insanity to harbor even one tiny ray of hope that he might have cared more for her than he did for that damn company. She was a fool.

Lindsey heard the muffled sound of his car engine, listening as it faded into the distance, and seemed to take her breath, her very life with it.

She stood with her hands flat upon the bulwark and rubbed them hard against the rough surface, as if needing to feel the pain to make sure that she was still alive. She felt dead, empty. Looking down through a blur, she saw a drop of water plunk into the dust on the stone of the bulwark. Then another drop, and another. Very quietly, she cried.

Michael drove almost blindly as his mind angrily repeated the scene of moments ago. He thought of what had been said and of many things that he wished he would have said. Finally he pulled the car to the curb and sat there with the engine purring. Slowly he reached up and switched off the key.

The whole idea was insane. Lindsey could no more begin to know what to do with Ingraham's than a baby with a rare steak. What a waste.

He clenched and unclenched his hands, trying to sort out his feelings.

Plans for his whole grocery chain project would now have to be reworked. Michael didn't like the idea of the change. His original plans were good; it was the way he wanted it. His mind just didn't want to accept anything less than that original idea.

And Beatrice—she was doing well now. What would the strain of dealing with Ingraham's do to her?

Well, what did he care? She'd made this crackbrained decision. She'd made it knowing how much he wanted and needed Ingraham's.

But he did care. Something deep inside acknowledged a grudging admiration for the daffy old woman. Beatrice knew exactly what she was getting herself into. She knew the odds, yet was willing to give it a try, anyway.

But Lindsey didn't. She was going full steam ahead, blindly.

It struck him then, as he pictured Lindsey, her blue eyes clouded with anger, her chin set stubbornly. He'd lost something far more precious than a promising deal here.

He'd lost Lindsey. He'd lost love.

She could get hurt in the course of all this, he thought. She had so much pride, so much spunk. And it was never going to work. What would happen to her when it all just collapsed around her?

He pinched his eyes closed as something akin to physical pain swept through him, and an emptiness that he'd never before experienced engulfed him.

Then, instinctively, he began to fight back. What did he care? he argued with himself. Lindsey Ryland was beautiful, but so were a lot of other women he could have. And they weren't half as contrary. They knew a woman's place.

The arguments fell hollow. Michael still wanted Lindsey. He wanted her physically and emotionally. He wanted her approval, her support, her entire attention, the way a man wants the woman he loves.

And Michael had always gotten what he wanted. The thought slipped unobtrusively into the midst of all the others. Yes, he'd worked hard, sometimes on impossible deals, reaching, always reaching, never giving in to defeat. And he wasn't about to start now.

A shrill ringing awoke Lindsey. With her eyes still closed, she hit out at the obnoxious noise, her hand waving in the air. Why wouldn't that horrendous ringing stop? Where was it? What was it? Her hand connected heavily with the bedside table, then with something cool and hard. There came a crash. The shrill ringing continued, but sounded muffled now.

Lindsey finally managed to open her eyes. Staring at the ceiling, she sought time and place, bit by bit remembering. She'd set the clock for six-thirty. Ugh! Her eyes were heavy and swollen from too little sleep and too much crying. The alarm clock's jangling slowed and then stopped altogether. Thank heaven for small favors, Lindsey thought.

Dragging herself from the bed, she stumbled into the bathroom. She turned on the light and squinted in the brighter light. After half a minute she ventured a look in the mirror. A pitiful creature looked back at her: hair like a bird's nest, face drawn, pinched around the mouth, and eyes that looked as though they'd spent all night reading the fine print of a contract in a smoke-filled room. Slowly, almost muscle by muscle, Lindsey's face crumpled. Tears welled up and spilled down her cheeks.

She was a mess. How could she face anyone, let alone the mammoth problems waiting at Ingraham's along with hordes of employees?

And Michael was gone.

At this thought she sobbed, her shoulders shaking uncontrollably.

She had to do something about this. She had to stop crying. She'd dealt with disappointment from those she loved before. She could do it again, she told herself as she sniffled. Her lower lip trembled, and she burst again into sobs.

Sometime in the middle of her shower, she was able to stop the tears. Control settled over her and a determination, however wavering. She would feel much better after several cups of hot coffee. She dressed, keeping her mind totally on what she was doing at that moment. She couldn't risk thinking of Ingraham's. Every time she did, she almost jumped back into the bed and pulled the covers over her head.

Still, Michael's image returned to haunt her. A resigned sadness settled over her. Going beyond her belief that Michael was only after the company—and she did believe that, didn't she? Yes, of course she did, she told herself, but perhaps his reaction wasn't totally unreasonable. Stupid, pig-headed, overbearing, but not totally unreasonable. She'd messed up plans that meant a lot to his business success and pocketbook.

And he'd never forgive her.

And he saw her as some sort of doll, shiny and beautiful now, to show off and enjoy. For a man who was uncommonly perceptive, Michael had a huge blind spot. Perhaps he was afraid to see further. But if that's all he ever saw, he'd tire of her eventually.

Why, she was actually feeling a bit sorry for him, she realized. How stupid! Mr. Garrity could certainly take care of himself.

I'll show you, Michael Garrity, she muttered to herself. I'm more than a pretty piece of fluff you can wrap around your finger to get what you want.

Apparently Jay had come home sometime in the early hours of the morning. Lindsey noticed his closed door as she went to Beatrice's room. Well, she didn't have time to be concerned over him now. He could stay out all night if he chose; he was a big boy.

She shared toast and tea with Beatrice and waited for questions. They didn't come. Instead Beatrice regarded her calmly and said, "You look nice."

"Thank you," Lindsey said, puzzled at Beatrice's lack of curiosity. Wasn't she going to ask about Michael? And talk about the company she'd been so concerned with these past weeks?

After a moment Lindsey asked, "Grandmother, just what am I going to do at Ingraham's today?"

Beatrice smiled. "You'll figure it out when you get down there."

"What kind of answer is that? We're supposed to be partners, remember? I think you'd better give me some hint as to where to start."

"At the beginning—that's where."

Lindsey cast her a darkly skeptical look.

"Just take a few days to get your bearings. Robert and Ivy will explain things. And here—you can take these papers we were discussing yesterday, see where these ideas may fit in."

"And that's it?" Lindsey felt she was beginning to paddle upstream.

"It's a start."

Lindsey looked doubtful. She ate her toast in silence for a minute.

"Aren't you going to ask about what happened with Michael last night?" she asked, unable to stand Beatrice's attitude of calm nonchalance.

Beatrice shook her head. "I know what happened."

"You know..."

"I went to the back bedroom, raised the window and watched you two."

Lindsey blinked. "You watched...you listened? A private conversation, and you listened?" She shook her head at the blatant audacity. But then, that was just like her grandmother.

"I wanted to know," Beatrice answered boldly. "And since you brought it up, Lindsey, I think you're being a bit unfair to Michael."

"Unfair..." Lindsey's voice rose. "Since you listened, you know what he said. All he was interested in was the company—all along."

"He didn't say that, Lindsey," Beatrice answered calmly. "Now, did he actually say those words?"

An adamant "yes" was on the tip of Lindsey's tongue, but she stopped. He hadn't actually said those exact words. "His manner was enough," she said. "He was mad because he couldn't have what he wanted—Ingraham Corporation. He'd thought he had it made."

"He's a businessman, Granddaughter. We threw him an unexpected curve. Anger was his first instinctive response. That doesn't mean it's how he truly feels."

"It's a good indication." Lindsey folded and refolded her napkin. "And he thinks I'm a pretty bit of fluff, designed to cater to him as a man. In the kitchen and bedroom is where he'd have me—and no, he didn't say that exactly, either, but I know Michael Garrity, believe me." Yes, she knew him, and she was the worse for it. She should have known. How could she have been such a fool over a man?

Beatrice sipped her tea. "Hmmm...I do believe you. And the kitchen and bedroom isn't so bad, as long as Michael knows who and what you really are. Wouldn't you say?"

Lindsey didn't know what to say. "I'd better be going." She gave Beatrice a light kiss. "Wish me luck."

"You'll do fine," Beatrice assured her.

Fine? Lindsey thought as she stepped into the hall. What a mess I'm into.

It was midmorning, and she was sitting at Beatrice's oversize desk, sipping stale coffee and up to her elbows in dusty ledgers and files. She heard scuffling and voices raised in the hallway. Seizing the opportunity to escape from the confusing ledgers, she stepped to the doorway to see what was going on.

A man in a gray uniform was entering Lyle Cummings's now-vacant office, pushing a file cabinet on a dolly before him. Another gray-uniformed man followed behind, carrying several boxes. Still another man behind him rolled what appeared to be, of all things, a portable bar. A telephone-company man following close behind ended the procession. Rampant whispering flowed from the large open floor of desks beyond.

Puzzled and exceedingly curious, Lindsey walked to the doorway. Voices floated to her just as she peered in. One voice in particular touched a nerve. No! It couldn't be!

Robert stood near the center of the room, stammering. "I don't know... we've never..."

Michael smiled charmingly at Robert. "Oh, I know it's unusual, but nothing says I can't, I'm sure."

Lindsey's eyes widened as her gaze fell on Michael. Dazed, she took in the scene of activity: two men moving the desk, another placing a file cabinet, the telephone-company man working with the wires and Michael Garrity standing next to that odd little portable bar, right in the middle of it all. Even in that moment, she felt her pulse quicken—with attraction.

"What is going on here?" Lindsey was aware that the activity stopped at her voice, but her eyes focused only on Michael.

"Good morning, Princess," he said smoothly. He shot her a charming smile. "I've decided I need to keep closer tabs on my investment here at Ingraham's. I'm moving in for a while." Moving the bar toward one of the men, he said, "Roll this over by the window. Thanks."

"You're what?"

"Moving in for a while. This office will do fine." He glanced around, frowning slightly. "It's rather drab for my tastes, but I'll make do."

"You'll make . . . You can't do this," Lindsey said, stepping farther into the room.

"Oh, yes, I can make do," Michael said easily, his steely eyes twinkling.

Lindsey's heart pounded. He was . . . the man was insufferable in his confidence.

"You cannot move into this office," she stated. "I'm manager here now, and I say you can't." She felt as though she was doing anything but managing.

"Oh, but I can, Princess. I own thirty percent of this company. It's only right that I keep an eye on my investment—especially now."

Lindsey opened her mouth then closed it. She stared at his steely eyes daring her. "You never give up, do you?" she asked in a quiet voice.

"Not until I've exhausted all my options," Michael replied in a voice equally as quiet. His gaze was unsettling. And the magnetism was still there, drawing Lindsey.

"Can he do this?" she asked Robert, who stood to the side, watching uneasily and fidgeting.

"I . . . think maybe it's possible," Robert said.

"It could get messy in the courts not to mention expensive, to try and get me out," Michael interjected.

Lindsey faced him hotly, and her mouth clamped tight against angry words that were too jumbled to find a sensible way to her tongue. His gaze held hers, and she winced inwardly as she felt her heart tug at her.

"Lindsey. . ." His tone softened, and he stepped toward her when suddenly a lilting feminine voice drew Lindsey's attention, along with everyone else's, to the doorway.

"Michael—Jan said I could find you here," said a beautiful woman. Dressed in a femininely cut suit, a sleek, wide-brimmed hat upon her dark hair, she exuded an air of sophistication that at that moment made Lindsey feel artless. Her hand resting against the doorjamb, the woman paused, her gaze sweeping the room, then returning curiously to

Lindsey twice. The second time the look held a hint of disdain.

"Hello, Gwen," Michael said. It comforted Lindsey slightly that Michael seemed surprised. Then he smiled widely. "Come in."

Lindsey had no intention to stand there and be politely introduced to this paragon of womanhood who, at the moment, was actually sneering at Lindsey while managing to smile at every single male in the room. Lindsey simply couldn't cope with it at this moment. And she didn't care if it seemed rude.

With motions calculated to be as smooth and graceful as possible, Lindsey turned, brushed past Miss Femme Fatale, giving her a polite smile, and walked with dignity to Beatrice's office, and closed the door behind her.

She looked at all the books on her desk, clenched and unclenched her hands then finally stamped her foot. Then she stamped both feet—as hard as she dared, not wanting anyone to hear her. Striding across the room, she jerked open the doors to the built-in bar. She pulled a soft drink from the small refrigerator then rummaged through the cabinets, looking for something to eat. Good grief, she was hungry. She simply had to have something sweet.

Finding nothing, she strode to the phone and called into the receiver, "Ivy!" The dial tone sounded in her ear. She couldn't remember what button she was supposed to push. Angry and frustrated and feeling like a complete imbecile, she began punching all of them.

Seconds later Ivy poked her head in the door. "Yes!" One look at Lindsey, and Ivy stepped into the room, closing the door softly behind her.

"Don't we have any snacks around here? We are in the grocery business, aren't we?" Lindsey growled, her temper growing at being seen by anyone at this moment. It had been years since Lindsey had experienced this feeling of inferiority, of complete ineptness. She couldn't stand to have anyone see it.

"There's a vending machine downstairs," Ivy said.

Aware of Ivy's curious stare, Lindsey averted her eyes. "Well, would you go and get me something?" She asked, softening her tone. She had no right to take her frustration out on Ivy, especially after the woman had spent most of the morning trying to help Lindsey and keeping up with her own work, as well.

"Sure, honey," Ivy answered good-naturedly.

Lindsey rummaged in her purse for money. "Here—get me anything. Several packages," she said gratefully. She simply couldn't risk facing Michael and that woman again.

"I eat when I'm upset, too," Ivy said.

"I'm not..." Lindsey stopped. "Just go, please."

"Lindsey, honey, I saw that woman from my desk. Well, I mean, Michael Garrity was causing quite a stir." Ivy paused. "She ain't got nothing on you, though. Take a look in the mirror."

After Ivy left, Lindsey rose and looked out the window. She waited to see if Michael and Gwen would emerge. Several minutes later they did. Lindsey had to push her forehead against the window and strain to look down and to the right as they walked toward the parking lot. Michael's hand moved along Gwen's back.

"Oh!" Lindsey said heatedly, slumping in dejection against the glass, wanting very much to go home and pull the bedcovers over her head. Her emotions were so jumbled; she'd never felt like this before—yes, perhaps she had. She'd experienced the same frustration as a child when she'd wanted to fit into Mona's world, but had never succeeded.

She thought longingly of the bedcovers again.

But she wouldn't, she couldn't, she thought doggedly as she settled again at the desk. Ivy brought Lindsey her snacks: four packages of chocolate cookies with cream centers. Lindsey ate every one of them as she pored over facts and figures that became more muddling as the time wore on.

* * *

It was nearing two o'clock when Michael returned to the Ingraham building. He'd declined Gwen's offer of lunch, having the perfect excuse of a previous luncheon date. He was glad. He didn't care to be bothered with Gwen's attentions, or intentions. He'd wished she hadn't come barging in this morning but then had decided to try to use it to his advantage. Perhaps a bit of jealousy would be good for Lindsey. Or maybe it had just screwed things up worse. Lindsey had been furious with him.

Nodding to the receptionist staring wide-eyed at him, Michael walked on to the office he had commandeered. It was spacious enough with fine carpeting and with a private bathroom, but the pictures on the walls were unimaginative and the drapes dated and dirty.

He called Jan to let her know he'd returned and to get his messages. Nothing pressing. For a moment Michael sat back in the chair, testing it, thinking he'd have to get another—this one was terrible.

Now that he was here, Michael mused, what was he going to do? Nothing inspiring came to him, but he didn't worry about it. Opportunities would come his way. They always had, and he knew how to take advantage of them when they came.

He wandered out into the hall and toward Beatrice's office—now Lindsey's, he corrected himself. The door was ajar. Looking in, Michael saw Lindsey behind the huge desk that was strewn with ledgers and papers. All he could see of her above the desk were her shoulders and head. She was sideways to him, leaning back in her chair, staring into space.

As his eyes swept over her profile, he felt his heart twinge with a mixture of pity and longing. In this unguarded moment Lindsey's face and posture reflected total dejection.

He pushed at the door and entered. Lindsey turned, and Michael's heart tightened even further to see her dull expression, her usually sparkling blue eyes devoid of life. As they gazed at each other, Michael expected at least some bit of anger, but there was nothing. This hurt more than the anger ever could.

"Hello, Michael," she said quietly. She could have been saying hello to a passing stranger, Michael thought, and concern rose in him.

"Hello." He walked closer, surveying the books and files upon her desk. Good grief, she'd been trying to take it all in at once. It was too much for her, the poor kid.

"Come to keep tabs on your investment?" she asked dully.

"You might say that." Michael's gaze took in her red-rimmed eyes, with dark smudges beneath. He longed to stroke the frown from her forehead, to pull her close and ease the strain.

She nodded toward the desk. "Your thirty percent isn't worth a whole lot at this moment," she said. Her voice was flat.

Michael shrugged. "Oh, I'd say that depends on how you look at it, Princess." Pushing aside a stack of folders, Michael perched on the edge of the desk near Lindsey's chair. It should have been enough to at least cause her to glare at him. That her expression remained almost blank worried him.

"You can look at it from a hundred different angles, and it's still going to read the same—bright red." Her eyes rested heavily on the paper-strewn desk.

Michael read the defeat in her voice, saw it in her face. Any minute she was going to say he could have it all.

And suddenly he couldn't let her do that. In that instant he saw quite clearly that if Lindsey gave up now, she'd be lost to him forever. She'd see it as a failure and connect it to him. Always. She could never love him. There would be no future for them.

"Ah, so you can tell the difference between red and black. When did you learn—this morning or this afternoon?"

"I'm sure it was somewhere in there," she said wryly with a very small smile. At least it was a reaction, and Michael, encouraged, pressed on.

"I think it's about here that I'm supposed to say 'I told you so,'" he said, watching her closely as he pretended to play with a letter opener. He caught a flicker in her blue eyes.

"Oh, don't let the opportunity pass you by, Mr. Garrity," she said, the tiny flicker of life in her eyes growing brighter.

Rising, Michael walked slowly to lean on the front of the desk. He looked straight into her eyes and smiled. "I told you so."

Lindsey returned the look. "You said that perfectly." Her eyes reflected a growing irritation. Michael smiled again; at least she was no longer indifferent. As he held her gaze, the energy began to flow between them. She looked away.

Slipping his hands into his pockets, Michael sauntered around the room, portraying perfectly a man who is looking over the goods he intends to purchase. He picked up an ashtray and pretended to look it over, ran his hands over the mahogany paneling thoughtfully then went to where he knew the bar to be concealed behind the cabinet doors and opened them and casually reached for a glass.

"Well, make yourself at home, Michael," Lindsey quipped.

He glanced over easily as he reached into the tiny refrigerator for ice. "Thanks," he said, smiling. He found the bourbon and splashed it into the glass.

Lindsey strode around the desk, came over and closed the doors with a hard snap. Michael grinned down at her; she was alive now, all Lindsey, all woman. He stepped toward her; she stepped back. She was up against the cabinet now, her blue eyes disconcerted as she realized her position, yet they were warm upon his own. Her lips parted slightly as she began to say something.

But Michael cut her off by covering her lips with his own. He hadn't planned it. It had just happened. The magic chemistry that flowed between them pulled him to her.

She struggled, yet a split second later she was responding, hungrily returning his kiss. Her lips were warm and moist, enticing Michael with their sweetness, an intoxicating sweetness that left him wanting more and more.

Almost without realizing it, he set the glass down on a nearby shelf. He had to hold her with both hands, had to stroke her firm curves. Her body quivered beneath his touch, warming his hands through the thin summery fabric of her dress. And in his mind there was no fabric there at all. Just silky, pale-apricot colored skin.

He stroked her waist, pulling her hips against his, trying to assuage the throbbing ache within his groin. Then his hands moved to brush the lovely roundness of her breast, to explore the silkiness of her hair and to delight in the softness of her cheek.

In those moments he kissed the woman he loved, and the world was only them and the wondrous magic that they shared. She melted into him, and he took all she had to give then sought to return it tenfold.

There was a flutter of movement, a voice, and as Lindsey's body tensed beneath his touch, everything came to Michael at once and brought him to reality. Lindsey, blushing profusely, struggled from his embrace.

"I'm so sorry..." Ivy Reed stammered. Michael turned to see her crouching on the floor and picking up the papers she had dropped. "I...I just didn't think..." Robert Boyle stood right behind her in the doorway, his mouth all but hanging open. Lindsey turned away from everyone, her hand to her cheek.

"It's all right, Ivy," Michael offered easily but didn't really feel much could be said in a situation like that one. "Lindsey and I were just...conferring."

Lindsey shot him a look full of daggers, and Ivy smiled, almost on the brink of a full laugh. Robert still stared.

"I'll come back later, Lindsey," Ivy said, backing from the room, forcing the still-in-shock Robert with her.

They were alone again. Michael raked his fingers through his hair and tried to think of something to say to Lindsey. Her back, flagpole-straight, was turned toward him. He could imagine what she was thinking at the moment: that he would do anything to get control of Ingraham's. The thought pained him. No matter how true the fact was that he'd go to great lengths to secure his business investment, he'd kissed Lindsey for himself, wanted her for himself. Ingraham's be damned.

But maybe in this instance her supposition would work for the best, Michael thought. Maybe it would be the prod she needed to get going on this company, to not give up right now at the beginning.

Opting to stay silent for a few more minutes, Michael picked up his glass and wandered over to the bar, intending to rinse it.

"I'll do it," she said sharply. "Please, just leave." Grabbing the glass from his hand, she opened the cabinet doors and plopped the glass on the counter.

Michael leaned against the cabinet. "Leave? Now? When we're supposed to be conferring?"

"Oh!" She turned to face him, her hands jammed on her hips. Her face was beautifully radiant in her frustration, and her blue eyes snapping with life. Michael stretched out a hand to touch her arm. "Don't touch me!" she said, stepping back, the look in her eyes growing wary, even fearful.

Michael knew what she felt. He felt it himself. If he touched her, he didn't think he could stop from pulling her into his arms—and more. He leaned again against the cabinet with much more nonchalance than he felt.

"Well," Michael said, inclining his head toward the desk, "now that you've seen all the red ink for yourself, are you ready to admit it's too much for you?" That ought to do it, Michael thought.

Lindsey's eyes widened. "Too much for me... You can go on wishing, Michael Garrity. You can go on trying your little tricks, your kisses, your maneuvering, but you're not getting Ingraham's."

Michael shrugged. "We'll see."

"Would you please leave," Lindsey said, striding to the desk. "I have work to do." Jutting out her chin, she looked very prim, proper and businesslike.

With a wry smile and a mock salute, Michael walked to the door. Opening it, he stepped through and closed it quietly behind him.

I must be losing my mind, Michael thought. He'd had the perfect opportunity to have Ingraham's. Lindsey had been ready to throw in the towel only minutes ago, and then everything would have been his. Garrity's grocery chain from Maine to Florida. But, no, he had to prod and poke her out of her defeat, to rile her so she'd get going. Now she'd probably see to it that he never got Ingraham's no matter what happened to the company.

Somehow that didn't seem so important, if in the end he could just get Lindsey.

He shook his head. Yes, he must be a little crazy. A woman could do that to a man, he'd been told.

With a sinking heart Lindsey gazed at the mess of files and books upon her desk. She remembered Michael's lips upon her own only minutes ago and grew heated. How could she let him do that to her, she thought angrily, when she knew his true intentions? She knew, and still he could melt her, make her forget everything but what it felt like to be in his arms.

Ready to admit that it was too much for her, Lindsey thought in disgust. Ha! He thought her some witless female playing a game that she would soon tire of. Well, she'd show him she had the fortitude to at least give it a try. Maybe she couldn't do with Ingraham's what Michael could, but she did at least have the courage to try and see what she could do, to not let Beatrice down—nor herself, for that matter. She was more than a pretty plaything.

She didn't have time to be mooning over Michael now, Lindsey thought resolutely. She had to begin on this company. She gave a loud sigh of disgust as she looked at her desk. She might as well get rid of this mess and begin on something she could understand.

Picking up the telephone receiver, she carefully chose the right button to summon Ivy. "Yes, Lindsey?" Ivy's voice came cheerfully over the line, obviously recalling the scene she'd witnessed minutes before. Never mind, Lindsey thought, letting her discomfiture pass as she thrilled to the realization that she'd chosen the right button on the telephone. So, one thing learned today.

"Get in here, Ivy. I have some instructions."

Chapter Eight

"Yes, Lindsey?" Ivy entered with rapid steps, her eyes bright with curiosity.

Lindsey stood behind her desk, closing ledgers with emphatic plops. "Get rid of this...this mess," she said for lack of a better word, denoting her opinion of all the muddling records and charts. With a puzzled look but no comment, Ivy began stacking the books and files.

Feeling somewhat as if she were springing from a high-diving board with no knowledge of the water's depth below, Lindsey took a deep breath, then let it out. Maybe it was frightening, but she was beginning to feel invigorated and alive again.

"Ivy," Lindsey said, "I want you to find someone to take over all your other duties. As of now, you are my private secretary." Ivy's eyes widened. "You know more than anyone else about the overall running of this company. Between the two of us, maybe we can make some headway."

"Yes—ma'am." Ivy's eyes twinkled.

Lindsey plunged on as thoughts like a rushing river tumbled through her mind. "I want you to get rid of that archaic coffeepot that turns out that detestable brew we've been calling coffee. Buy a new, no, two new coffee makers—the best! And throw out those revolting Styrofoam cups—I don't want to see a single one. Buy some mugs—really delightful ones." For emphasis Lindsey threw her used Styrofoam cup into the trash. "And have this done on all floors, in all departments."

Ivy grabbed a notepad from the desk and began scribbling. "Yes, Lindsey. Anything else?"

"Call that slipshod janitorial service that's supposed to be cleaning this place and tell them I expect to see these offices sparkling by tomorrow morning. I want to see my face in the tile hallways—or they're fired. And charge all that other stuff I told you to buy."

Ivy scribbled upon the pad.

Lindsey raked the hair from her face. "Call around and get information on having our interior painted, all the paneling refinished. Arrange appointments for me to meet with the representatives of three of the companies that look the most promising."

"Right!" Ivy raised an eyebrow and held her pencil poised.

"That's it for now."

Ivy gave a sharp nod, her lips twitching into a smile. Her arms loaded with ledgers, she strode from the room.

Lindsey didn't sit down. Absently she toyed with a pencil and considered what she was about. Appearances count. That was something she'd learned long ago. To make money, it helped to appear to have money. Never niggle when you're short of cash. Aristotle Onassis had said that, and since he had become extremely wealthy, he ought to have known. Yes, appearances count, Lindsey thought again, sinking her teeth into the idea—and it was something she knew, something she understood. So she would begin with what she knew.

Michael was totally correct. She didn't know much about running a corporation—but she did know how to look the part. And she was adept at learning the rest. Hadn't she been rubbing shoulders with some of the most successful businessmen in the country for the past few years? She'd absorbed a bit of knowledge by simple osmosis.

Reaching for the telephone, she punched the buttons for Robert's office, and was immensely satisfied when she heard his voice on the line. She'd remembered his extension!

"Robert, compile whatever information it takes and tell me how much money we're going to need in the next week, where we need it most, and ideas on where we can get it. And we're not closing any more stores."

Robert mumbled something about not being sure. Lindsey smiled into the receiver and her voice gentled. "Just work with the figures, Robert. I'll worry about what to do with them." His mumbled reply registered relief. Figures were his world.

Dropping the receiver into its cradle, Lindsey bent to retrieve her purse from the desk drawer. Straightening, she found Michael leaning against the jamb of the open door.

It took her by surprise. She hadn't expected to see him. She'd just pulled her mind back together after that mortifying encounter only minutes ago, and seeing him now made it all come flooding back. Worse still, she felt the heat slip across her cheeks, betraying her embarrassment.

Why in the world hadn't he left? Any other man would have.

But Michael Garrity wasn't any other man. Here he was, leaning his tall frame casually against the doorframe, as if nothing had happened between them at all. Didn't anything daunt the man?

One fleeting look, and she averted her eyes. She felt the attraction—still. The only way she knew how to deal with it was to keep her distance.

Keep it light, Lindsey, she told herself. Don't let your emotions cloud your thinking. She could be as casual as he.

If she could keep thinking of what she must do, she wouldn't be able to dwell on the remembrance of Michael's warm kiss, the stroking of his strong hands, the way he had made her nerves sing with heat, her heart with joy.

"Still keeping an eye on your investment?" Lindsey asked as she checked her purse for her car keys. Michael was surveying her again in his pointed manner. He smiled.

"What's going on? I just saw Ivy overseeing the disposal of the coffeepot and cups. Even plucked the cup from my hand—and I wasn't finished with my coffee. Said something about you hating Styrofoam."

Lindsey snapped her purse closed. "Yes. A little quirk of mine." How would she get past him? He still blocked the door and showed no sign of moving. Well, she wasn't afraid of him, she told herself, striding toward the door. Oh, how dare he be so damn handsome! How dare he look at her, as if he were the rat and she the cheese. Well, the rat part fit. "I'm leaving for the day— Please." She raised an eyebrow.

"Leaving? Already?" Michael didn't move. He checked his watch. "Several hours early, aren't we?"

Lindsey's temper began to simmer. He was playing with her. Well, she wouldn't fall into his game. She would remain calm, aloof.

"Not all business is done in the office. A fact I'm sure you're aware of." She deliberately moved her gaze past him and down the hall. "My, is that another one of your lady friends come to call?"

It worked. Michael whirled and stepped slightly from the doorway to follow Lindsey's gaze, giving her enough room to pass through the door.

"Oh, my mistake. It was only Toni, our receptionist." Shooting Michael a wide smile, Lindsey breezed past, leaving him to step quickly after her. She admitted to being pleased that he continued to pursue her. "I'm gone for the day," Lindsey tossed to Ivy without stopping. "You go ahead and leave as soon as you can to do that shopping, then call it a day."

"I'll walk out with you," Michael said, falling in step beside her.

Lindsey shrugged. "Suit yourself, but I thought you were here to keep an eye on your investment."

"Oh, I am. I am." Michael gave her one of his most self-satisfied smiles, and Lindsey looked away.

He stood close as they waited for the elevator. The air between them fairly vibrated, and Lindsey was extremely aware of his every movement. Did he feel it, too? The elevator doors opened with a whoosh.

As if in answer to her unasked question, Michael said, "You can act as indifferent as you want, Princess. But we both know there's something hot between us." He spoke low as he stepped beside her into the elevator.

Lindsey started and looked up at him. Had he read her thoughts?

They were alone as the elevator doors slid closed, so intimately alone. Fearful of what could happen, and more of her own reaction than Michael's, Lindsey stepped a safe distance away.

"Yes, I know something sparks between us," Lindsey said. "It's called lust."

"You don't believe that."

His words hung in the air. "No," Lindsey said softly. "I'm not sure what I believe." She needed to speak honestly and openly, to explain her feelings and to understand his. "But I don't like the way it makes me feel out of control. Or the way you want to use it."

Michael regarded her thoughtfully. "Not use it, Lindsey. Experience it."

"You'll do anything to get Ingraham's." Lindsey spoke quietly but firmly.

"Maybe I'll do anything to get you. Have you thought of that?"

Lindsey regarded him for a moment. "And with me comes Ingraham's?" She raised a questioning eyebrow.

Michael gave a half smile. "Perhaps. I've never stopped at half measures."

The elevator door opened, and they said nothing more. Michael walked Lindsey to her rented car and opened the door. She slid behind the wheel. Closing the door, Michael propped his hands against the open window.

"Why is it so wrong to want both you and Ingraham's?" Michael said, and his thick brown brows knitted above cloudy gray eyes. "Isn't it the American dream to have it all?"

Lindsey studied his face, her heart giving a tug at the earnestness she found there. He wasn't kidding, wasn't playing games at this moment.

"Which do you want more?" she found herself asking.

"You." Michael's tone was deep and hard. "Can you believe that?"

"I want to." Lindsey could hardly get the words out. "But then Ingraham's and I are inseparable, aren't we?" Turning her head, she started the car and shifted into reverse.

Michael watched Lindsey drive away. He considered following her, but quickly tossed the thought aside. He'd irritated her enough for one day. He didn't want to take a chance on pushing her so far that he pushed her away for good.

His heart thumped heavily with a mixture of elation and disappointment. He rubbed the back of his neck and walked slowly to his car. Women! You couldn't live with them, and you couldn't live without them, so the old saying went. And this woman was tying him in knots.

Michael couldn't remember a time when he'd felt more confused. Why had he prodded the way he'd done? She'd been ready to give in; he knew she had. Ingraham's would have been his now. And, damn, he still wanted it. He would have taken over Ingraham's, Lindsey would have calmed down and seen he loved her, and they would be spending many warm and happy hours out at the beach house. But an inner instinct had spoken to him, telling him it wouldn't be quite that simple.

The Princess had guts, Michael thought with grudging admiration. She had to be scared—but she was determined. Companies were often saved on this alone, Michael mused.

The thought didn't sit well. He didn't want Lindsey to succeed, he realized, and as the light dawned, he knew it had little to do with his own business plans. He wanted to marry her. He wanted her as his wife, waiting for him at home, supporting him, cheering him in his business successes. If she made it with Ingraham's, she wasn't likely to be content with that. And she wouldn't need him.

His mind turned away from the thought. It was too hard to take.

Lindsey's image—her eyes so blue—floated before him. Minutes ago she'd looked at him with those eyes. It had been good those few minutes. They'd been honest with each other. He'd been able to break through her protective barrier. She cared for him. He gave a half laugh, remembering. Her kiss told her true feelings. He'd broken through the barrier once, and he'd keep on doing it until Lindsey became his.

Handing her credit card to the clerk of the exclusive boutique, Lindsey's eyes strayed to the line of carefully covered suits and blouses hanging on the rack beside her. New clothes for her new part. She'd chosen styles that fit the business executive image yet were definitely feminine. She was satisfied with her choices, even mildly proud. Style was something else she knew quite well.

Her mind conjured up an image of herself sticking out her tongue at Michael and jeering. See, I'm not stupid, she thought. Then she remembered his remark about fashion magazines. Well, knowledge of this sort could come in handy if one knew how to use it.

As several clerks carried her purchases out to the car, Lindsey's eyes lit on a display of hats. One with a sweeping wide brim caught her attention. Shaking back her silky hair, Lindsey adjusted the hat upon her head, critically examining the effect in the mirror. The hat was made of some sort of straw and dyed a dark navy, complimenting her pale complexion.

She elevated her chin slightly. Ha, Mr. Garrity! she thought. Her expression fell and she stood regarding herself in the mirror. You idiot, she scolded the reflection that looked out at her. Can't you forget the man for more than five minutes?

She swept the hat from her head, almost as if to sweep Michael's image from her mind. "I'll take this, too," she told the clerk.

It was nearly seven. Lindsey was bone tired, relieved to turn the car into the drive of Ingraham House. That relief turned to horrified dismay when her gaze fell upon the silver Mercedes parked beneath the portico.

Michael.

Not again! Couldn't she get away from the man? she thought, her temper rising. Doggone it, she was too tired to deal with him and his insanity of harassment—or her own jumbled feelings at the moment. Had her heart actually picked up tempo in anticipation? No. Emphatically no! It was anger. How dare he come now to her own home after what he'd said to her last night. After the way he embarrassed her in the office today!

Wriggling from the seat, she struggled to pull several of the suits on their hangers from the back, and all the while heated words that she intended to level at Michael Garrity tumbled through her mind. She kicked the car door closed and stamped up the steps.

Soft light fell from the living room and there came the low murmur of voices. Could it be Beatrice? Lindsey wondered anxiously. Her grandmother wasn't supposed to be going up and down the stairs yet.

Closing the front door with a bang, she strode across the hall.

"Lindsey?" Beatrice, elegantly dressed for formal dinner, smiled at her from one of the tall, wing-back chairs. The golden glow of the nearby lamp was kind to her face. Resting his forearms on his thighs, Michael sat on the edge of the sofa. He, too, was dressed formally in white shirt and black tie. It was a cozy scene, with brandy glasses before them, the atmosphere easy.

Lindsey's gaze skimmed from Beatrice to Michael, who regarded her closely, then back to Beatrice again.

"Grandma, you weren't supposed to come downstairs yet." She spoke low, banking the fire of anger. She didn't want to lose her temper in front of Beatrice. She didn't want to risk having her grandmother upset. She didn't move to go in the room, just stood, holding the suits with one hand over her shoulder.

"I'm bored upstairs," Beatrice said, waving the air. "And I didn't break the rule. Michael carried me down and will carry me back up." Her gaze fell to the clothes Lindsey carried. "You've been shopping, Granddaughter?"

"Yes . . . I needed a few things."

"Pressing business away from the office?" Michael said with a twitch of his lips.

"You might say that." Lindsey stepped back.

"Lindsey," Beatrice said, "Michael is staying for dinner—I've convinced him. A celebration—your first day at Ingraham's and my first meal in ages in the dining room. Hurry and freshen up and join us."

Lindsey blinked. She hated to disappoint Beatrice, but she simply could not enter that room with Michael, could not go through an evening acting socially polite as if no friction existed between them, as if last night or this afternoon had never happened. Even as she felt his gaze now, it warmed her blood, and her nerve endings tingled. No, she had to get away and be alone.

"I'm sorry, Grandma. I'm terribly tired. I'm going to my room and turn in early." Quickly, not waiting for a reaction, Lindsey pivoted and walked to the stairway. She was on the landing when Michael's voice reached her.

Turning, she saw him standing at the foot of the stairs. A soft lock of golden-brown hair fell across his forehead, and his piercing gray eyes focused pointedly on her. Slowly, almost hesitantly, he placed a foot upon the bottom stair, resting a hand upon the newel post. For an instant his face blurred before her eyes, and she realized she was blinking back tears.

"Lindsey, let's call a truce." Watching her, Michael spoke low, choosing his words. At the moment she resembled a wary gazelle on the verge of flight. "Come have dinner with us."

She gave him a dark look. "Must you turn up everywhere I go?" Lindsey complained in a raspy whisper. "I would hardly be surprised to find you in my bathroom when I stepped from the shower."

"It would be interesting, you must admit." He allowed a low chuckle.

"I am not in the mood for jokes. I am tired. Tired from getting up before the chickens, tired from drinking that detestable coffee at the office, tired from trying to read squiggly figures that don't make any sense—but most of all tired of seeing your face every time I turn around." She gestured with one hand. "You can persist in this campaign of harassment, but it's not going to get you Ingraham's."

She was beautiful when angry—a cliche, but terribly apt at the moment. He raised an eyebrow. "But will it get me you?" he asked slowly.

Lindsey opened her mouth then shut it. "Oh!" she said.

"Okay, Lindsey, I know I lost my temper last night. I know we don't see eye to eye on this issue, but I fully understand you've made up your mind. You and Beatrice have a perfect right to your decisions. And it doesn't make any difference to how I feel about you, to the way I feel inside every time I look at you. We were enjoying something very good. Let's go back to it. I can even help you with Ingraham's, if you'll let me."

She studied him warily. "I'm glad you're finding some understanding. And I thank you for the offer of help, but I'd rather do it myself."

Michael saw her distrust, yet he also saw her wavering. She wasn't so sure of that distrust any longer.

"Lindsey, I can help you a lot—money, knowledge..."

"I know that, but your helping would be taking over."

He looked at her, knowing the truth in her words. Why was it so wrong to want to take a burden from someone you love? To live their life, he heard his conscience whisper. But he didn't want to hear it.

"Lindsey, you are the most foolish, most stubborn woman I've ever met."

"Only *you* can surpass me in those traits. Good night, Mr. Garrity." She turned away, her shoulders rigid.

Quickly, Michael spoke, wanting to hold her in his sight as long as possible. "I remember our kiss this afternoon, Princess. Don't you?" Hesitantly she turned back toward him, and Michael allowed his desire to show plainly in his eyes.

But she was not to be softened. "Yes, I do. And it is an episode I intend to forget." She stamped up the stairs.

Michael watched her go, cursing beneath his breath. Why was he bothering? She was shoving everything he offered right back in his face. The poets were right when they said love was blind.

The next morning was a repeat of the morning before— without the tear-swollen eyes. Lindsey had fallen into a deep, dreamless sleep shortly before nine o'clock.

The shrill ringing of the alarm echoed in Lindsey's head. Her hand slapped at the sound; then came the crash and merciful quiet. She dragged herself into the bathroom, bypassing the mirror and stepped straight away into the shower. Turning off the water, she had the ridiculous urge to peek from the shower to make sure Michael wasn't waiting outside.

Michael again, already filling her thoughts. He'd said he wanted her and Ingraham's—her most of all. That was important. Lindsey would never play second fiddle to anything in a man's life. It wasn't so unreasonable that he still wanted Ingraham's. But was he telling the truth? Lindsey had begun to believe that he was. But it didn't solve all their problems.

Selda had brought the rest of her clothes and the hat box from her car the night before. Lindsey chose the suit that matched the hat: a white dress with a wide navy blue belt and soft white jacket with pushed-up sleeves. Adjusting the hat in the mirror, she felt pleased with herself.

Okay world and Michael Garrity, here I come, she thought.

Again she had a light breakfast with Beatrice.

"Love the hat," Beatrice commented with a smile.

Lindsey smiled in return. "There's something about them, isn't there?"

"Oh, yes," Beatrice said. "I always used to wear a hat to important business meetings. They have a way of making one feel so capable." Beatrice buttered a muffin. "You refused Michael's offer of help."

Lindsey looked at Beatrice. "Yes—his kind of help would be taking over. He wouldn't be able to help it. It's the way he is."

Beatrice nodded in agreement. "I asked him here last night, Lindsey. I hoped you two... I don't want Ingraham's to come between you."

Lindsey sighed. "I don't think it's all Ingraham's between us, Grandma. It is Michael's stubborn nature—oh, all right, my stubborn nature, too," she amended at Beatrice's glance. "Now I'd just like to drop the subject of Michael Garrity."

"As you wish, Granddaughter," Beatrice said placidly, though her eyes betrayed a sharp sparkle. Taking a drink of tea, she changed the subject. "I telephoned several old friends yesterday, prominent business people in Jacksonville. I used the guise of reporting about my health, and leaked, so to speak, that my granddaughter, Lindsey, was now in charge of the company, and major changes were taking place. You should begin to receive invitations to various parties and luncheons in the near future. People will want to check you out."

Lindsey nodded. "Fine—that sort of thing I can handle, no problem." Her mind twirled around the idea.

Beatrice smiled. "Tell me what went on at the office. What are your plans?"

At first Lindsey was shy about telling Beatrice her idea of improving Ingraham's image, but gradually she warmed to the subject and was thrilled at Beatrice's wholehearted approval. "Ah, you're not mine and Thomas's granddaughter for nothing," Beatrice said.

Lindsey smiled. "This granddaughter of yours better get to the office." She gave a mock sigh. "Why do business hours have to start so early?"

"Why, Lindsey, it's after eight o'clock."

"That, Grandmother, is exactly what I mean. Ten is the earliest acceptable hour for a human to rise," she quipped with a light wave as she left the room.

As Lindsey passed Jay's door, she noticed that it was ajar. She'd been so busy yesterday that she hadn't given him a thought, and last night her mind had been too occupied with Michael. A light snoring sound drifted into the hall.

Lindsey stopped, irritated. If she had a spoon and pan in hand, she'd rip right in there and bang them over his head. If she had to get up and face the world, Jay Fordham could do the same. Out all night, heaven knows where, sleeping all day, eating her food—well, Beatrice's food. It was about time Jay straightened up and did something. It appeared that Beatrice was right, and Lindsey was going to have to give him a nudge.

Now is as good a time as any, she thought vehemently. And she didn't have the time to be gentle about it.

"Jay," Lindsey called loudly, pushing the door wide. There was no response. Jay lay face down, spread diagonally across the bed, with the sheets in a knot at the foot. He still wore his clothes: thin cotton pants and designer sailing shirt. His feet were bare. A pillow covered his head, but his nose stuck out, emitting gentle snores.

Stalking to the side of the bed, Lindsey said, "Jay!" Still nothing. She picked up the pillow and leaned close. Then she jerked back up when her nose detected the strong reek of fish and alcohol. Fish and alcohol? What in the world had he been doing?

Leaning only inches from his ear, she yelled, "Jay, wake up!"

Immediately Jay rose with a start, and Lindsey jumped back to keep her nose from meeting his head. With her hand on her hip, she surveyed him. His eyes didn't want to focus, even to open.

"Wh-what?" He grabbed his head. "Oh..."

"Serves you right for drinking," Lindsey said.

"Aw, Lindsay... I didn't get drunk—it was the combination of oysters and beer. Just didn't sit well."

"Where have you been lately?"

"Chad Albert and Shawn Keen are in town." Jay rubbed his face then reached for the pillow.

"Oh, no, you don't." Lindsey ripped the pillow from his arms and threw it beyond the bed. "Chad and Shawn? I thought you had better taste. Now get up. You're done lazing around here."

"Get up? What the hell do you mean?"

"Just what I said. Get up. You have one hour to shower and get dressed and get down to Ingraham's." Lindsey walked to the door.

"Ingraham's?" Jay croaked. "What for?"

"To go to work, Jay." And she left him gaping at her.

Michael's car wasn't in the lot when Lindsey pulled in, and a whisper of disappointment tugged at her. How in the world could she possibly be disappointed? The man was insufferable, and he'd been hounding her. No, it was a relief he wasn't here, and that was it. But her heart didn't believe it.

She couldn't take time to sort out her emotions at the moment, though. There was too much waiting to be done.

So it began. With Ivy at her side, Lindsey went through every office, personally meeting the employees. She conferred with several men about the building repairs and chose one, arranging for the work to begin immediately. While walking through the offices, she noticed the shining floors and dust-free desks and shelves. Everything looked much better. Apparently the janitorial service had taken her at her word. It gave her confidence a high boost. At least a few people were taking her seriously.

Jay managed to show up about midmorning, looking bleary-eyed and reluctant, though dressed in style.

"I want you to go see a man for me," Lindsey told him, shuffling through the papers on her desk for the name and address. "Tell him we're going to be opening up our warehouses again. He's a supplier—some of the best produce in Florida. At least he used to be. Find out what he can do for us."

Jay stared open mouthed. "Lindsey..."

"You need to go to work. I'm offering you a job—and I need you, Jay."

Watching his eyes, Lindsey realized it was perhaps the first time anyone had ever really needed Jay.

"But I don't know anything about any of this," he protested.

"And I do?" Lindsey countered. "Look, you've dealt with restaurant maître d's, hotel clerks, tailors and wine merchants for the finest in merchandise and service all your life. You can deal with this—and I want the finest possible produce. Find out what you can, okay?" She waited.

Slowly Jay reached out and took the paper from her hand. "Okay."

Lindsey sent out for sandwiches for lunch and spent the time choosing new carpeting and drapes for all the offices. After the salesman had taken the measurements and left, she lingered in the office Michael had so obstinately commandeered, vaguely sensing his presence. A bottle of his favorite whiskey sat on the portable bar, and she thought she caught the faint scent of his after-shave. Telling herself his opinion didn't matter one whit, she couldn't help thinking he'd like her choice of carpet and drapes.

She and Ivy pored over the advertising layouts for the coming weeks. They were boring.

"What we need is a symbol," Lindsey said, tapping a pencil against her chin. The layouts were spread across her desk, and she shifted them and reshifted them to get a better look.

"I thought the Ingraham's emblem was the symbol," Ivy said. "I'm afraid what we need is new artists with new ideas. Maybe we should hire an advertising firm."

"We can't just fire these people, Ivy. Besides, I want to keep this in-house."

Ivy shrugged, looking doubtful. "Okay."

For nearly an hour, they each tossed out ideas but came up with nothing satisfactory.

"I know," Ivy said at last, "why don't we use a half-naked woman—it sure works for the sports magazines."

Lindsey laughed. "Yes, but it's women who do the shopping."

"Okay." Ivy shrugged. "A naked man, a real brawny one." And they both laughed.

Hearing a knock, they looked to the door. The receptionist stood there. "A messenger just brought this," she said, walking to the desk and handing Lindsey a small package.

"Thank you." Lindsey looked at the small package. Her name, and Ingraham's Offices, was all that was written on it. Absently she sat down and gently tore away the brown paper to reveal a sturdy plain white box. Her curiosity rising, she lifted the lid and pulled away tissue paper.

An exquisite stained-glass rainbow lay within. The colors were vibrant, the glass unusually delicate for such a work, and the surrounding metal was of fine brass.

Lindsey knew immediately who had sent it—Michael.

Her heart thumped rapidly. With shaking fingers she picked up the attached chain and held the rainbow toward the window. Light sparkled through the colors. It was beautiful to her, almost beyond words.

Michael. Oh, Michael.

Lindsey gazed past the rainbow and out the window. Sunbeams filtered brightly here and there through the heavy clouds. A summer rain was coming. Lindsey's gaze was drawn back to the magical colors of the "suncatcher" still swinging within her grasp.

Her mind drifted to that evening she'd spent with Michael, the dinner with soft candlelight, the hours they'd spent talking. She could almost smell the fresh rain scent again and Michael's cologne as he brushed against her while they shared the magic of the rainbow stretched across the sky.

"There's a card," Ivy said softly, passing Lindsey a small envelope.

Handing the rainbow to Ivy, Lindsey turned her back and opened the envelope. Her gaze flowed over the words Michael had written.

Can't be there today, Princess, so I send this as a reminder of me. Wouldn't want you to forget. See you soon. Love, Michael.

He'd underlined the word love.

She turned and looked at the suncatcher Ivy now held toward the light. Something spoke within her. That's it, she thought excitedly then breathed aloud, "That's it!"

"What?" Ivy looked puzzled.

"A rainbow. That's what we'll use—on everything. We'll plaster it everywhere. It will be our symbol." Ivy looked skeptical, but that didn't daunt Lindsey. "Here." She scribbled upon a note sheet. "This is what I want you to tell advertising. And I want to see sample rainbows before they go ahead with one. Samples of all their work.'' She handed the note to Ivy, taking the suncatcher. She heard her office door close softly, while once again her gaze was captivated by the magical colors of the glass rainbow as she held it in the air.

Facing the window, Lindsey rocked back in the leather chair. The rainbow suncatcher swung gently in her fingers, its colors somewhat darker now that the clouds had thickened in the sky outside.

She reached for the card and stared at Michael's words. Ah, Michael, she thought. I'm afraid I love you, too. What are we going to do about it?

She dropped the card to the desk, and again swung the rainbow, marveling at its exquisite workmanship—and at Michael for sending it. She smiled, giving a light chuckle. He was one persistent man, that much was certain.

Was she in love with him? Only two days ago she'd thought so. Then with his stubborn stand, she'd been so angry and disillusioned. What was she feeling now?

She wanted to believe in Michael. Could she? She thought about that question for a long minute. Gradually a yes whispered through her being. Yes, she thought more firmly. Oh, she wanted to. It would be like being set free.

Michael was a hard businessman, but honest and forthright. He'd said he wanted both her and Ingraham's. That wasn't so unreasonable. No, it was very, very human. Certainly not sinful. And he'd said he wanted her most of all. But did that change things? Not really, she thought with a shake of her head.

She had to finish this job with Ingraham's. Come good or bad. She had to do it for Beatrice. How could she have said no to her grandmother? But more, she thought, she had to do it for herself.

She'd never held on to anything, never completed anything that truly mattered. Her adult life had been occupied with making sure that she stayed away from responsibility, from entanglements, never allowing herself to get involved.

Involvement was just too risky, could end up being too painful.

Yes, she gave away a lot of money. Deep inside, she wanted to help people in some way, and this was the only method she could use to do so, the only way that didn't involve her on a truly personal level. And she supposed it was a compulsion to make up for all the wealth she'd enjoyed in her own life, while she knew others weren't so lucky.

Maybe that's what she felt about Ingraham's, too. A way to pay back her grandfather and grandmother—herself, too, for all those idle years. And Ingraham's had been Ingraham's for nearly seventy years. Didn't that count for something?

Yes, she had to do it for herself. And without Michael's help. She wasn't quite sure why that was so important. Perhaps in part because she knew it was perfectly true—give Michael an inch in helping and he'd take a mile. He'd take the whole company.

She wanted Michael, and she believed she loved him. But she didn't want him to think of her as simply some pretty bauble. Her ego—her pride, she supposed. He'd gotten her ire up, that's what he'd done. And what he thought mattered. It mattered a great deal. She wanted his respect for her abilities, and not just for knowing what dress to wear with what shoes, or knowing how to smile to make a man feel comfortable, or how to cover a squabble at an elegant party.

She was going to make a go of this company. Or at least give it her best try.

Still swinging the rainbow, she buzzed Ivy.

"Yes?" Ivy's voice came over the line.

"Order some large, very colorful arrangements of flowers to be delivered to the advertising department. Perhaps it will give them inspiration. And we'll have those offices painted first." She paused, her eyes fixed on the rainbow, but her mind seeing Michael's eyes. "And send someone in to hang my rainbow at the window."

Chapter Nine

Four days later Lindsey reclined against the soft leather of the Rolls as Sandy drove her to the airport. She was off for a week's tour of all the Ingraham's stores. She would have preferred to drive, to take a train, a bus, a horse and carriage—anything but fly—and sometimes, Lord be with her, she would be flying twice in one day. But there simply wasn't time, and she was determined to visit each store. It had to be done. So she pushed her fears into a back closet of her mind and locked the door.

She thought about the Ingraham's stores in Jacksonville. She'd already begun changes in them. Things that didn't take actual money. She'd had to fire a few people, and this had been hard, but they'd been thieves. Lindsey had no patience for that.

The information Robert had come up with hadn't been encouraging. Money—they needed it. It was barely two months until their loan came due at the bank. Where was the money going to come from? Robert had no suggestions and was having heart palpitations over her expenditures for the remodeling. She'd been charging it all. It was amazing what one could have with the simple signing of a name, Lindsey mused.

She'd arranged to have her New York apartment sold, her furnishings packed and shipped south. She'd cut the tie for good now, and there was no going back.

Then she'd done the only other thing she could think of for money. She'd called Stanley and instructed him to liquidate the majority of her stocks. He'd moaned and groaned as Lindsey explained things, and in the end he agreed to sell, but not all. He intended to protect her from herself, he said. The money this would bring was but a drop in the vast ocean of debt, but it was something anyway.

Gazing out the window, Lindsey watched the scenery and tried to keep her spirits up. It was a losing battle, and she found herself sinking. She was preparing to fly alone to cities where she would be alone, to face store managers, employees and problems—alone.

Her thoughts returned to Michael, as they invariably had the past two days. She hadn't seen him or talked to him. Beatrice had made a point of announcing that Michael was in Pittsburgh.

And Lindsey had found herself starting whenever the telephone rang or listening expectantly whenever footsteps approached.

She missed him terribly.

She squirmed beneath the thought, not wanting to admit it, yet knowing the truth.

She missed the strong set of his shoulders, his confident grin, his bold, leering gazes, his digs at her ability. She missed his manly scent, which stirred her senses, and his steely gray eyes that seemed to caress her every time he looked at her.

Oh, how could she be feeling this way? she derided herself. Michael Garrity was a stubborn male chauvinist, a womanizer, a money-grubber and company stealer who harassed her incessantly and who thought she was a beautiful doll with an empty brain.

Yes. Yes, he was all of this, Lindsey thought, giving a wistful sigh. And yet, life was so...so...dull without him! How it hurt her pride to admit it.

She pictured him, his slightly lopsided, confident grin, the way he shot flirtatious looks through his slanted eyes, eyes that managed to say so much and to make her blood flow hot in an instant.

Michael Garrity—he was vibrant and exciting and made Lindsey feel overwhelmingly alive. In fact she'd never felt so alive as when she'd stepped on that plane with him, and her whole life had changed.

Catching her reflection in the window, she saw she was smiling. Her gaze fell to the car telephone. Perhaps he was back in town. Perhaps she could speak to him. Hesitantly she stretched a hand toward the phone. She let her hand drop. What in the world could she be thinking? She simply wouldn't call him. He probably wasn't even in town.

But she could find out, her mind whispered.

Again she stretched her hand to the telephone, this time gripping it firmly. She obtained Michael's number from the operator and stared long seconds at the receiver. Should she? She didn't consciously answer the question, only dialed.

"I'm sorry, Miss Ryland, Mr. Garrity isn't in at the moment," his secretary said, "but I expect him any moment. May I give him a message?"

"No...no, thank you," Lindsey said hurriedly. "It's not important."

She hung up quickly, relief and disappointment warring within her. Whatever could she be thinking? What would she have said to him?

Sandy carried her bags to the airline counter. Lindsey had managed to keep her luggage down to two garment bags and one suitcase, but only with quite a bit of squeezing. Min-

utes later she walked through the security check and toward
the boarding gate.

The flight loaded right on time, and the plane was only
sparsely occupied. Lindsey found her seat by the window—
first class. She'd economized on luggage but hadn't pro-
gressed any further with budgeting as yet. With a wry in-
ward smile, she realized that if matters didn't improve with
the company soon, she'd learn about economizing rather
abruptly.

The plane's engines rumbled as they sat there—and sat
there, Lindsey thought, checking the time, wondering at the
hold up. Minutes later the stewardess announced a short
delay. "But we'll only be a few minutes more," she said.
"And we'll be arriving in Mobile on time."

Ten minutes later the plane rocked slightly, and there
came the murmur of voices and sounds of movement from
the front of the plane. The engines revved, and the stewardess's pleasant cultured voice called instructions.

Lindsey closed her eyes and gripped the arms of her seat
as the engine noise grew louder, and the plane began to roll.
For an instant she thought she heard Michael's voice telling
her to relax and that he'd hold her hand. Then her eyes flew
open. *It was Michael's voice. It was Michael!*

He smiled as he slipped into the seat beside her and ran his
fingers through tousled hair. "Whew—almost didn't make
it."

Shocked speechless, Lindsey stared at him. She blinked
once. It simply couldn't be. She didn't believe in fairy tales.
But he was here beside her, smiling at her with his sexy see-
through-her-clothes smile. His strong hand reached out and
took hers and pressed it tightly. "Just hold my hand, Princess, and we're up, up and away."

"How...?" Her words trailing off, Lindsey looked at him
in wonder. Her heart pounded; she couldn't take her gaze
from his. Touched by the bright sunlight, his gray eyes
sparkled with a thousand facets.

"A man in my position can do small things like hold up a plane—especially when his girl calls and wants him."

"His girl? Calls and wants you!" Her words came out in an indignant whisper. Oh, of all the nerve! Oh, yes, this was Michael all right. How in the world could she have believed she missed him? She moved to jerk her hand from his, but he held it tight. "You're crazy, you know that?"

"The word for a person in my profession would be eccentric." His eyes caressed her. "You did call my office, didn't you?"

"Yes," Lindsey admitted reluctantly. And she was glad he was here, terribly, wonderfully glad. The revelation in her heart shocked her, dismayed her. She didn't want to feel like this; it was too dangerous, and she couldn't let on. She just couldn't! It would give him an edge over her. "But I did not say I wanted you."

"Oh." One small word, saying absolutely nothing. But his eyes spoke. They were warm upon her, twinkling and lively. For a heart-stopping moment, Lindsey felt herself responding, her being tuning to his. His gaze never left hers, and his hands stayed in place, but her body quivered with his caress. "We're in the air, Princess," he said softly.

Turning her head, Lindsey looked through the window to see fluffy white clouds and crystal blue sky. Michael rubbed his rough thumb over her fingers. He'd done it again, occupied her totally so that she hadn't been aware of takeoff.

"Would you like something to drink?" the stewardess asked, smiling at them both.

"I'll have a Jack Daniels, and the lady..." Michael stopped as Lindsey softly cleared her throat. "What would you like, Lindsey?" he asked slowly.

"Red wine will be fine." He'd actually asked her preference without choosing for her. It was a major stepping-stone. And it frightened Lindsey, for it drew them one step closer together, and she wasn't at all sure that was to the good.

They looked at each other, questioning, speaking without words. What were Michael's intentions? Lindsey wondered. What were her own?

He'd missed her. He couldn't believe how much he'd missed her. He'd almost called her several times but had managed to check the impulse. It would be better to let everything lie awhile, he'd thought. And apparently he'd been right.

She'd called him. The thought filled his heart almost to bursting and, allowing his gaze to flow over her, he smiled widely. She'd actually called him. That meant something.

When Jan had told him, Michael had moved, and fast. Jan had looked at him as though he'd lost his marbles when he began rattling off instructions, stepping out the door at the same time. He'd just come in the night before and was leaving again. But Lindsey had called him, and he wasn't about to let the opportunity slip by.

"Why are we flying to Mobile?" Michael asked, his gaze taking in Lindsey's silky hair, the deepening blue of her eyes.

She raked back her blond hair and raised an eyebrow. "I know why I'm going. Why are you going?"

"When a beautiful woman like you summons, I come running."

"I did not summon you!"

"My secretary told me Lindsey Ryland called. Was she mistaken?"

"Yes, I called..."

"See," Michael interrupted.

"I telephoned," Lindsey corrected, her voice rising.

"Why did you telephone?" Michael asked. Color touched Lindsey's cheeks, and her expression registered relief at the stewardess's interruption as she brought the drinks. The stewardess retreated, and Michael took a sip of whiskey. "Why did you call, Lindsey?" he repeated.

"I..." Fear and confusion darkened her china-blue eyes. She looked away, her fingers playing upon her glass. "I wanted to tell you about the improvements in Ingraham's," she said.

He smiled. "You wanted to tell me about the improvements as you rode to the airport?"

"It was my only free time," she said, lifting her chin.

"So, what are the improvements?" he asked, trying to keep his grin down. He reached for her hand, and she didn't tug it away. The energy flowed between them as he caught and held her gaze. He knew she wasn't thinking about improvements.

"I...I've ordered new carpets and drapes." Her eyes grew darker. "And the whole interior of the building is being remodeled." Her voice dropped a notch; her lips parted, moist and inviting.

Watching the pulse throb beneath the tender skin of her neck, Michael leaned closer. "We've got a new ad campaign going—a new symbol..." Her voice trailed off, and she took a deep breath as Michael leaned even closer. Her gaze had dropped to his mouth, and her heavy lids, trimmed with thick lashes, hid her eyes. She smelled of jasmine and warm sunshine. Placing a hand on the satiny smoothness of her neck beneath her hair, he pulled Lindsey to him, her lips to meet his own.

She came to him willingly, her lips soft and pliable, sweet and intoxicating, and he was inexorably drawn to her. He kissed her softly, fleetingly. "Did you get my message?" he whispered huskily, his lips remaining bare inches from hers.

Her eyes searched his, and he read the desire there. Again he teased her lips. "Did you?" he prodded.

Lindsey's moist lips curved slightly. "I...it's the most beautiful rainbow I've ever seen," she breathed as her gaze focused heavily on his mouth.

Her look and the timbre of her voice churned his insides with a fiery desire. He pressed his mouth to hers, demanding, searching, savoring the taste of her, the warmth of her, as his tongue explored the recesses of her mouth. And she responded. Desire grew to a painful ache as his chest seemed to burst with both lack of air and a hunger too long denied.

Reluctantly dragging his lips from hers, he buried his face in the rich tresses of her hair, his breath coming in short gasps. His heart pounded, and his hand shook as he stroked her cheek.

She allowed her head to lie upon his shoulder, and Michael felt her quivering against him.

"I missed you, Princess." Michael found that his voice was husky. He held his breath, waiting. So much he wanted to hear...

The intensity of his longing surprised him.

"I missed you, too, Michael."

Her voice was a bare breath of a whisper. But it was enough; it was everything at this moment. He felt a damp drop fall on his shirt, then another, and realized Lindsey was crying. And his own eyes moistened.

They were in the air again, and it was dusk now as their plane prepared to land at New Orleans. But Lindsey wasn't afraid. Her mind was filled to overflowing with Michael. She kept smiling at him and he at her, with those silly, secret smiles she'd often seen lovers share. And now she, herself, was experiencing the magic.

Just when the barriers had lifted between them, Lindsey wasn't sure. Perhaps it had happened when she'd admitted to missing him. In that moment, with his arm around her, she'd realized how much he added to her life.

He'd toured the Ingraham's grocery store in Mobile with her but had remained quiet. Lindsey found this almost as unnerving as his constant taking over and bossing around. Yet she'd been quietly pleased to see surprised approval register on his face more than once.

They'd enjoyed a leisurely lunch and had fallen to talking business. They'd tried not to, both of them had, but somehow little comments kept cropping up. Several times their talk had become heated as they compared viewpoints, but Lindsey was no longer intimidated, and Michael considered her views seriously. And of course, Michael being Michael, he'd made certain she knew his mind strayed often to more intimate subjects.

After lunch they'd returned to the store for a conference with the head managers. Her visit had been an intentional surprise, but the managers had responded well. Lindsey clearly explained what she demanded from her employees and the changes she intended to make for the benefit of all. They sold service as well as a commodity; friendly service would go far to compel people to return again and again to Ingraham's. And if the stores prospered, so would the employees.

"You have a way about you, Princess. There's no denying it," Michael said with admiration in his voice as he opened the door of the rental car for her. "I do believe in your gentle way. You could convince me the moon was blue."

Remembering those words now, Lindsey smiled inwardly. Michael checked her seat belt then traced his thumb over her lips. Desire and intent were written plainly in his steel-gray eyes.

And Lindsey answered him with her eyes. She was hesitant, yes, but thoroughly caught up in the magic that sparked between them—the magic of love.

Was this real? Or was it part of Michael's campaign to obtain the corporation he needed and wanted so badly? The questions came unbidden into her heart, and she pushed them away. She wouldn't allow them to spoil this wondrous time in her life. Sometimes there were no guarantees against heartache, but to win the prize of love, you simply had to risk and to trust that love would find its own. She chose to love Michael and therefore to believe in him.

"Let's cancel your hotel reservation and let me make another for us in the city," Michael suggested as they made their way to luggage pick-up after landing at the New Orleans airport. "I know a fabulous hotel in the old quarter." He studied her, his eyes clouding with apprehension, yet leaving no doubt as to what he was asking.

"I'd like that," Lindsey said softly. Her heart soared at the look of joy that spread across his face.

While she waited for their luggage, her luggage, actually, as Michael had brought only a small bag of essentials with him on the plane, Michael went to make the arrangements. A boyish grin swept across the strong planes of his face as he fairly skipped away to find a telephone, and Lindsey's heart swelled. Oh, Lord, it was so good. Please let me know love. Make it real, make it last.

The hotel was a continuation of her dream, graciously elegant, speaking of a rich and varied past. If walls could talk, Lindsey thought as she stepped through the wide glass doors onto thick crimson carpeting. The spacious lobby was quiet in the dinner hour.

The desk clerk was efficient and pleasant, never batting an eye as Michael registered them as Michael Garrity and Lindsey Ryland into a one-bedroom suite.

"A suite, Michael, for one night?" Lindsey asked as they turned from the desk, though the question was the least of many swirling around in her mind.

Michael took her arm, and electricity seemed to slip up her limb and streak across her shoulders.

"One night, yes, but a very special night." His steely gray eyes focused heatedly on her own.

Her breath caught in the back of her throat, and a smile tugged at her lips before she averted her eyes. She wanted him. Her entire body felt a magnetic pull toward him, aching with longing and anticipation. And fear.

She was surprised when Michael handed the bellboy several bills and the key, telling him to take their luggage on up to the suite. Taking her arm, he guided her toward the lobby doors. "Let's walk," he said huskily, his gaze warm. "This city is beautiful at night, and I know a good place to eat. You are hungry, aren't you?"

"Famished!" Lindsey said, giving a laugh. She hadn't noticed until that moment.

They strolled down the lamp-lit sidewalk, arm in arm. Lindsey breathed deeply of the humid air scented with the sweet fragrances of summer. The area was familiar to Michael, and he pointed out various architectural designs and spoke of the shops that had been in the district for generations. Leaning close, smiling, he caressed her lovingly with his gaze, as if she were the only thing of any import in his life. Occasionally, and no doubt on purpose, his arm brushed her breast, and his thigh met hers, sending Lindsey's nerves tingling. And the longing grew.

They went to an old, cozy and inviting restaurant to dine. There were photographs on the walls of famous people, mixed in with family-type photos, checkered tablecloths, bentwood chairs, and candles in the middle of the table. Their host was apparently the owner, and he knew Michael.

"Ah, so glad to see you, Mr. Garrity," the older man said with a soft native New Orleans accent and a wide smile. His gaze sparkled as he looked at Lindsey. "Ah—so beautiful! Mr. Garrity always brings the most beautiful women into my restaurant."

Lindsey smiled, her eyes widening at Michael. "Oh, he does?" Jealousy nibbled at her heart.

Michael for once wasn't quick with an answer, but their host, sensing a possible error, said, "Yes, but you are the most beautiful ever! Congratulations, Mr. Garrity."

"Thank you, Felix," Michael said, a wry chuckle beneath the words.

"The most beautiful women?" Lindsey commented as the older man led the way. "You come here often, Michael?" She sought to keep it light, to tease, yet it hurt to think of him bringing her here, where he'd brought so many other women before her.

They were seated before Michael answered, his eyes studying her over the candlelight. "This is one of my favorite places in New Orleans," he said. "I wanted to share it with you."

Looking into his gaze, Lindsey's blood flowed warm, like heated honey.

Felix returned, bringing wine. Instead of ordering Michael told Felix to choose from the menu the finest of the evening's offerings. Thoroughly pleased, the older man strode away to the kitchen.

"You've made his night," Lindsey commented.

Michael poured her wine. "And now just wait. You'll taste the best food of your life." His gaze lingered again on hers then moved downward, focusing on her lips.

They dined on creole bouillabaisse, shrimp jambalaya, and dandelion-lettuce salad with sharp seasoning, and Jumbles. There was so much that Lindsey fell to taking small bites just to taste it all. When they'd finished with their meal, Felix brought flaming coffee, a rich creole concoction heavily laden with spices, sugar and whiskey.

As they walked back to the hotel, Michael held her close, his arm around her shoulders. His voice was husky when he spoke, and Lindsey found that her body quivered at his tone. She longed to touch his skin. Her mind tried to imagine the feel of it against her own. It would be smooth and stretched taut over his firm muscles.

Michael broke away long enough to retrieve the room key from the desk clerk then pulled her to him again and guided her to the elevator. A husband and wife and their two young children joined them. Lindsey was vaguely aware of their presence, yet her mind was totally taken up with Michael.

In the elevator Michael faced her, his gaze heavy with desire. Lindsey read his intention of a kiss; then his eyes shifted. Following his gaze, Lindsey smiled and choked back a chuckle. The two young children stared at them unabashed.

Lindsey walked ahead of Michael into the softly lit suite. Slowly, her pulse fluttering, she slipped out of her light suit jacket and tossed it on the nearby couch. Nervously her gaze flitted around the room, taking in at once its colors of green and blue, the small, lovely marble fireplace in the romantic style of years past. The soft light illuminated a watercolor painting of a woman tenderly holding her tiny baby.

Oh, how could she have forgotten? The thought startled her. She'd never been in this situation, never given it a thought.

Michael touched the bare skin of her upper arm, and she whirled to face him, wide-eyed. She didn't know what to say.

Michael sensed the change in her immediately. "Lindsey?"

No words would form. She wanted him. But she had to tell him. It would be cheating not to. But if she said anything, would he pull away? Confusion tugged at her, and her body clamored, demanding fulfillment.

"Michael...I'm...we're..." she stumbled. His brows knitted in confusion above those fascinating steel-gray eyes. He stretched a hand toward her, but Lindsey turned away in embarrassment. "I don't have any birth control," she said finally in a whisper.

The air was heavy with silence for long seconds. Then Michael's arms wrapped around her, and he buried his face in the hair at her neck. Savoring the embrace, Lindsey melted against him, closing her eyes and rubbing her hands over his. His breath was moist against her skin, his chest rock hard against her back.

Gently turning her to face him, he stroked tendrils of hair from her face, his fingers playing lightly against her skin. Tenderness filled his eyes. "That's all right, Princess," he whispered. "I love you." His words were a low whisper. Then he kissed her.

And nothing else mattered. Lindsey's body was taking over, drawing her into a world where only she and Michael and their love existed.

His heart beat against her, and his heat beckoned. He nibbled Lindsey's ear, sending fire leaping within the deep recesses of her body, a throbbing between her legs. She relished the sensations as they flowed in waves from her head to her toes.

This was a new unknown magical world for her, and she experienced each sensation with wonder. The way her heart fluttered, the way her legs weakened, the way every bit of her body seemed to throb in longing. And the way it all felt so wonderfully good.

Never, never had she been this attracted to a man.

What made the difference? she asked herself as Michael's lips seared her skin, his tongue flitted within her ear, and as impossible as it seemed, the fiery sensations grew within her body. She'd known many men equally as handsome, perhaps even more so, many of them suave and sophisticated, expert in romancing a woman. Yet none had ever touched her, made her so completely aware of her own femininity. None had ever kindled this overwhelming desire.

Love, came the whisper in her heart. Love makes the difference.

She heard a muffled groan and realized it came from her own lips. Michael's hands stroked downward, pulling her tightly against him. He sighed, and the very sound echoed within Lindsey.

"Ah, Princess, what you do to me . . ." he murmured.

Then quite gently he cupped her cheeks and studied her face. Lindsey couldn't keep her hands from him. She rubbed her fingers over the fabric at his waist, longing to touch his skin. His eyes grew dark as he held her gaze, questioning. Then his expression changed and he smiled his lazy, seductive smile. At the look, Lindsey's breath caught in the back of her throat.

With a swift motion Michael scooped her easily into his arms and headed toward an adjoining door. Lindsey snuggled against him, testing the effect of her light kisses on his neck. He shivered at the caress, and joyful triumph leaped in her heart.

He stopped inside the bedroom and kicked the door shut. Blurred by desire, Lindsey's gaze skimmed the room, her vision lighting first on the bedside lamp then moving to the wide bed, its covers turned down and waiting.

I love you, Lindsey thought, amazed at the total knowledge, yet too afraid to say the words aloud.

Slowly his mouth descended to possess hers in a fiery kiss. He demanded and she gave. "Michael . . . Michael," she breathed, pulling at him as he broke away. Then his lips teased her skin, edging downward toward her breasts. Her blouse was open; her bra had slipped free, and pushing it aside, Michael cupped and kneaded her delicate globes.

Lindsey couldn't breathe. Her head swirled, and she felt she would shatter from the exquisite sensations. Tenderly, Michael's movements slowed. Lindsey found that somehow she'd unbuttoned his shirt, and her fingers stroked over his skin, which was taut and firm the way she'd imagined. Smiling down at her, he slipped completely from his shirt.

Her gaze roaming over his strong frame, Lindsey took a deep breath. When her eyes again met his, she discovered his grin had widened. Then he was kissing her—with passion, with tenderness, with love.

With languorous movements Michael removed her clothes, then more hurriedly, his own. The lamplight reflected warmly in his gray eyes and touched his tanned body with a golden glow. Tentatively Lindsey stroked his thigh, marveling at his reaction to her touch.

He kissed her fleetingly then pulled back to allow his gaze to roam over her face. An involuntary smile of pure joy touched Lindsey's lips and leaped within her heart when he smiled in return. Was he, too, experiencing the wonder? Or was it simply her own mirrored in his eyes?

Michael caressed her with his hands, with his eyes and with his lips, every motion drawing a response from her, and she gave in return. He explored her breasts then tasted a trail to her navel, and moved downward to the meeting of her thighs then even farther to the sensitive pulsebeat behind her knee.

Her movements became rhythmic against him, pleading. She ached for fulfillment. He slipped between her legs; then his heat touched her, searing her. Michael's movements slowed. Gently, tenderly he moved, pushing farther within. Like tiny, hesitant sparks of a kindling fire, Lindsey felt passion fill her being. Slowly at first, then faster, she matched Michael's rhythm. She clung to him, desperate with the need to be close to him, to become a part of him.

Michael...oh, Michael. Her heart breathed his name again and again. Lovingly she gave herself to him, every hidden facet, without thought of return, simply overwhelmed with the giving.

Together they soared into passion. Higher than the eagles, higher than the clouds, higher and higher, beyond the rainbow.

Leisurely they descended, wrapped together in the mellow glow of love. Gradually Lindsey became aware of Michael's skin against her own, of his lips teasing her neck. Purposely he moved within her, and Lindsey's breath caught. She moved with him, luxuriating in the sensation. They kissed, chuckled as they looked deep into each other's eyes, boldly caressing each other, then kissed again and again.

This is heaven on earth, Lindsey thought. This is life.

Tears escaped her tightly squeezed eyelids. Michael tasted their salt as he fluttered kisses across her cheek.

"Lindsey?" His voice betrayed concern. He turned her face to the lamplight and stroked the tears away with his thumb.

"I never knew..." she managed in a choked whisper. "I never knew, Michael."

He crushed her to him, rocking her, kissing her temple, her hair. "I didn't either, Princess," he murmured. Continuing to hold her close, he stroked her back, occasionally kissing her hair.

Slowly Lindsey relaxed. Satiated by the warm glow that burned between them, she lay in Michael's embrace, drifting between wakefulness and sleep. Doubts, like clouds, tried to float across her sunny happiness. She and Michael weren't married—nothing new in this day and age, but Lindsey craved a secure, permanent love. Was there truly such a thing? Had it meant to him what it meant to her? By making love with him, she'd given herself to him before God as surely as if she'd pledged herself in a ceremony.

The thought was scary, and she snuggled closer within Michael's arms, burying her face in his shoulder and breathing deeply of his scent. He was here now, and nothing was between them.

Lord, make it right, she prayed. Please make it right.

Michael watched Lindsey's face relax. Carefully pulling back the sheet, he gazed at her body, bathed by an apricot glow in the soft lamplight. She was more beautiful than he'd imagined, softer, too, more rounded in all the right places, he thought with a smile.

He stroked her silky shoulder, and she cuddled closer. Michael's heart swelled. The Princess had a way of making the man in him feel taller, the boy within freer.

Her naïveté surprised him. He'd just assumed... Well, Ty's report on her linked her to not a few world-class playboys. He'd assumed she was experienced.

Raising himself slightly, Michael stretched his arm and turned out the lamp. Lindsey tensed against him. "Michael?"

"Shush...go back to sleep," he crooned, tucking the sheet around her.

"Oh, Michael, I haven't called Grandma. No one knows where I am. She may..."

"Shush..." He stroked her hair, holding her tightly to him. "Nothing's going to happen tonight."

"Uhmmm," she murmured, relaxing against him. She was asleep again.

I love you, Lindsey, Michael thought. He'd wanted to tell her, a thousand times tonight he'd wanted to. When he'd spirited her away to the restaurant instead of directly up to the room, he'd wanted to tell her. For some insane reason, he'd suddenly got cold feet. He hadn't been all that hungry, but he simply hadn't been able to face her intimately. Dinner had been wonderful. There was such a magic about her. And his need had grown until he could hardly wait.

Remembering, he moved against her, and she pressed against him. Michael savored the sensation. Tonight she was his, he thought. But what about tomorrow, when all the bold facts of the world again closed in? Would she love him? He knew she did now, and it felt so damn good. But would she be able to trust him in the light of day?

Would the specter of Ingraham's step between them again? On his part, he'd pretty much given up wanting the company. But his need and desire for Lindsey overshadowed everything else. Would she believe that? And what would happen when her plans for Ingraham's came crumpling down around her ears as they were sure to do eventually? Would she blame him?

Caressing her sleeping form, Michael vowed he'd have to find a way to make it last.

Chapter Ten

Michael slid gently from beneath Lindsey's sleeping frame. She stirred but didn't waken. Quietly he left the bed and went to take a shower. Wrapping himself in the thin complimentary bathrobe, he realized he was going to have to do something about his wardrobe. From the sitting room he telephoned the bell captain and arranged for his suit to be cleaned and pressed and the rest of his clothes laundered. Spurred on by Michael's promise of a large tip, the bell captain assured him the clothes would be ready in a little over an hour.

The next call was to room service. Michael ordered a large breakfast, a bouquet of yellow roses, and *The Wall Street Journal*. The bell captain tapped at the door, and Michael handed him his clothes.

Peeking into the bedroom, he saw that Lindsey still slept. The urge was strong to join her, to kiss her awake and savor her love again, but he wanted to call Ty about a few matters of business.

With a sigh of regret Michael again closed the door and returned to the couch to place the long-distance call to Ty's apartment in Jacksonville because it was too early for him to be at the office. A woman answered groggily; then Ty's voice came across the line.

"Late night, Ty?" Michael teased.

"Look who's talking," Ty countered. "Jan said you took off after Lindsey Ryland like a man possessed. Did you catch her? And where are you?"

"I'm in New Orleans. I need you to take care of a few things." Michael waited while Ty moved to the telephone by his desk and located a pad and paper. He gave instructions then listened to Ty's report from the past week when he'd been away.

"If you're not careful," Ty teased, "we won't need you around anymore."

"I'm beginning to believe it—and it's fine as long as the checks keep rolling into my account."

"Listen, lately more checks have been rolling out of your account," Ty quipped,

Michael lowered his voice. "How is the buying going on the Ingraham's stock? Are you finding most of the people?"

"We're coming along," Ty said. "It'll be awhile yet, though."

"Okay. Just make sure my name stays out of it."

"No problem. No one will connect you. But it's hard to keep the buy-up completely secret, you know."

"I know." Michael raked a hand through his hair. "One more thing—keep a discreet eye on Ingraham's."

"Will do," Ty said, then added, "You found her, I take it?"

Michael grinned broadly into the receiver. "Yeh, I found her."

"Good luck, buddy."

"Thanks, Ty. I need it."

* * *

Lindsey awoke slowly. She reached out for Michael, smiling, remembering. Her eyes flew wide when she realized he wasn't there. Her heart constricted tightly. Michael wasn't there. She listened but heard nothing. Had he left her? Had he simply got up and left her?

Dragging the sheet around her, she hurried to the door, opened it and looked into the sitting room. She stilled, joyous relief flooded her when her gaze fell upon Michael standing out on the small balcony. A breeze fluttered the sheer curtains.

Apparently hearing her, he turned. Their eyes met, and Lindsey's heart soared at the warmth written in his gaze. This is what the poets write of, Lindsey thought.

A knock sounded at the door. "Room service," came the call.

With a wide smile Lindsey ducked back into the bedroom. Quickly she opened her suitcases, searching for her robe, humming as she moved.

She slipped into a satin rose-colored robe then gave her hair a hurried brushing. The face staring out from the mirror was that of a woman in love. Yes, she thought, amazed. A woman in love. She felt filled with it. She felt feminine, womanly.

The door opened and Michael stood there, though all Lindsey could see was a tall vase of magnificent yellow roses that appeared to have Michael's legs.

"Roses for my Princess," came his muffled voice from behind the flowers.

Laughing, she threw herself at him. "Oh, Michael, they're beautiful!"

"Hey..." he chuckled, balancing the vase. Somehow he managed to hold both the vase of flowers and Lindsey. His lips came down on hers in a long kiss, setting her pulse to hammering.

Breathless, Lindsey drew away. "I...I have to take a shower."

His gaze held her, and Lindsey wavered then pushed herself from his arms. "Oh, Michael, it's terribly late already."

Quickly he caught her hand. "Come to breakfast first."

Midway through breakfast, Lindsey broke out in laughter. Thoroughly unaware that he was the cause, Michael stared at her. They'd bantered easily over the meal, flirting, sending caressing gazes to each other. But through it all, Michael's eyes had been irresistibly drawn to his financial newspaper. He'd take a bite of food, converse with Lindsey for an instant; then slowly his gaze would slide downward. He poured a second cup of coffee and opened the paper wide, laying it beside his plate, still trying to talk to her and read in glances.

"What's so damn funny?" Michael broke out after a full minute of Lindsey sitting there chuckling.

"You—you are dying to read that paper! I am sitting here, in a beautifully sexy gown—nothing underneath I may add," Lindsey teased wickedly, "and you can't keep your eyes from that newspaper."

"Oh, and that's funny?" Michael rose with a glint in his eyes.

"Yes, that's funny, Mr. Don Juan." Laughing, Lindsey snatched up the paper and ran behind the couch. "You always bring the most beautiful women into my restaurant," she taunted, imitating Felix's voice from the night before.

Lindsey was quick but not quite quick enough; but then, she didn't want to be. Grabbing her by the arm, Michael managed to pull her over the back of the couch and across his lap. He nuzzled her neck, turning Lindsey's giggles into deep sighs. An instant later Michael ripped the newspaper from her hand.

"Now, let me look at my paper, woman. I haven't been in my office in five days, don't intend to be for many more, and somehow I still have to run a business."

"You don't?" Lindsey stared at him wide-eyed, her heart picking up tempo.

"Don't what?" His eyes searched hers.

"Don't intend to go back for a while."

"No." He shook the paper open. Lindsey discovered that his lips were trying to twitch into a smile.

"Oh," she said. She pushed her head closer to look at the newspaper. "Let me see, too." This was his world, and she needed to learn. "Does it say anything about Ingraham's?"

"I hate to tell you, Princess, but Ingraham's at this point doesn't rate the Wall Street Journal." He gave a chuckle as his eyes scanned an item. "I thought Phillip Brinson was about to do that . . ."

"Phillip Brinson?" Lindsey echoed, reading the item Michael referred to. It pertained to some stock manipulation, apparently the legal sort, though questionably so.

"Where did he get the money?" Michael mused aloud.

"From Cynthia," Lindsey answered.

"What?" Michael stared at her.

"I said from Cynthia."

"You know about Brinson—about this deal?"

Lindsey acted nonchalant, but she was bursting with excitement. "Yes, sort of." She let it hang.

"Well, who's Cynthia?"

"Joe Malone's daughter. She and Phillip have been lovers forever. They keep it hush-hush because Joe doesn't like it. Phillip is trying to win him over. Cynthia's mother is helping by supplying the money for Phillip's deals. But so far he hasn't made much; he keeps losing." She took the story further, elaborating on Phillip's future plans if his current deal succeeded. "But poor Cynthia won't get her wedding if the weather turns sour."

Michael's mouth did all but hang open. Seizing her chance, Lindsey perused the paper, giving incisive comments about many of the articles, as well as supplying tidbits of gossip here and there. In minutes Michael was discussing the articles with her, explaining where his interests lay, what certain business trends could mean to him and to the economy in general.

Catching sight of Michael's watch, Lindsey jumped up, despite his protests, and headed for the shower. She wanted to visit two local Ingraham's stores today, she hadn't called Beatrice yet, and her scheduled flight out was for four-thirty in the afternoon.

Would Michael come with her? He'd said he wasn't going right back to Jacksonville. She wanted to ask, but her pride wouldn't let her.

Michael cared for her, but as he'd pointed out, and as his preoccupation with business even this morning proved, he was a torn man. His finesse in the financial world was his life; it was what made him the uncommon man he was. He thrived on the challenge, pitting his brains against others', his daring against the odds. The Ingraham's deal meant so much to him. And yet he wanted Lindsey, too. Which way would he lean? But then would he have to choose?

There were too many questions whirling around in Lindsey's head; she couldn't sort out her feelings. Only that last night and that morning had been the best hours of her entire life. The thought was somewhat fearful. She was vulnerable now, more than she'd been in years. She wasn't at all sure how to handle it.

Stepping from the shower, she wrapped herself in a large towel. What would she say when she was all dressed? "Well, so long, Michael." "It's been nice." How about, she thought, "I've enjoyed your company."

The door opened, and Michael's image was reflected behind hers in the mirror. His hands went around her, pressing her against him.

Lindsey's heart hammered; her body betrayed her. There wasn't time, she couldn't...people depended on her... Beatrice...she shouldn't. But just this moment, just for one moment, she thought, she'd savor what it felt like to be in his arms. Leaning her head back against his firm shoulder, she closed her eyes. The moment lengthened. Michael's breath came softly against her neck, and Lindsey felt herself swirling away into her desire for him.

Scooping her into his arms, he carried her to the bed. She looked into his luminous gray eyes, and all thought of the world beyond faded. This was where she wanted to be, where she needed to be.

They regarded each other. His eyes never wavered, seemingly absorbing her. Lindsey watched, spellbound as their color darkened, and she could actually see them fill with heat.

"You're beautiful," he whispered huskily, his eyes mirroring his words.

Lindsey stroked his cheek, wondering at the shattering beauty of her feelings, sensations she could never begin to put into words. Was this love? Was this why there were no words to totally describe that elusive fairy tale called love?

Michael turned his mouth into her palm then caressed her skin with his lips, proceeded up her arm and across her shoulder as his hands began a gentle searching of the rest of her body.

"Michael..." Lindsey whispered then eagerly lost herself in the delicious heat that swirled within her body. This was love, this was life. She moved against his hard frame wantonly, her heart swelling when he moaned with pleasure. Michael, her mind called, Michael. Their bodies moved in feverish need against each other as Lindsey gave to him, received from him.

Minutes later, her body still pulsing, her mind still reeling, she lay snuggled into his possessive embrace. Repeatedly he kissed her hair, and once Lindsey thought she heard him mumble, "I love you." Fear tugged at her heart, but she denied it, for now. For this moment was too beautiful to be clouded.

"Oh, Michael, I have to get ready now. I've got to visit both those stores and make my four-thirty flight."

"You'll make it, Princess," Michael said. "And don't worry about the flight. We'll be taking my plane. I arranged it this morning."

Lindsey opened her mouth, but nothing wanted to come out. "We...you're going with me?" she managed finally.

"Yes. I'm a stockholder, after all," Michael said, giving his brilliant self-confident grin.

Lindsey didn't know what to say, or even what she felt. Her heart rejoiced. Six whole days. They would be together six whole days. Her mind raced ahead, picturing the nights.

During the following days Michael watched Lindsey with a sense of amazement, and at times with concern, and sometimes with a twinge of apprehension. One minute he was convinced she didn't have a snowball's chance in hell of making a go of Ingraham's, and at other times he marveled at her forethought and thought that things were looking exceptionally promising. Either one worried him.

She was one hell of a woman, he decided, way beyond her years. But then, he was prejudiced—he was in love with her.

He watched as every time before she would enter one of the Ingraham's grocery stores panic played upon her face. He saw her doubts, her terror. But she would have rather died than tell him, just like the first time they'd met, and she'd been terrified to fly. Yet she'd done it, anyway, because it had to be done. She was like that; she faced things. Head on, even if at times it would be more prudent to go around.

But always, by the time she'd walked through the glass doors of the Ingraham's store, she was in command: she was elegant; she was discreet and kind; she was capable, even shrewd. She had an ingenuity when it came to relating to people. She could read them, and before they knew it, had them eating out of her hand. If they'd given awards for this sort of thing, Michael would have made the presentation.

They'd visited ten more Ingraham's stores in five days, and the cities seemed to flow together as one; Natchez,

Vicksburg, Jackson, on up to Columbia and Charleston. Their world was limited to the two of them, with an occasional intrusion by Ingraham's, but by unspoken agreement this was kept separate. When they were alone, which was ninety percent of the time, they spun a realm of their own, complete.

And with every day, Michael hoped to strengthen the link binding Lindsey to him.

Stopping in Atlanta, they prepared to go home. They'd missed a few stores, but Michael had talked Lindsey into letting the remaining ones go. "You simply can't do it all in one trip Lindsey," he argued, more for himself because he'd been away from his office in Jacksonville far too long—and there was still one more place he wanted to take Lindsey before they returned.

It hadn't been too difficult to convince her. Lindsey missed Ingraham House and Beatrice—and Selda's cooking, she confessed.

They'd spent the night in Atlanta after visiting the stores there. Waking early, Michael lay looking at Lindsey. In sleep she resembled a young cherub—a sexy young cherub. Pale silky hair tumbled across her creamy rosebud complexion, and her full lips parted slightly in sleep, inviting Michael's kiss—which he did, gently savoring her sweetness.

Lightly he traced his palm over her rounded breasts, down to the feminine curve of her stomach.

He'd already decided to ask her to marry him. Surely she would say yes. Surely she wanted to be with him and get the hell out of Ingraham's, he added in irritation. Why did it bother him? It was irrational, but somehow her involvement in Ingraham's threatened him.

"A quarter for your thoughts," came Lindsay's soft voice.

Michael looked down into her china-blue eyes. "The phrase is a penny," he said huskily.

"Inflation," she quipped.

She filled his senses, even bone tired as he was now. Her gaze stayed on him, and he saw the questioning look flicker across her face; the same look he'd seen often the past days.

"I'll be glad to get home and brew myself a decent cup of tea," Lindsey sighed as she sipped the last drop from the thick restaurant cup. Looking at him, a trace of sadness fell across her features.

"There's one more place you're going before heading home, Princess," Michael said. "Perhaps you can have your tea there—and some of the best biscuits made in the South, as well."

Her blue eyes widened. "Where?"

Tossing the money for the check on the table, Michael stood. "I'm taking you home to meet my mama," he said, reaching for Lindsey's arm, drawing her beside him.

"But," she sputtered, "Beatrice is expecting me, Michael. Today."

"You can call her while I load your luggage in the car." He kept on walking, pulling her along at a brisk pace. "It's not a long way, only about an hour or so—great for a Sunday drive. And one more day away from Jax isn't going to shake the world from its axis."

He wasn't about to take no for an answer. Somehow it seemed to cement his dream of making her his if he took her home to meet his family. How, then, could she say no?

He shot her a grin. "You'll love the hills in August. We'll actually be able to see the stars tonight."

"Tonight? But what about..." Looking at him, she let the comment drop. Slowly her lips curved into that little smile that sent Michael's body to swelling. "It sounds fun, Michael," she purred.

Laughing, Michael pulled her to him and kissed her hard, right outside the restaurant and in full view of a busload of touring senior citizens who applauded loudly.

* * *

Michael had rented them a Ford convertible; a summer wind tugged at the scarf Lindsey had wrapped around her hair. The sun warmed her shoulders through the thin fabric of her blouse and lit the golden highlights in Michael's hair. Kenny Rogers's country music played softly on the radio.

They headed north out of Atlanta, crossing the Chattahoohee River and turning onto a blacktop state highway. It wound its way through forests, past farms, one-store towns and roadside stands.

At first Lindsey relaxed, glad for the chance to put the concerns of Ingraham's Corporation behind her for a while, glad to have one more day with Michael.

At her pleading he stopped and bought famous Georgia peaches from one of the roadside stands. Lindsey raved over the fruit. "I haven't had one of these in so long, Michael." He joined her, and they laughed over the mess they made with the fresh juice dripping down their wrists.

As the time wore on, Lindsey found she became more apprehensive. "Did you call your parents, Michael? Let them know you're bringing me?" What would Michael's mother think of her? What in heaven would she think of a woman who had been boldly sharing her son's bed for the past week?

He took her hand and laced his fingers through hers. "They're used to me dropping in whenever I get the chance."

"Oh, Michael. You shouldn't spring a stranger on them—especially on your mother. A woman likes to be prepared for these things. There—" Lindsey pointed "—there's a station. Pull over and call and let them know."

Michael chuckled. "We'll be there in fifteen minutes," he said as he zoomed past the gas station and telephone. "I'll tell them then."

"Oh, Michael!" Lindsey wailed. A minute later she asked in a low voice, "Are you going to tell them we've been traveling together for the past week?"

"I imagine the subject will come up." Michael glanced sideways at her. "Why?"

Lindsey rolled her eyes. "Why? What will they think?"

"They'll think that I'm in love with you," he said, squeezing her hand.

Lindsey stared at their clasped hands, unwilling to meet his gaze. Her heart fluttered. Again he'd said he loved her. It was wonderful—and frightening.

Fifteen minutes later they passed the local high school and entered the limits of the small Southern town. There was a tarnished statue of some historical figure on a green lawn next to the library. Michael turned down a street beside a prominent, thoroughly typical Southern mansion and kept going several blocks through a quiet neighborhood. Children skated on the sidewalk, laughed, played tag; older folks and couples sat upon porches. A man about Michael's age looked up from polishing his car, called to Michael and waved. Michael waved in return.

Another block and he pulled into the cinder drive of a huge old house with a wide front porch, complete with rockers and a swing. An ancient elm shaded half the house, and several rose bushes rimmed the porch. The air was quiet and cooler than Atlanta's and smelled of fresh-mown lawn.

Michael had barely stopped the car when he opened the door. "Come on—Dad's in the garage," he said with an eager smile and pulled her along the drive beside the house.

Lindsey's heart raced. What would they think of her? Good heavens, she thought, you've danced with royalty, flirted with American senators, dealt with eccentrics on New York sidewalks, and you're worried about meeting these people?

Yes, she was, terribly. To her they were the most important people she'd met in her whole life.

The old wooden garage door stood wide. A tall, sinewy man looked up from where he worked at some sort of saw. "Michael!" It was a joyous call, filled with welcome. He tossed aside the piece of wood he held and wiped his hands on his coveralls then opened his arms wide.

Michael and his father embraced, pounding each other's back. Lindsey held back, uncertain. But an instant later Michael was pulling her forward. "Dad, I'd like you to meet Lindsey Ryland."

"Hello," Lindsey said as her hand was enveloped by Mr. Garrity's large rough one. His eyes, older, but just like Michael's, smiled down at her, coaxing her to smile in return. Her timidity faded.

"Welcome, Lindsey." His raised eyebrow and a glance at Michael revealed surprise. "Come on in. Dori," he called as he ushered them toward the back door of the house.

Dori was Michael's mother. She was tall, at least a head taller than Lindsey, well shaped, with thick salt-and-pepper hair cut short, complementing her face. She wore a colorful apron over a smart soft-gray dress. Her hands showed evidence of hard work, but moved with uncommon grace, just as she did when she walked. Her eyes watered as she looked at Michael, hugging him, then feasting her eyes upon him again.

When she was introduced to Lindsey, her eyes widened noticeably, but she recovered quickly. She smiled easily while Lindsey felt her penetrating assessment. Michael had his father's eyes, Lindsey discovered, but his mother's way of sizing a person.

They stood in a large country kitchen. Dori urged them to sit at the table and turned to prepare coffee while she fired questions and comments to them. "We've been to early church." "Would you like some peach pie? This one is freshly baked." "Your father managed to spray that old peach tree once or twice this season—good fruit this year." "How long are you going to stay, Michael?" "Are you from Jacksonville, Lindsey?"

The kitchen door slammed, and into the babble ran a small boy, about seven, Lindsey judged. The boy threw himself into Michael's arms. "Uncle Mike! Uncle Mike!" he shouted.

Michael hugged the boy warmly then introduced him to Lindsey.

"Hi," Kory said shyly, snuggling into Michael's lap. "Grandma, can I have some pie, too?"

Lindsey remained quiet while Michael and his parents talked, only speaking when spoken to. She watched Michael with a sense of wonder, seeing a side of him that she'd had no idea existed. There he sat, in slim jeans, a soft cotton shirt, his professionally styled hair slightly tousled, and allowed a small boy to squirm upon his lap and play with his expensive watch. Often Michael stroked the boy's hair and would interrupt his conversation any time Kory spoke to him. There was so much about this man she didn't know, she realized. And yet, she thought, her heart warming, there was so much she did know.

So many memories, long buried, surfaced. She felt out of place here, as when she was a girl and Mona would drag her along to Paris, Monte Carlo, or to visit friends in Miami.

Yes, she felt out of place, but she wished she could belong here. This was a family. It had been her heart's desire as a child to have a family such as this. And the longing, the hurt, the insecurity returned. But she wouldn't let on. She didn't want to spoil Michael's time. Quietly she listened to the talk, careful to keep her hands relaxed, her composure serene.

It was harder when the conversation turned to what they'd been doing and how they came to drop in. Michael explained who Lindsey was and their touring of the past week. His parents were quite polite, but Lindsey felt their close scrutiny. Michael caught her eye, and Lindsey blushed, knowing surely his mother could read the heated look.

"My goodness, little gal, you don't look half old enough for such a responsibility," Michael's father said.

"I don't think age has much to do with such a thing, Mike," Dori said to him. "Her grandmother needs her—and my, look at the opportunity." She smiled at Lindsey, and Lindsey's heart tripped.

Michael's father chuckled. "That's true... We tried to raise all our children to believe the sky's the limit. They could do anything they set their mind to. Michael, more than the others, took the advice straight to heart. Has he told you about the time he risked his last—his only—two thousand dollars on wheat futures? Him—a snub-nosed kid of twenty from up here in the hills . . .''

Michael and his father fell to reminiscing, and during their talk Lindsey began to discover just what Michael Garrity was made of.

The whole family gathered for Michael's visit, except a younger brother who was away at the seminary. There was an older brother who grabbed Lindsey in a bear hug, and his wife and children, and a sister, Della, who was Kory's mother. Lindsey liked her immediately. Della was widowed and studying to be a lawyer. "I'm like Michael in some ways, I guess," she said with a wink. "I want a few of the finer things in life, but I don't want to pass the time working in some diner waiting for the right man to bring me those things."

Michael's youngest sister, Roxanne, came racing in the back door and threw herself into Michael's arms to hug him enthusiastically. She was attractive, slight, with pale golden-brown hair. At eighteen, she was the youngest of the Garrity children.

After a moment Michael extricated himself and introduced Lindsey. Shock was the first thing Lindsey recognized on the younger woman's face. It radiated from her round eyes. Roxanne looked almost as if she'd been slapped. After an instant she held out her hand to Lindsey in a decidedly icy greeting.

Why, she doesn't like me, Lindsey realized, dumbfounded as she shook Roxanne's hand, and their eyes met. Roxanne's were gray-green and cold as a January wind. In fact, Lindsey thought, the emotion could very well be hate.

Chapter Eleven

Lindsey felt as if a cold blast of air had touched her shoulders. Roxanne gave her a plastic smile, murmuring words of polite greeting. Then she dropped Lindsey's hand, gave her a dismissing glance and pulled Michael away with her as she chatted excitedly.

For a moment Lindsey felt like one of those raw American tourists lost on a bus with only French-speaking people. What in the world was she doing here, anyway?

Della touched her arm. "Come on. I'll help you get your bags." Going out to the car, she linked her arm companionably with Lindsey's. "I think I'd better explain something."

Lindsey shot her a searching glance.

They stopped beside the car, and Della leaned close, her voice a conspirator's tone. "My fascinating brother Michael has never brought a woman home with him before." She looked pointedly into Lindsey's eyes.

Lindsey leaned against the car, not saying anything.

"I'm talking of not even a girlfriend from school—he never brought any home. And now he's not only brought you home, introducing you to Mama—I think Dad's met a few of Michael's girls—but he's admitted to being with you the past week."

Lindsey opened her mouth, but Della held up her hand. "No. I wasn't asking. I was just explaining this highly unusual set of events so you would understand."

Lindsey inclined her head slightly. "I see." At least the explanation was a crack of light in the dark curtain.

Della gave a small smile as she seemed to consider her next words. "About Roxanne." She paused. "Roxanne is the last child—the unexpected surprise of Mom's and Dad's middle age. A blessing, yes, but she has her problems. One of them is the need to be the center of the universe. She's pretty, the youngest, and Michael especially has spoiled her rotten since she was born. She's possessive of him, wants him to return here to live—which he never will, of course." Her eyes darkened. "Perhaps Michael should tell you these things, but sometimes men can be very blind about a woman's needs." She waited for Lindsey's reaction.

"Thank you, again, Della. It helps, it really does."

Della nodded and, grinning, moved with Lindsey to the rear of the car. "I like you, Lindsey. I think we're going to be good friends." She looked into the trunk. "Good heavens! Is this luggage all for you?"

Reaching for a bag, Lindsey chuckled. "Yes. I confess! But I'll only need this one for tonight. And this one's Michael's."

Walking back up the drive, Lindsey stopped. "You know, Della," she said slowly, shyly. "I've never had a girlfriend before."

"I can imagine." Della caught her eyes and grinned.

"Well, thanks," Lindsey said.

"Sure. Now, tell me—what's it like to be rich and oh-so-beautiful?" Della joked as she led the way upstairs.

Della led her to a spacious bedroom in the back. "It used to be Michael's, but Mama redid it to be a guest room," she said, plopping Michael's bag down beside Lindsey's.

Looking out the window, Lindsey saw little Kory pumping high in a wooden swing hung from a large elm. His cousins chanted him on. Michael and the rest of the men grouped outside the garage. Sunlight filtering through the tree's leaves reflected off his brown hair. Roxanne clung to his arm.

Della was rummaging in the closet. "Ah-ha!" she called in triumph. "Here it is." She held up a photo album. "Let me show you Michael as a little boy."

They were sitting on the bed, laughing, when Michael appeared in the doorway. "Here's where you got to."

Lindsey started at his voice, her heart fluttering as her gaze met his. For those seconds everything else faded away.

"I, uh, think I'll go see if Mama needs me," Della said, smiling knowingly as she left.

With lazy strides Michael crossed the room and sat beside her. Almost before she realized it, he'd pushed her back to lie on the bed and leaned above her. Then his mouth was on hers, almost roughly parting her lips, demanding in the motion.

Lindsey's blood ran instantly with heat. She clutched him to her, so grateful to have him near her at last. When finally he dragged his lips from hers and buried his face in her hair, Lindsey realized his hand had slipped beneath her blouse and his leg was thrown over hers. She had shamelessly pushed her throbbing body as close to him as she could.

Even as she struggled to control her breathing, Michael did the same.

"I've missed you these past hours, Princess," he said huskily, his moist breath teasing her neck. Moving her hair with his lips, he nuzzled her ear.

"Michael." The call came as a demand.

At the sound of the voice, Lindsey froze, her mind struggling to return to the world. Very slowly Michael broke the kiss and turned his head toward the doorway. Blinking, Lindsey followed his gaze.

Roxanne stood there with one hand on her hip. "Mom wants you," she said in a cutting voice.

Humiliation swept Lindsey as she looked squarely into Roxanne's glaring gaze. Michael didn't move his body from Lindsey's, and she felt him tense.

"Have you ever heard of knocking, Roxanne?" Irritation threaded through his voice.

"The door was open." Roxanne pouted, hooking her thumb through the belt loop of her jeans. "Mom wants you."

"Fine. I'll be there in a minute. Now close the door on your way out," Michael barked.

"But..." Roxanne scowled. Michael's jaw worked, and his anger was clearly visible. "Okay!" Roxanne cried, slamming the door behind her.

Long seconds ticked away. Michael didn't look at her; he didn't move his body from hers. Lindsey traced his profile with her eyes, her heart aching with a sense of loss, yearning for him to come back to her.

He brushed the hair at her temple. "I'm sorry." He gave a sigh. "My baby sister is a mite jealous of us, I'm afraid. She'll get over it."

"It's okay," she said, touching his cheek.

"I..." Letting the words trail off, he kissed her, but they both held back. "We'd better go down and see what Mom wants," he said as he slipped from the bed.

Dori wanted Michael to start the barbecue fire; it was a tradition. Michael, his father, brother, and little Kory went off to buy charcoal. He didn't ask Lindsey to go.

The women chatted in the kitchen as each woman pitched in to prepare the large meal, laughing, bumping into one another. Dori supervised. It appeared that this, too, was tradition. Lindsey felt like a fish out of water. She'd never done this at home. The only real family she'd ever visited was Jay's, and the Fordham's had a full house staff. Everyone played or relaxed until called to dinner. Only heaven knew what steps the food underwent from kitchen to table.

Female conversation filled the room: styles, colors, flowers, gossip, many questions for Lindsey. Somehow she found herself at the counter, looking at a small basket of tomatoes, with a cutting board in front of her and a knife in her hand. Chopping tomatoes was easy, she decided, quite proud as the bowl before her filled with the juicy red fruits.

A moment later Roxanne plopped four onions on the counter near Lindsey. "Here, chop some of these for Mom's barbecue sauce. And a few slices for Daddy." She smirked, turning away. No one else was paying Lindsey the slightest attention.

That little stinker, Lindsey thought, regarding the onions uncertainly. Well, she'd cut the onions. She wasn't about to let Roxanne have the least satisfaction or say anything at all. They'd only fuss over her and possibly scold the young girl, and that wouldn't help the way Roxanne already felt. And Lindsey couldn't bear them to think her inept at such a small thing. Besides, how hard could it be?

It wasn't hard, but Lindsey was slow. And because of that, the onion fumes began to sting her eyes unmercifully. She blinked again and again. Tears welled up to blur her vision, and that only made the slippery white balls harder to slice.

Roxanne slipped beside her to wash something in the sink. "About done?" she asked, her voice mockingly sweet. "Mom'll need these chopped finer than that for her special sauce," she advised.

"That's fine—be just a minute." Lindsey didn't look at her but felt her gaze. The next minute Roxanne bumped Lindsey's arm, hard. The fine edge of the knife Lindsey used sliced neatly into her finger.

Instinctively a sharp intake of breath was the only sound she allowed. For a split second she and Roxanne looked at each other. The younger girl's face was a careful mask, but Lindsey could almost smell her dislike. She'd done it on purpose, Lindsey realized, aghast.

Roxanne moved away, and Lindsey quickly moved to the sink, putting the cut under cool water.

"What in the world . . ." Della's voice came from behind her. "Have you cut yourself . . . here," she handed Lindsey a paper towel. "I'll get a bandage."

Lindsey wrapped the paper towel around the cut, squeezing it to stem the blood, which still wanted to flow.

Dori was hovering around her. Taking Lindsey's finger, she gently unwound the paper towel. "Oh, my, that's quite deep," she said.

"It's not so bad," Lindsey said. "Quite clumsy of me."

"I almost always get my finger when slicing," Michael's sister-in-law said, smiling comfortingly at Lindsey. "Della, get that bigger Band-Aid."

In minutes Lindsey's finger was bandaged. She turned back to finish the onions, and talk went on. Roxanne had left the room.

"What happened?" Noticing Lindsey's bandaged finger, Michael reached for her hand. It felt cold.

"A duel with a knife, and I lost," Lindsey quipped. She smiled, but Michael saw something leap within her eyes, something that he couldn't read. He felt shut out. He didn't like the feeling.

He did chuckle at the thought of Lindsey cutting tomatoes and onions. He was pretty sure that it wasn't something she had a lot of experience at. As if reading his thoughts, she smiled in return then turned abruptly away as a shadow slipped into her blue eyes.

Michael knew no one but himself noticed Lindsey's unease. Through dinner and into the evening, it was the same. Lindsey seemed to have retreated behind a pleasant mask, even from him, Michael realized with a stab to his heart.

Several times he observed Lindsey and Roxanne glance at each other, as if they shared an uneasy secret. He was going to have a serious talk with that baby sister of his, he decided. Her childish, selfish jealousy had gone far enough. He wouldn't tolerate Lindsey being hurt.

Finally things began to quiet down, and Michael managed to get Lindsey alone outside. "Told you we'd see the stars from up here."

He hugged her to him, her back against his chest, while they both stared up into the velvet night sky lit by tiny diamond stars. She relaxed in his arms, and a throb of longing stirred in his loins. She smelled of warm roses and soft spring breezes.

With relief Michael sensed Lindsey gradually returning to him, her reserve melting like an ice cube fallen upon the stove. And he found he couldn't keep his hands still. He stroked her stomach over the fine fabric of her slacks and pulled her firmly up against him. Giving a deep sigh, Lindsey laid her head back upon his shoulder. When he nuzzled the warmth of her neck, she took a sharp intake of breath.

"Michael..." Her voice was a whispered protest.

"Ummm..." He slipped his hand beneath her blouse. Her heart beat rapidly. Michael's thoughts turned to more erotic subjects than stars.

"Michael." She caught and held his hand from going farther. "Michael, I..."

There came a rustle of movement, and Kory appeared in the light from the porch. "Uncle Mike—look what I found."

Michael broke away from Lindsey. "What'd you find, bud?" He bent down to see that Kory held a large toad. "Well, that's a fair-sized fellow," Michael admired generously, his mind working on ways to get rid of his nephew quickly.

"See, Lindsey..." Kory held the toad higher.

"I don't think Lindsey is interested in toads," Michael said hurriedly, restraining Kory by the shoulder.

Lindsey smiled. "Of course I am. I've eaten sushi—I can look at a toad," she shot at Michael. She bent closer to Kory. "Why, he's quite a catch, Kory."

"Here." Kory jammed the toad toward her.

Lindsey didn't flinch. She simply held out her hand, and Kory plopped the fat ugly frog on it. Michael watched, his heart swelling. Lindsey was something. Just when he thought he had her figured out, she did something to amaze him. Would it always be like this? Would he even get the chance to find out?

Lindsey handed the toad back to Kory. "Thank you for showing me."

"Sure."

"Why don't you take him in and show Grandpa now, Kory," Michael said, raising his gaze to Lindsey. He wanted to hold her to him, he wanted to kiss her, and he definitely wanted Kory out of the way.

"Yeah, I bet Grandpa will be surprised." Kory skittered away, calling for his grandpa. Michael was already reaching for Lindsey.

Stepping back into the shadows, he pulled her up against him, but she pushed at his chest.

"What's wrong?"

"Michael, where will you be sleeping tonight?" Lindsey asked.

He started to joke, but something in the shadows of her face told him the question was not an idle one. He looked at her, but the light was too dim for him to read her expression.

"With you, Princess. Something wrong with that?"

"Yes . . ." Lindsey pushed herself from his arms and turned. "We're here at your family's home. I just think it would be better not to."

"Why?" Irritation pricked him, but he kept a lid on it.

"Your parents are of another generation. I think it would be polite on our part to observe that. And we don't need to parade our relationship in front of your family's noses."

"You mean Roxanne."

"She's not happy about it." There was a hurt catch in her voice.

"I'm not concerned with whether Roxanne's happy about it or not." This nonsense had gone far enough, Michael decided. Reaching out, he turned Lindsey and gripped her shoulders. "I love you, Lindsey. I brought you here to meet the other people I love in this world."

She looked at him for a long minute, her expression blurred by the shadows. Then she came into his arms and laid her head upon his chest. She felt so good to him.

"Mom and Dad are quite taken with you," Michael said softly.

"They'd be taken with an elephant if you brought it home," Lindsey mumbled into his shirt.

Michael gave a half chuckle. "Probably..." He held her to him, needing her warmth, her closeness, reluctant to make a sound or move that would break the spell that bound Lindsey to him.

Minutes ticked by. Then Lindsey stirred and looked up at him.

"I still would rather that we slept apart tonight, Michael. I'm not yet ready to bare our relationship for everyone to see. It's ours. It's private."

"Now, that..." He brushed his thumb across her velvet lips. "I can understand. I may not like it—but I understand." He kissed her, giving her all he had to give.

A thousand times at least, Michael thought with raw humor on the trip home to Jacksonville the next day, he'd started to ask Lindsey to marry him. But, damn it! There had never been time. Not the right time, anyway. He wondered at himself. How could anyone with the nerve he had in taking risks in business be such a coward when it came to this?

Before he knew it, it was late morning, and they pulled to a stop before his building in downtown Jax. Sandy had met them at the airport with the Rolls.

Reluctantly Michael turned to Lindsey and pulled her into his arms. Remembrance of his insane urge to make love to her on the car's smooth leather seat flashed through his mind, and an involuntary smile lit his lips.

"What is it?" Lindsey asked curiously.

"You," Michael whispered. "I want you." He enjoyed the color that crept into her cheeks and knew she felt the same. His male ego soared at the knowledge. "Have dinner with me tonight."

She nodded. "Yes—but come to the house. Beatrice will like that. I can't leave her alone again so soon."

"Okay—but we will have time alone," he instructed.

"Yes." Lindsey grinned. "Yes."

Michael stepped from the car's air-conditioned interior into the humid heat of the city. For a moment he stood and watched the white Rolls drive away.

Tonight. He'd ask her tonight. And she'd say yes. She had to. They'd get all that nonsense about Ingraham's out of the way. He didn't care what happened to the company anymore. He only wanted Lindsey to be his.

Lindsey couldn't keep the small smile of contentment from her lips. The pressure of Michael's arms around her seemed to linger, and she allowed her mind to remember their times together over the past week.

Perhaps it wasn't all going to end now, after all. Perhaps it was just beginning.

Beatrice sat in the shade of the awning on the back patio. No, she wasn't supposed to be going up and down stairs yet, she admitted to Lindsey, but Jay had brought her down this morning and would carry her up in the evening. He'd been doing it every day, she reported. She was still adamantly refusing to install an electrical chair to take her up and down the stairs. She looked sharp, vital, and overjoyed to see Lindsey.

Jay was with her. And here was the old Jay again, handsome, smiling charmingly, dressed in a tan summer suit. And there was something more, some added sense of confidence and coiled eagerness.

Lindsey hugged them both, glad to be home. This was her home now, she realized. Slipping from her shoes, she curled up on the chaise, and the catching-up began.

Beatrice had not been idle. "The telephone is the greatest invention on earth," she commented. She'd been spreading the word of Lindsey's taking over management and the changes that were being implemented. "Of course, I embellished a bit."

"Embellished!" Lindsey laughed. "You were out-and-out lying."

Beatrice shrugged. "We're moving again. That's what counts. People are finding out Ingraham's is far from dead."

Reportedly, the Ingraham's offices had been visited by numerous trade people, all interested in selling their wares. Lindsey was astonished when Jay announced that the warehouse would be ready for opening within the week. All he needed was her go ahead on his arrangements. And that wasn't all. He had approached his father for a sizable loan to invest in Ingraham's. The elder Fordham approved of Jay's endeavor, and the funds were being transferred. Lindsey doubted she could have been more shocked if Jay had told her he was flying to the moon. Watching her expression, he grinned widely and took her hand. The three of them talked rapidly about the best places to funnel the money. It wasn't enough to pay the loan at the bank, but it could be used as an overture or to go toward the overwhelming debts.

Finally, after several glasses of iced tea all around, Beatrice bluntly asked Jay to leave. "I want to talk to Lindsey alone."

With a knowing look, Jay kissed Beatrice's cheek. They'd grown close, Lindsey realized, pleased.

Lindsey studied her grandmother's face. "You look good, Grandmother."

"Ah, and so do you, Granddaughter." There was a wicked twinkle in Beatrice's eyes, and Lindsey knew the unspoken comment concerned Michael.

"Yes, Grandma. I'm wonderful."

"So tell me about Michael," Beatrice ordered.

"He's coming to dinner tonight," Lindsey said, shifting her gaze to the river. She wasn't sure how much she wanted to say to Beatrice. She needed to slow herself down, to think.

"Quit fiddle-faddling around, Lindsey. You've just spent a week with the man and have gone to meet his family. Are you in love with him?"

Lindsey took a breath. "Yes."

"And he loves you?"

"Yes . . ."

"You believe that, Granddaughter?"

"Yes, I do."

"Then are you going to marry him?"

"He hasn't asked me."

Beatrice waved the air impatiently. "If he loves you, he will. What will you say?"

Lindsey regarded her for a moment. "I'll say yes."

"Then what about Ingraham's?"

"I don't believe Ingraham's is a problem any more," Lindsey said slowly. "Maybe it never was. We've come to know each other this past week. He understands now how important this is to me. We'll continue to do everything we can to bring Ingraham's around, Grandma—you and I—and Jay."

Beatrice patted Lindsey's knee. "Nothing, Granddaughter, is more important than your happiness. Please know that. I'll understand if you choose to do otherwise—but I can't help but believe you handling Ingraham's is in the best interest of your happiness."

Lindsey hummed to herself as she slipped into a delicate cream satin dress with thin straps. Definitely not office style, she mused, surveying her image in the mirror, her lips curving into a pleased smile. She shook her head then fluffed her hair around her face. I'm a woman in love, she thought wonderingly. How magical it is.

Still, there were doubts. Was this love true? And what about Roxanne? Would she be able to cause trouble? Would Michael really understand about her need to continue with Ingraham's, as she had told Beatrice he would?

She pivoted from the mirror. Perhaps love was like this. Perhaps its very preciousness left one continually open to wild fancies of insecurity. Well, it was nonsense. How could anything be more real than this? As for Roxanne—she was a child. She would accept, or at the very least, they wouldn't have to be around her often. And, yes, of course Michael would understand.

As Lindsey slipped on her sandals, a knock sounded at the door. "Come in."

Jay let out a low whistle as he entered. "You look super."

"Thanks." Lindsey laughed, standing and testing her sandals. "You don't look so bad yourself." Jay was dressed in black tie and would definitely turn a feminine eye.

As was Jay's habit, he pushed his hands into his pockets. "I wanted to thank you—for the chance you've given me at Ingraham's," he said. "Thanks for pushing me."

"I think I need to thank you. You've really gone to work. And the money Jay. You know how much we need that." She hugged him enthusiastically. "But mind—we'll make it strictly legal."

He hugged her in return. "You know, I never would have thought I could even begin to do something like this—but I'm not half-bad. Of course, with my looks, name and charm, it hasn't been all that hard."

Lindsey playfully slapped at him. "So glad to see the old Jay again."

"Lindsey..." Jay's expression turned serious. "This thing with Garrity. Well, I'm glad for you. I just wanted you to know. I've talked to a lot of people down here now, and the word is he's a pretty straight arrow."

"Are you saying you're ready to like him?"

"I didn't say that." Jay gave a half grin.

Lindsey touched his cheek. "Thank you for caring, dear friend."

He offered his arm. Lindsey took it, and they went downstairs. Selda was just letting Michael in the door. Lindsey's breath caught in her throat at the sight of him: his brown hair warmed by the dimly lit hall and his male form accentuated by the elegant black suit. He looked up, and a hint of irritation crossed his features when his gaze touched on them. Smiling indulgently, Lindsey removed her arm from Jay's and went to meet him.

Her heartbeat picked up a quickened tempo. He'd said they would have time alone, she remembered. Suddenly she was eager for dinner to be over.

The talk at the table was light and gay—or what Lindsey caught of it seemed to be. Her mind kept slipping away, drawn by the magnetic energy that swirled between her and Michael. His eyes seemed to dance in the candlelight, to caress her, to beckon to her. Often in midsentence she would find herself stumbling around for the words she'd intended to say, but they had escaped her.

There appeared to be an unspoken truce between Jay and Michael, each painstakingly deferring to the other, no barbs thrown. Lindsey felt Beatrice's gaze, but her grandmother refrained from saying anything.

Right after they'd finished dinner, Jay rose. "I'm sorry to leave this cheerful gathering," he said, smiling smoothly. "But I have a date. Mustn't keep her waiting."

"A date?" Lindsey said in surprise. He'd never said a word.

"Uh-huh." Jay kissed Beatrice's cheek, then Lindsey's. As he rounded the table, he said, "Can I see you for a minute, Garrity?"

Mystified, Lindsey watched Michael and Jay leave the dining room. She glanced to Beatrice, who only shook her head, also in wonder. Lindsey found herself listening for the sound of blows. Those two had been entirely too cordial to each other all evening.

Jay led the way, not stopping until he reached the front door. Michael waited, wondering what was to come.

Fordham looked at him a moment, sizing him up. "If you hurt her, Garrity, I'll bust your face in. I can't ruin you financially. I wouldn't kill you. But I can sure as hell mess up your face."

Michael took in the younger man's earnest expression. He had to admire the young Adonis, in fact, he was even grateful that the woman he loved had such a good friend.

"I love her," Michael said, extending his hand. "I promise you, I'll do everything in my power to make her happy."

Fordham took the offered hand, shook it firmly then turned and left. Whistling, Michael slowly returned to the ladies.

They looked at him expectantly, of course. "Conversation between gentlemen," he said lightly, managing to keep a straight face.

Damn, she's beautiful, he thought for the hundredth time that evening, looking at Lindsey. Her blue eyes seemed to glow more vividly than ever before. They rested on him warmly, and for a split second Michael forgot everything else. He couldn't wait to get her alone, to feel her silky apricot skin beneath his hands. And yet—he quivered inside, nervous about the proposal. Would she say yes when he asked her to marry him?

Inside, he tried to quell the crippling uncertainty. Every man in the world must feel this way before taking the giant step. Of course she would say yes. Her eyes told him so. Didn't they?

They talked and shared the ambrosial after-dinner coffee Lindsey had made. Feeling expansive, Michael took Beatrice's hand and led her in a slow waltz to the soft music from the stereo. She was exceedingly light and thin in his arms, but followed his steps unfalteringly, seeming to glow with the gay activity. Then Lindsey was in his arms, and he swirled her around, their eyes only on each other.

With a knowing look at Michael, Beatrice announced that she was ready to retire. Michael grinned at her, his gaze issuing a silent thank-you.

"Grandma, are you feeling all right?" Lindsey asked, her voice echoing immediate concern. She hadn't seen the glances exchanged between Michael and her grandmother.

"I'm fine, Lindsey. I'm just ready to relax in bed with my books and brandy." She lifted her hand to Michael. "Michael, would you do me the honors?"

Michael walked hand in hand with her to the stairs then lifted her in his arms. Against her protests, he carried her all the way to her room. "Must take advantage of this opportunity of holding a beautiful woman," he teased as he lowered her to the bed.

She cocked an eyebrow. "You have a gifted tongue, Michael." It was a subtle warning. They looked at each other.

"I love her, Duchess," Michael said.

"I very much want you both to be happy, Michael." She pressed his hand. "Now tell Lindsey I won't expect to see her until tomorrow morning," she said in dismissal.

Saluting smartly, Michael left the room. Closing the door softly behind him, he broke into a near run, skimming the steps on his way down the stairs.

* * *

Lindsey was stacking the coffee cups and saucers on the silver tray when Michael returned. He stopped in the living room archway, and she straightened to face him. How handsome he was. His eyes appeared dark silver, warming her with their gaze. With lazy strides he walked to the stereo and started the music. Then he swept her into his arms, whirling her around and out into the spacious hall.

His arms were strong around her, and his steps led hers flawlessly. Her vision blurred as the light dusted Michael's face in an ethereal glow. Lindsey felt as though they danced atop a rainbow, high above the world in a colorful sphere all their own. She was his princess. He, her prince.

Michael grinned then he laughed. She laughed, too, giddy with high emotion. *I love you, Michael,* her heart whispered. *Oh, how I love you.* And she never wanted it to end.

Suddenly he was whirling her toward the end of the hall then right through the swinging door into the kitchen. Selda stopped in midmotion, a dishcloth in one hand, a pan in the other. She looked at them as if they'd lost their minds. And, indeed, Lindsey felt she had, and was never more glad of it. The feeling was euphoric, a once in a lifetime experience, and she intended to savor every precious second.

"Take care of Beatrice, Selda," Michael called as he whirled Lindsey through the kitchen. "The Princess will be out for the evening."

"Well, my stars . . ." Selda commented, wide-eyed.

Then, scarcely missing a step, Michael opened the back door and swept Lindsey out into the soft warm night.

Their waltzing came to a stop beside the bulwark of the river. "Oh, Michael," Lindsey laughed as she gasped for air. "I . . . I can't breathe."

He gave a breathless chuckle and reached again for her arm. "You...don't need to breathe...only to kiss me." But they were both so winded that they could do nothing but fall together, each trying to steady their breathing while hampered by laughing.

Slowly the laughter died. Heat stole through Lindsey's veins. Michael drew her close, and she wound her arms around his neck, looking up into the shadows of his face. A bold moon rising to the east dusted them with faint silver light.

His gaze surveyed her, taking account. Lindsey had become used to it, even welcomed it. It was his way.

The throbbing began low in her abdomen, flutteringly light at first, then more forceful. "Michael." His name whispered from her lips before she realized it. Then his lips crushed hers, demanding fulfillment. Lindsey opened to him, aching with the need to give, to take, to become a part of him.

His scent, his very essence, filled her nostrils. She raked her fingers into his thick hair and pressed against his strong frame. His body throbbed into hers, and her heart seemed to keep tune to the rhythm. Michael, her heart whispered. Michael, it cried.

Breaking the kiss, he pressed his mouth to her ear and into her hair. Then he kissed an erotic trail down her neck. Lindsey couldn't seem to get her breath. Clutching at him, she heard a moan and realized it came from her.

Suddenly Michael stilled. Lindsey's heart pounded loudly in her ears. It was the only sound she was aware of. Something blurred her vision, and she realized it was tears.

Cradling her cheeks in his hands, Michael turned so the moonlight bathed her face.

"I love you, Princess." His voice cracked. "Will you marry me?"

Time stopped. Lindsey couldn't seem to get any words out. Michael's eyes were very dark, very shimmery in the moonlight. Please, Lindsey thought, I want to look at those eyes the rest of my life.

"Yes," she managed at last, the word a husky whisper. She tried again, her face breaking into a wide smile. *"Yes!"* Then she threw herself against him, and he clutched her to him.

"Oh, Lindsey...Lindsey," he murmured into her hair as he rocked her back and forth.

It was their moment in time, and Lindsey seized it, holding it within her heart. For all the years to come, she thought, she wanted to remember the rapture, the very smell of this moment. She pressed into her memory Michael's strong embrace, the roughness of his cheek against hers, the heady scent of his after-shave, the beating of their hearts, and the full moon smiling romantically down at them.

Michael pulled away. "When?" he demanded. "How about day after tomorrow?"

Lindsey laughed joyously and stroked his arm. "Whoa . . . you have to tell your parents—your family."

"I think they're ready and waiting, Princess."

A shadow crossed Lindsey's joy. "What about Roxanne, Michael? Maybe we should wait—give her time." Though she couldn't imagine how that would help. Roxanne plainly didn't like her.

"Look, Princess, I love my sister. I'd die for her," Michael said ruefully. "But I will not live for her. And you're marrying me—not my family." He kissed her softly, keeping his hands on either side of her face. "Now—what do you say?"

"Give me five days at least." Lindsey laughed softly. "We have to find a minister—a church wedding, please, Michael. And I have to find a dress, and shoes, and the food, and people have to be invited. . . ."

"Okay, okay," Michael said grinning. "Sunday afternoon—no later." He hugged her to him, rubbing his hands over her back. "Oh, Princess, there's so much I want to show you. My beach house—we'll live there. You'll love it. It's a great place for kids. We can fish and swim—Damn . . ."

"What is it?" Lindsey asked.

"I'm supposed to go north next week, and it can't be put off. Not much of a honeymoon for us right away, I'm afraid, but I'll make it up to you, Princess." He spoke earnestly. "And you'll come with me, anyway. I can snatch time away here and there. Ever seen Pittsburgh? And I want to show you how my stores are coming along. Then New York—I need to see a man there about a company I'm thinking of investing in..."

He was talking so fast that Lindsey could hardly keep up. She laughed and he stopped. "Pittsburgh is one city I've missed," she said, smiling. "I'd love to see it." She dropped her voice to a sensuous tone. "Especially with you—" She slipped a finger between the buttons of his shirt and ran her fingernail across his skin. "But, Michael, I can't leave Ingraham's for a while. We're making too many changes, too many things I have to see to. Maybe I can get away on the weekend."

"Ah, honey, you don't need to worry about that anymore. I can give you the names of several competent people you can get to run it for you. I want you with me, Princess." He hugged her to him. "Besides, I'm going to be keeping you awfully busy."

A coolness touched Lindsey's shoulders and slipped down her spine. She pushed away from his chest and looked up at him.

"I don't want someone else to run it, Michael. I want to do it."

He stiffened. Even in the dim silver light, Lindsey could see his eyebrows knot together.

Chapter Twelve

As Lindsey watched Michael, a flicker of foreboding touched her joy. She tried to ignore it. Maybe she was just imagining his displeasure.

"It'll be all right. Why, you're a big wheeler-dealer with your own jet to bring us together whenever we wish. And it'll only be for a while, until things get halfway straightened out at Ingraham's." She allowed her voice to slip into a sultry tone.

Michael didn't say anything for a few seconds. "But why bother?" he said finally. "Get someone else to do the work. You and Beatrice direct from behind the curtain. I want you with me—all the time."

Slipping from his embrace, Lindsey turned and leaned her forearms on the bulwark. The river lapped gently below. What was happening here? she wondered.

"You know Ingraham's Corporation can't possibly afford anyone of the caliber it would take to do the job," she said.

"Yes...but Garrity Corporation can," Michael countered, raising his hands as a plea for peace when she would have spoken. "Now, don't go jumping the gun on the old argument of 'Michael's after the company.'" He cupped her elbows, turning her to face him. "There's nothing wrong with a loan between family members. And that's what I'm talking about."

Looking at him, Lindsey realized that her fears of his ulterior motives had faded days before. Michael Garrity was a man who was above such things. But still, he didn't seem to want her to continue with her efforts for Ingraham's. Perhaps, even after all the long and intimate hours they'd spent together, he still didn't understand what it meant to her.

"No, there's nothing wrong with it," Lindsey said slowly. "But I don't want it like that, Michael." She regarded him earnestly. "This is something I have to do on my own...not with you standing behind me to call the shots, to pick up the pieces from my mistakes. Can you understand that?" She searched his eyes for an answer.

"Yes, Princess, I understand. You've wanted to prove you have a brain underneath all that beautiful hair. Well, you've proved it a hundred times over." Michael gestured with a wave of his hand. "I've watched you—you surpass the word *diplomat*, you're audaciously inventive, and you've got more courage than any woman I've ever met. You don't need to prove anything to me—to anyone, anymore."

"I know I don't." She paused, searching for the right words, wanting so much his understanding, and more perhaps, his approval. "But I haven't succeeded—I've only just gotten my feet wet. I want to see what I can do. And actually, it doesn't matter so much anymore if I fail—except for the disappointment it would be for Beatrice. But it's the excitement of trying. And the satisfaction of seeing the job through to the finish."

Michael looked at her for long seconds. Then he turned away, raking his fingers through his hair. "If it's the challenge and excitement you want, Lindsey, you'll be a part of all my business dealings. I want you with me—board meetings, trips, business lunches, dinner, and parties where half the deals are made. I want you beside me."

"I want that, too. Why does my carrying on with Ingraham's have to change that?"

"Because you won't have time," Michael said irritably. "Right now you've just told me you can't get away to go to Pittsburgh. What if I didn't have to make the trip and planned a wonderful honeymoon? You wouldn't have time for that, either?"

"Well, you apparently don't have time for one," Lindsey countered, matching his tone. "But I suppose it's perfectly acceptable that we can't enjoy a honeymoon since you have business in Pittsburgh, but not acceptable if I have business. Can you tell me why?"

"Because I'm the husband," he said tersely, his voice rising. "Because I want you beside me, not stuck in some business meeting or seeing to some crisis at Ingraham's when I need you, when I want you." His voice rose.

"And I'd love to be with you, included in all your business, but that's just what it is—your business. It's not the same thing for me. Michael, Ingraham's is something I need to do myself."

"And what am I supposed to do while you're doing all this wheeling and dealing?" Anger edged his voice. "What am I supposed to do in the evenings when I come home? Sit in the chair and wait for you? Do you think you can fit children into all this?"

"I'm not suggesting forever, Michael," she said, still hoping he would understand.

"Damn it, Lindsey! Listen to reason."

"I haven't heard any yet. All you've presented is warped macho male views." Her patience was wearing thin.

"All I've presented is good common sense."

"Oh!" Lindsey whirled and clenched her fists against the bulwark. "You're not listening."

"I am listening. And damn it! I want you with me—not caught up in corporate maneuvers! I want my woman within touching distance. I want to go to bed with you every night and wake up with you every morning."

Silence stretched between them. Lindsey was so mad that she couldn't think of a coherent thing to say. He wanted her. Well, she wanted him, too—but not to be at his every beck and call, to accommodate her life totally to his. He wanted all the giving on her side. He didn't want a wife, she thought indignantly, he wanted a lap dog! And he wasn't listening. He simply wasn't listening!

Anger vibrated between them, almost as if it were a tangible wall, invisible but solid. Lindsey wouldn't turn around, yet her body listened for his, detecting his breathing, seeming to feel his heart beating.

She heard the movement before his hand rested upon her shoulder.

"Lindsey," he said, his voice low. "Let's go to my apartment. We can talk more there."

It was an effort at conciliation. Even as she recognized it, her hurt wouldn't let her give in. And she knew he had more in mind than talking. Even at that moment his touch reached through the barriers of pride and anger, sending a quivering of longing pulsing in her veins. But she couldn't, she wouldn't. Could she? Her shoulders remained unyielding.

He removed his hand. "Okay," he said passionately. "But I'm not letting up. I love you. I want you."

The sound of his retreating footsteps faded into the night, taking with them her very breath. Her rock-hard anger dissolved as salt into water. Panic took its place. She couldn't let him go.

She began to run, heedless of her pride, only knowing her need to be with him and to love him and allow him to love her. He was opening the door of his Mercedes just as she rounded the corner of the house. Something, her footsteps or an inner sixth sense, must have told him she was there, because he stopped then slowly turned. Lindsey hesitated, wondering at the wisdom of her actions but knowing she wanted to be with him. He was the man she loved. It had to be right.

She could easily see his face in the amber glow of the portico lights. His expression softened, radiating warmth. He smiled slightly and held out his hand. With rapid steps Lindsey crossed the distance between them and put her hand into his. They grasped tightly. The light in his eyes and the magic that enfolded them erased all doubt as to the wisdom of her choice. She was following her heart, and it spoke truly.

Michael's apartment was quiet. There was no sign of Elwin, although there was a light on in the living room and another in the hall. With a firm grip on Lindsey's hand, he led her straight through to the bedroom.

He didn't turn on the lights, leaving only the dim light from the hall to fall into the room. Lindsey was glad. For some unfathomable reason, she didn't want to look at him or for him to see her eyes.

Pulling her to him, he kissed her, a kiss that quickly turned rough and demanding. She answered in kind, welcoming it as the perfect balm for soothing the hurts and worries of minutes before.

Pressing herself against Michael's long, lean form, she wrapped her arms around his neck and dug her fingers into the thickness of his hair. She clutched him to her, at the same time clutching at their passion, wanting it, needing it.

His hands eagerly roamed her body, touching, kneading, familiar with all the right places. She fumbled several buttons loose on his shirt and slipped her hand beneath the fabric to stroke the smooth skin stretched over taut muscles. But somehow the sensual comfort she'd experienced by the action in the past eluded her now.

In reaction, wanting desperately to recapture the warm magic they'd shared before, she pulled his shirt open, thinking that if she could just press her skin against his the breach between them would be healed. As eager as she, he unzipped her dress, pushed the straps from her shoulders and the bodice to below her breasts. His movements were hasty, and Lindsey heard fabric rip.

But even when they lay in bed, their heated bodies seeking each other, a shadow tainted their sweet passion. And neither of them could get beyond it.

Finally Michael stilled, his body quivering against her as he held her tightly against him. His moist breath touched her cheek, and his heart pounded hard against her. Lindsey closed her eyes tight against tears that seeped through her lids.

"It's no good, Princess." His voice was husky with frustrated desire and sorrow. A moment later he slipped from her embrace. The bed dipped as he rose, and Lindsey heard his quiet movements within the room, visualizing a closet when she heard a door creak. Then, wrapped in a dark robe, he stepped into the beams of light from the hall and left the room.

Tears spilled down her face. Her body throbbed with denied fulfillment. Oh, Lord, she wanted him, needed him. Why couldn't they put aside the world for just a little while? What was wrong with them, anyway? She searched her heart, her mind, but nothing made sense. She was hurt, angry—at herself and Michael—and totally confused.

The bed was cold without him. Sitting up, she managed to discover a bedside lamp, then its switch. It gave off a soft amber light. Her gaze skimmed the room, flowing over the Spanish print coverlet of the wide bed, the antique chest of drawers, the hand-hooked cotton rugs. The warm colors, the excellence, the earthiness, all breathed of Michael, and Lindsey's heart ached.

Agitated, unable to lie in the bed and wondering where Michael had gone yet fearful of facing his return, Lindsey got up. Spying his white shirt crumpled at the foot of the bed, she put it on. Floor-length draperies covered part of one wall, concealing a sliding glass door. Opening it, she stepped out on the terrace and breathed deeply of the humid late August night air.

Moving to the edge of the terrace, she leaned against the parapet and gazed out at the city, a magnificent sparkling jewel stretching as far as the eye could see.

How many lovers were out there tonight, loving, laughing, fighting? she wondered. Her mind pictured Michael's face as it had been that night in New Orleans in Felix's restaurant. His eyes, glowing warmly in the candlelight, had spoken boldly of his love, of his desire.

What if she lost him now because of her need to finish what she'd started with Ingraham's? Did she need that more than she needed him? Surely nothing was worth losing Michael. Except losing herself. That thought dropped quietly, yet firmly, into the midst of all the others.

Somehow she feared that if she took the easy way out now with Ingraham's she may just end up losing all she'd discovered about herself. She couldn't truly fathom why, except that it had to do with sticking to what she'd started. She'd spent so many years of her life running from responsibility, from facing anything. Now she had, and still was, facing this challenge. And she had to see it through. It didn't matter if the whole situation was a bit fantastic. It didn't matter that her chances were as slim as a reed. It just mattered that she tried.

Could she make Michael understand? Or even if he did, would he accept it? Why, why, was he being so stubborn?

So deep in thought, she didn't hear Michael approach and jumped when he spoke from behind her. "You improve that shirt."

She whirled to find his familiar gaze moving over her body. She couldn't help remembering what his body looked like beneath the long, dark robe.

Crooking a questioning eyebrow, he held a wineglass toward her. Sparkling liquid filled only about a fourth of it. He remembered even the small things like her custom of drinking only minute amounts of wine, she thought, her heart swelling with love as she took the glass. Sipping from a small glass of his favorite whiskey, he joined her to lean against the parapet.

They didn't say anything for several minutes, but Lindsey felt their minds and bodies communicate. The very air between them crackled.

"We've got a problem, Princess," Michael said, breaking the silence. "Can we talk about it?"

Lindsey nodded, and her voice came hoarsely. "Yes."

"I'm sorry about before..." His voice trailed off. It was the apology of a man unaccustomed to failing in bed. Lindsey's heart tugged at the little boy she saw within the big, strong man.

"It wasn't your fault," she hurried to assure him. He frowned and reached for her to draw her within the shelter of his arms.

"I love you, Lindsey."

"And I love you, Michael."

"But not enough." It was a combination of question and statement. She felt his body tense.

"Couldn't the assumption be reversed, Michael?" she asked gently. "Perhaps it doesn't have anything to do with loving enough. Maybe it has to do with things within ourselves that are beyond our control."

Silence enveloped them again. Lindsey sipped her wine then leaned her head on his shoulder. "Why are you so against the idea of me running Ingraham's?" she asked softly, the question out almost before she realized it.

Michael stroked her cheek with his thumb. Downing the last of his drink and absently setting the glass on the parapet, he gazed out into nothingness. "I want you with me. I want you to come into my world, because I can't...you won't let me into yours."

"It's not that I want to keep you out of my world, Michael," she protested. "I welcome you—I did on our trip. I just have to keep enough distance to prevent you from taking over."

"So you said." His chuckle was harsh.

"It's true, Michael. You're a leader—it comes as naturally to you as a baby's crying for milk. You didn't think I noticed during those days we toured the stores, but I did— you nearly exploded several times trying to keep your mouth shut. And even then we ended up in some pretty heated arguments. Oh, Michael, you couldn't be any other way...and I wouldn't want you to be. But I want my own chance. I want to experience a little of what you have had for the past years. Remember how you felt when you risked that money on that first deal your father was talking about? I'm tasting that now, and I want to see it through."

Michael was quiet, seemingly digesting her words.

"What if you get so involved with Ingraham's that you can't get out? You may find you enjoy the corporate challenges much more than you would being my wife." Lindsey recognized a tremor in Michael's voice. Why, he was afraid—afraid of losing her to Ingraham's. That's what this whole thing was about.

"I love you, Michael." She looked long into his dark eyes. "I don't want to make Ingraham's my life. I never will. This is simply something I must see to the end, whether I fail or succeed. And I want so much for you to understand." She continued to look at him, allowing her eyes to speak all the love and assurance that filled her heart.

Slowly he brought his mouth to hers and kissed her gently. He pulled back, and as she gazed heavy lidded at his mouth, the tingling warmth of desire stirred deep within her body.

Then he was kissing her again. She melted into him, parting her lips, welcoming him into her. She pressed her palms against his chest then rubbed them sensuously across his shoulders beneath the robe and then moved to the taut cords at the back of his neck, savoring the feel of sleek skin and firm male muscles. His lips massaged hers, pressing and releasing, pressing again, drawing her, enticing her.

No, they hadn't reached total understanding, but by the very act of loving enough to try, the wall of lingering hurt and anger had been dissolved. Love filled Lindsey's being, radiating out to join her to Michael. And as a leaf responds to the slightest movement of the breeze, so did their bodies respond, each to the other.

Michael lifted her easily and carried her back to the bed. Stretching beside her, he gazed at her a long time. Lindsey smiled at his inspection, at the heated glow reflecting in his eyes. With his gaze locked to hers, he unbuttoned his shirt, now stretched across her breasts. Then he parted it slowly, teasingly.

A fever flowed through her veins, sweeping her away into that special sphere vibrating with passion. They fondled and caressed each other. Michael's gentle but firm touches brought her higher and higher. With both his hands and his lips, he worshiped her breasts and their delicate nipples then moved to her stomach then lower to her sensitive inner thighs.

Her breath caught in the back of her throat, and she felt her feminine muscles throbbing, aching for fulfillment. Instinctively she moved in rhythm against Michael, pleading with the motion.

In answer he covered her with his body, slipping between her legs. Lindsey gasped in relief, in pleasure, in heated desire as he filled her. He moved slightly, testing her response. Then they were moving together, and Lindsey's conscious world ceased to exist. She was swept into the wonder of giving herself to Michael, of receiving from him. He filled her completely, mind, body and soul.

Michael woke and lay watching Lindsey sleep peacefully in his arms. The lamp was still on, allowing him to see her silky skin and the gentle smile that touched her lips. His

heart swelled, and he gave thanks for the moment—as well
as for those of before.

They'd reached an understanding of sorts, he supposed.
More, perhaps, an impervious draw. She was adamant
about continuing on at Ingraham's. He hated the thought.
He wanted her with him, to cheer him on, to support him.
Yes, it was jealousy. He couldn't stand the thought of
Lindsey being in an arena that he considered his.

What if she branched out from Ingraham's? His imagination ran wild, picturing her buying into other corporations, her photograph plastered on the front page of the
business section of the newspaper. He could see her, dressed
in a smart suit with one of those elegant hats she'd taken to,
sitting in a high-backed chair at the head of a long boardroom table. She'd look cold and calculating—and unreach-
able.

Stop this nonsense, he told himself firmly. He looked
again at Lindsey and smiled. She couldn't ever be that
woman in his imagination. Then the doubts shadowed his
thoughts again. People did change, often drastically.

They hadn't talked of marriage since their fight. Did she
still intend to marry him on Sunday? Well, he still did.
They'd work out some kind of compromise—and hopefully, once they were married, Lindsey would become less
and less enchanted with her corporate endeavors.

Lindsey watched as the new Ingraham's sign was hoisted
into place above the grocery store parking lot. She was
pleased. She'd helped with the designing and had ordered
the signs before she left on her tour of the other Ingraham's stores. The first one had gone into place only an hour
ago at the other Ingraham's grocery across the city. This was
only the second of many more to come. It would take the
next several months, though, to fabricate and install them.

In a matter of minutes the sign was secure, the giant boom
lowered the workmen to the ground, and they drove away.
Lindsey stood looking at the sign. Ingraham's was printed
in bold bright blue lettering with their new emblem, the

rainbow, above and behind the letters. It was eye-catching and fresh—very appealing.

Glancing at her watch, she moved hurriedly to the car. It was past ten o'clock. How could it be Wednesday morning already? she moaned inwardly, a smile tugging at her lips. Sunday was coming, racing toward her, and there was still so much to be done. Thank goodness Beatrice was handling everything; she was an expert at coordinating. She was meeting with the florists and caterers today and had already begun inviting people by telephone. That afternoon Lindsey was to break away from the office and try on wedding gowns that were being delivered to Ingraham House for her inspection. More were scheduled to come tomorrow, along with a seamstress to make any needed alterations, or even to change the design completely if Lindsey wanted.

Then it would be back to the office. There were thousands of things to see to there. She was amazed at the people who were trooping to see her. Beatrice had definitely been busy with her propaganda campaign. There were sales representatives from numerous food lines, sales reps for office supplies, and even a man who was interested in having an Ingraham's grocery open in his small community. And a man who wanted to talk to her about trucks, wonder of wonders. What would she know about such things? She'd pass him along to Jay.

As she drove past the Garrity building, Lindsey's heart sang. She was in love. She was to be married—to the handsomest, kindest, most romantic man in the universe.

Yet a hint of unease pierced her happiness. She and Michael remained at their impasse over her choice to continue with Ingraham's. He was adamant about them marrying on Sunday. He said he would be patient and that they would work it out. Lindsey agreed. All couples had things that they couldn't agree on fully; these things were worked out eventually, especially when two people were as much in love as she and Michael. But doubts continued to pop up at the most inopportune times—like now, she thought irritably. Get away from me! she ordered the nagging thoughts firmly.

She was going to marry Michael, the man of her dreams, and that was it.

The atmosphere at Ingraham's offices was amazing. There had been only a slight increase in the store's profits, and Robert wouldn't positively confirm that increase as yet, but the air fairly crackled with new life and vitality. It was as if the people of Ingraham's had been shaken up and polished right along with the windows and floors.

Lindsey touched the gleaming elevator walls and inhaled the fresh, clean smell, as well as the smell of paint and cleaner. Workmen were everywhere.

The receptionist greeted her with a friendly smile, as did several other office employees on her way down the hall. The polished floors glowed; the new carpet and partitions in the work areas pleased the eye. Several rainbow motifs hung from the ceiling or adorned freshly painted walls. The offices hummed around her as people enjoyed their work with a new purpose.

Chuckling inwardly, Lindsey thought of the bills. They were deeper in debt than ever before, yet everyone was happier. Surely something could be said for that. And now there was hope.

She peeked into the office Michael had commandeered weeks before. Her heart dipped, he wasn't there. Not that she'd expected him. He was in the same boat as she, over at his own office. Four days away, and too much to do. Her blood warmed as she remembered their last night together. They'd come so close, their bodies, their minds, their hearts. Now Lindsey understood the meaning of the "two shall become as one." Their love had done that.

"I need you to call several shops and have them deliver a few briefcases to Ingraham House for me to look at," she said, stopping at Ivy's desk. Her voice softened. "I want something out of the ordinary, Ivy. I'm looking for a very special one for Michael." She handed Ivy some notes she'd made on what she was looking for. "I simply don't have time to go shopping. I think I'm drowning."

"Ah, yes, but ain't it great," Ivy quipped with a grin. "Messages on your desk."

Placing the back of her hand against her brow in mock despair, Lindsey left Ivy chuckling. Tossing her purse on the myriads of papers upon the desk, she strode to the window and opened the drapes wide. Sunlight streamed through the sparkling glass and lit upon the colors of the rainbow suncatcher that Michael had given her.

Her gaze moved past the rainbow and in the direction she knew Michael's building to be. He was there. And she could hardly wait for the evening, when she would see him.

Several trucks rumbled past, heading around the corner for the back doors of their warehouse, Lindsey realized with satisfaction. With a sigh she turned back to her desk. She had to take care of business if she was even to get away for her dress fitting session, much less later for dinner.

Leafing through the pink message slips, she was pleased to see that Ivy had been able to get an appointment for Lindsey to meet with Adam Hendry, the president of the bank that held Ingraham's loan. Thursday, two o'clock. Wasn't that when she was supposed to try on shoes? Yes, she saw by her appointment calendar. Well, it would have to be changed. This appointment meant life to Ingraham's. Somehow, someway, she was going to have to convince Adam Hendry to give them an extension on the loan. She pushed from her mind any thought of what the consequences would be if she failed to do so.

Just after lunch, which for Lindsey was half of a turkey sandwich eaten while she perused reports from two of the stores she'd been unable to visit, Jay knocked lightly then entered with Robert behind him.

Lindsey looked up and smiled. "So how are things down in the warehouse?" she asked Jay. She stood and moved toward the wall cabinet. "Would you two like something to drink? I'm glad you're both here. I need to talk to you." She looked from one to the other as it finally dawned on her that they were unusually quiet—at least Jay was.

Robert pushed at his glasses, avoiding her gaze. Jay gave a half smile then reached for her hand. "Come sit down," he said. "There's something we have to tell you."

Lindsey cast him a puzzled look, slowly doing as she was bid.

Jay pushed aside some papers and seated himself on the edge of her desk. Taking her hand, he glanced around at Robert, who then moved to a chair closer to the desk. But Robert still avoided her gaze and fiddled with his glasses.

"What is it?" Lindsey said, her heartbeat picking up.

"Robert heard a bit of gossip yesterday and managed to check it out this morning," Jay said. He kept his gaze on hers, and she saw pain in his eyes. "We think you'd better know."

Lindsey glanced quickly at Robert then returned her gaze unwaveringly to Jay and gave a nod.

"A company called Directco has been buying up the scattered Ingraham's stock for the past couple of months. They've managed to secure most of it." Jay's voice was low and very precise.

"Oh," Lindsey sighed sadly. "Grandmother and I so much wanted to buy that ourselves." She looked to Jay. "But maybe we can later. Maybe at the right price Directco will sell to us. It may be expensive, but . . ." She left off speaking as she watched Jay's expression.

"Lindsey," Jay said gently, "Directco is Michael Garrity."

She sat very still, looking into Jay's blue eyes. Her first reaction was that she'd heard him wrong. But his expression told her otherwise.

She looked at Robert. "Can you be sure of this?" she asked sharply. "Do you have anything on paper?"

He cleared his throat again. "Ah . . . no, nothing on paper. But yes, I'm sure. It was done very quietly and with great effort to hide who owns Directco, but I knew a few people. There's no doubt." He fidgeted. "I'll be able to have something on paper in a few days."

"There's been some mistake," Lindsey said. She felt very still and cold.

"I don't think so, Lindsey." Jay's voice was filled with pity.

Rising with a quick motion, Lindsey turned to the window. She didn't want to look at the two men, didn't want the humiliation of them observing her pain. And she had to think—everything was a jumble.

"Thank you," she said, managing with superhuman effort to keep her voice even.

She heard Robert leave but knew that Jay remained. He stepped behind her. She felt him reach out to touch her and was glad when he didn't.

"Lindsey, I'm sorry," he said.

She nodded. "Please, I'd like to be alone to think."

"I don't want to leave you like this . . ."

"Thank you for caring, Jay. But I'll be all right. I just need a few minutes to myself."

He left, and she stood looking out the window, her gaze again moving beyond the rainbow suncatcher in the direction of Michael's building.

Pain such as she'd never known, swept over her. The pain of betrayal. Heartache. There truly was such a thing—physical and real. She pressed her hand to her heart, seeking relief. Then she slumped into the chair, her legs quite suddenly weak. For a few seconds she thought she may faint. The queasiness passed.

Then her mind rebelled. How could this be? It didn't fit; the image of Michael didn't fit with such treachery. Her Michael, the man she'd given herself to, wouldn't do such a thing.

He hadn't told her about owning thirty percent of Ingraham's in the first place, her memory reminded her. She hated the thought; it stabbed like a knife into her chest.

That didn't matter, she countered, not now. Not after their time together, their giving to each other. And they were to be married. Why would he be intending to marry her, if he'd done such a thing? No, she thought hotly, it just couldn't be. Robert and Jay didn't have anything on paper. There was some mix-up, some misunderstanding.

Even as her mind whirled with the thoughts, she reached for her purse and hurried from the office. She would see Michael, and he would explain. Her heart hammered in her chest as she clung desperately to the thought. He would deny it and say he wasn't the one. There'd been some goofy, weird mistake. She strode down the hall, faintly hearing Ivy's call, but took no time to answer.

The elevator in Michael's building opened directly into a wide reception area. Holding her purse tightly, Lindsey stepped onto the floor and looked hesitantly around. A pleasant-faced young woman sat behind the desk. To the right of the young woman was a door. The nameplate on it read, Ty Connors. Lindsey quickly swung her gaze across the wide area to another door on which the nameplate read, Michael Garrity.

"May I help you?" the young receptionist asked.

"I'm here to see Mr. Garrity," Lindsey replied, walking toward the door.

"But wait," the woman called, rising to try and waylay Lindsey. "You can't just go in there."

Lindsey didn't wait. She opened the door, swinging it wide. Michael turned quickly from where he stood at the window, holding a folder and some papers. Immediately his face broke into a wide, welcoming smile.

"Well, hello, Princess."

Lindsey's heart answered the warm greeting. She strode rapidly across the thick plush carpet of his large office, her gaze fastened on his. His smile slipped.

"What's wrong . . ."

"Michael . . ." She looked at him for a moment, seeing his puzzlement, praying that everything was a simple mix-up. "I've just learned about a company called Directco buying up the remaining Ingraham's stock." Something flickered across his face, and Lindsey felt her lungs tighten. "Michael, are you Directco?"

Chapter Thirteen

Michael's face flushed. As Lindsey watched his expression, the abhorrent truth struck her like a blow to the chest. It was there on his face—the surprise. And the guilt.

"Where did you hear this?" he asked, his eyes narrowing.

Guilt—still the guilt was there. Lindsey struggled for breath as her world collapsed around her. "It's... it's true, isn't it?" The fact fell like stone.

"Lindsey, it's not what you think," he said, his voice striving to placate her.

It grated on her. He'd turned on the charm, was wanting to get out of this. He'd been doing this behind her back, and still he thought he could get out of it. Slowly she backed toward the door as, to her consternation, tears blurred her vision and rolled down her cheeks. Michael was coming around the desk toward her.

"Lindsey, let me explain...."

"Oh, I bet you'd like to explain," she said, biting out the words. "Just like you explained that owning thirty percent of Ingraham's didn't mean anything to you—that was after you got around to admitting you even owned it. Come to think of it, you never admitted it. You only mentioned it when you found out I already knew. And now how fortunate you already owned that of-little-consequence thirty percent. Now you own nearly half the company."

Betrayal, hot as a poker, burned within her. And pain and anger.

"Explain?" she threw at him. "Are you going to deny you were buying up this stock in secret?"

"I can't deny it. Only it isn't what you think." His voice was firm and hard.

"No?" Lindsey sneered. "I'm sure you have a very good explanation. You always do, Mr. Garrity." She turned and headed rapidly for the door. "Well, you can just save your silver-tongued explanations for those who haven't caught on to you."

"Lindsey, just listen to me," he called to her.

But she couldn't stand to hear. She wanted to get away from the painful truth, to block it out. And to get away from the man who was causing it.

"No, I don't ever want to hear what you have to say again," she called back. At the door she stopped and turned again to face him. "I'll go ahead and bankrupt Ingraham's before I let you have it."

Standing stock-still, Michael watched her go. The elevator doors opened then closed. Jan stood just inside the doorway, looking at him uncertainly.

"Is there anything I can do, Michael?" she asked.

"No," he answered her, turning his back. "Just shut the door when you go out." A few seconds later his office door closed softly.

By any stretch of the imagination, or by any scale that could be used, Michael had never felt such regret, such self-loathing, such pain. A pain that went bone deep. He was frozen to the spot, staring through the thin draperies to the St. Johns river, yet his mind's eye still saw the disappointment, the pain, the wrath pouring from Lindsey's eyes.

And she wouldn't even let him explain. Would it have made any difference if he had? Would it have been any different if she'd heard the whole truth? he wondered helplessly.

The fact was, he'd started buying up that stock when Lindsey and Beatrice had decided not to sell. And it had been his plan to buy out Ingraham's, force them to sell it to him. They were both being so foolish, he had defended himself. He had thought to protect them from themselves, and to get what he wanted. Yes, it was underhanded, but for good reasons—at least they'd seemed so then.

But then he'd fallen deeply in love with Lindsey Ryland, and he hadn't been able to keep business and pleasure separate. And suddenly he'd known he couldn't do what he'd intended. But still he'd bought the stock—intending to give it to Beatrice as a present. It was going to be a surprise. Beatrice had spoken of her passionate desire to have Ingraham's be strictly family owned again. It would take her years to get enough money to buy that stock—providing Ingraham's ever did come out of the red. Years that Beatrice just may not have. He'd decided to help both Beatrice and Lindsey have their dream.

And, he admitted, perhaps he'd hoped to bind Lindsey tighter to him and in this way mingle their lives so he wouldn't feel so threatened.

If she'd only listened, he thought, growing angry. He would have made her understand. *If she'd only listened.*

After all the time they'd spent together, didn't she know him? Damn! All that time, and after what they'd shared with each other—he'd shared all he'd known how to give to her—and she still could think he would hurt her, that he didn't care for her.

He shook his head, as if trying to shake away the hurt. His throat swelled, and he choked back tears. If she could

think that of him, he didn't want to explain, he thought
pridefully.

Michael heard the door open behind him. He didn't turn
around, wanting whoever it was to go away.

"Michael." It was Ty. "Jan told me what happened."

Michael gave a slight snort. "Guess you're off the hook
for being my best man on Sunday."

"Why don't you go after her and explain?"

"She wouldn't listen." Michael turned to face Ty. His
anger came out in his words. "And I'm not about to tie her
down to get her to listen. If she can think me capable of
buying up that stock behind her back, just so I can get a
hold of Ingraham's . . . well, there's no place for me in her
life. I'm not going to crawl to her with explanations."

"You *were* buying it up behind her back to take over Ingraham's," Ty pointed out. "At least at first. Try to put
yourself in her place. What would have been the first thing
you thought?"

"If she loved me," Michael insisted stubbornly, "she
would have at least given me a chance to explain before she
started throwing accusations."

"Look, people have used her, have wanted things from
her all her life," Ty said. "And the secrecy we kept would
look fishy to a lot of people. In fact, it is exactly what is
done when you want to buy up a company without others
knowing."

"It shouldn't to the woman who's supposed to love me,
to have faith in me," Michael replied hotly.

"Maybe it shouldn't—but how much do you love her?
Can't you forgive her and give you both a chance? It's a
misunderstanding. People in love get crazy. Most of us take
a long time to feel secure with the person we love—mostly
because love can hurt so damn bad, and we're all scared. We
all walk the edge, ready to bolt if things look shaky.
Granted, this is a pretty big misunderstanding, but not one
that can't be overcome."

"Since when did you get so smart about love? Aren't you the man with a new girl every other weekend?"

"I know," Ty admitted, almost sadly. "But I haven't been as lucky as you to find that special one. Now that you have, you'd better do all you can to keep her."

"There's more than one woman for a man," Michael quipped bitterly. "And besides, maybe a new woman every other week or so is better for the health." But even as he said it, he didn't believe it.

Lindsey didn't know how she made it home. A guardian angel must have guided her way, because she couldn't remember the drive at all. Tears had blurred her vision, and her mind kept picturing the hard, cold look on Michael's face.

She was angry, and she was confused. She was hurting more than should be humanly possible and still be alive. Stopping the car beneath the portico, Lindsey just sat there.

Michael. Her heart ached at the name. He wasn't real. What she'd thought they'd had was fake. Why? How could he have done this to her? All along, when they'd made love, and she'd given herself so completely to him, he'd been buying up that stock. It had been a lie, *all a lie.* And now a big part of herself was missing; she may never be whole again.

She had to move, she thought. She got out of the car, slammed the door and strode up the stairs and into the hall. She had to fumble for a moment with the doorknob; the stupid thing was stuck, and Lindsey could hardly see it through her tears. Damn, the tears, she thought. Michael Garrity wasn't worth tears. She cried harder.

Beatrice called from the living room, and from her blurred peripheral vision, Lindsey caught sight of mounds of white draped over the furniture and several people milling around. Beatrice appeared in the archway.

"Lindsey, we're ready." Beatrice's face slackened. "Oh, my God, what's happened?"

"I . . . I can't talk now, Grandma." Sobs choked Lindsey's throat. "Send the dresses back. There's not going to be a wedding. I'm so sorry . . ."

She ran across the hall and up the stairs to her room to throw herself across her bed. For the first time since she was a very small child, she wished herself dead.

A little time later there came a rapping at the bedroom door. Insistent, it finally succeeded in penetrating Lindsey's consciousness. She looked around, puzzled. How long had she been lying there? She felt woozy, and her head was swimming. The rapping came again; then the door slowly opened.

Beatrice entered and came to sit on the side of the bed. Calmly, saying nothing, she took Lindsey's hand.

Looking at her grandmother, Lindsey's eyes widened. "Oh, Grandma—how did you come up the stairs? Did you call Sandy? You didn't walk . . ."

"I guess I can walk up the stairs now once in a while if I so choose."

Lindsey's heart fluttered and guilt assailed her. "Oh, I was only thinking of myself," she said remorsefully. Impulsively she sat up and hugged Beatrice to her. "Please take care of yourself. The doctor said no stairs for six months. Please . . ."

Beatrice pulled away and, holding Lindsey's hands, looked her full in the face.

"Now, Granddaughter, suppose you tell me what's happened between you and Michael."

Lindsey looked away. How could she tell Beatrice? It was going to be a great blow to her, too. Her mind squirmed, trying to think of a way around the true explanation. There was none. Beatrice was bound to find out the truth sooner or later; it was best she heard it from Lindsey.

"Michael has been secretly buying up the scattered Ingraham's stock these past weeks using a company name called Directco." Lindsey watched the stunned disbelief slip into Beatrice's eyes. Her heart thumped with her own pain and with concern over the older woman's reaction.

Beatrice looked away for an instant then back at Lindsey. Her expression had changed to one of intense interest. "How did you find out?"

Lindsey haltingly told her the story, how Jay and Robert had come to her with the information they had discovered, and what had transpired at Michael's office.

They both sat quietly. Lindsey looked down at her hands, remembering the look of astonishment that had come across Michael's face when she'd confronted him, then later his expression of clear, hard anger. Now, in the quiet of the moment, she remembered something else, something that her senses had taken in and processed but that she'd been too distraught to recognize at the time: Michael's face had also registered pain.

Beatrice touched Lindsey's hair. "I'm sorry, Granddaughter."

Lindsey leaned against her, grateful for her grandmother's quiet, strong presence. They sat quietly a few moments; then Beatrice said, "I'm going to my room to rest now, Lindsey." She looked suddenly tired.

A calm strength came over Lindsey; she had Beatrice to consider. She put her arm around her grandmother's shoulders. Beatrice looked at her with concern, and Lindsey smiled softly. "I'm okay, Grandmother. I'm a tough old bird—just like you."

Beatrice slipped her arm around Lindsey's waist, and they walked to the older woman's room. Lindsey helped Beatrice settle against the pillows and spread a light cotton cover over her legs.

"I'll have Selda bring you some tea, Grandma."

"Don't fuss, Lindsey." Beatrice's diamonds gleamed as she gave an impatient wave of her hand.

Lindsey grinned. "It gives me something to do." She turned to leave but stopped at her grandmother's call.

"Think about Michael, Granddaughter. Think about the man you know him to be. And always remember, lovers' quarrels can be corrected—by both parties." Beatrice's face was very white, and her blue eyes were intense.

"Yes, Grandmother," Lindsey answered quietly. "I will." Softly she closed the door behind her.

Lindsey herself made the tea. She had Selda take a pot upstairs to Beatrice, while she took her cup outside. She leaned against the bulwark of the St. Johns and watched the dark water flow. The sun warmed her shoulders, and a light breeze ruffled her hair.

She felt calm, terrifyingly so. Maybe she was dead and didn't even know it, she thought with a sad inner chuckle.

She thought of Michael. Deliberately, and though the pain of loss stabbed her heart, she remembered their week together, that wonderfully romantic week when she'd thought she had come to know him. But that Michael was gentle, kind, terribly romantic, and honest, strong and true. He wouldn't have slipped behind her back, doing something he knew would hurt her so badly.

At first she countered with calling herself a fool, simply too stupid to see what was underneath her nose. Then her self-confidence asserted itself. The reality was that she was a shrewd judge of character. Then had he been a master at deceiving her? Surely there would have been some give-aways, slipups on his part. And she had been skeptical, she pointed out to herself, highly distrustful of Michael's motives at first.

Yes, at first, she sighed, and then...oh, Lord, it had been beautiful. How could anything so beautiful have been wrong?

If the Michael she had come to know was real, how could she get around the fact that he had bought up Ingraham's stock in deliberate secrecy? Could there be two Michaels within the same man, one her wonderful hero, the other a contemptible snake?

Or was there a perfectly innocent reason he'd been buying that stock as he had? The thought came as a whispering doubt.

Lindsey sighed. Maybe she should have listened to him first. She owed him that much. Then her anger stirred. The fact remained that even if she knew nothing else of Michael Garrity, she knew he was capable of talking the moon into changing colors. She just couldn't take a chance on his breaking her heart again. She'd had enough pain.

And he had gone to great lengths to keep his purchasing of Ingraham's stock a secret—stock that gave him nearly equal controlling power in the company.

And yet . . . she still wondered.

The days passed. Somehow, for Lindsey, the sun didn't seem to shine as bright, no music was able to stir her soul, and even the vital hum at Ingraham's seemed to slow. She removed the rainbow suncatcher from her office window. She tossed it into the trash but later retrieved it and tucked it into a drawer. Still, the Ingraham's emblem became a reminder every time she looked over the company ads.

All the necessary people were alerted to the canceled wedding. Beatrice handled it all, appearing unembarrassed. "What do I care what people say?" she quipped when Lindsey apologized for causing the whole mess. "I'm too old to care about such things."

Still, Lindsey worried about her, and about Michael's family. They must be hurt and confused, as well.

Lindsey worked ten-hour days. She kept the appointment with Adam Hendry on Thursday, though she was conscious of her red-rimmed and puffy eyes. Dressed in her most elegant and inspiring business suit and a wide-brimmed hat, she waltzed into his office at the bank with an air of far greater confidence than she was truly feeling.

Astonishingly, he told her that Ingraham's loan could be extended easily. And he personally invited her to a party at his house, a week from Friday. "You and Beatrice will be receiving a formal invitation, of course," he said, his face jovial. "I've known your grandmother for a good number of years—and remember you as a girl of ten or so." In short, he was sweet, he was cordial, and he all but kissed her hand.

Lindsey paused on the sidewalk in front of the bank. She was still rather stunned by her interview with Adam Hendry. The day was shiny bright, and the sun gleaming off the waiting white Rolls that Sandy had pulled to the curb. The bank was no longer breathing at Ingraham's door, and the other creditors could be put off—for a while at least. The store's profits were definitely on the incline, slow, but a definite rise.

Then why didn't she feel happier than she did? Her heart squeezed. Because she no longer had Michael, that's why. The painful thought sat like a boulder upon her chest. It was not helped by the growing suspicion that perhaps she'd been unfair to him, the certain knowledge that she should have listened to an explanation before flying off the handle as she had. And there was the terrible fear of what could happen to her if she did listen to his explanations—only to be the fool again.

She reached for the telephone that afternoon to call him, but pride, hurt, doubt, confusion, and numerous emotions she wasn't even sure of stopped her. She stayed in bed most of Sunday, the Sunday that was to be her wedding day, not wanting to face anyone.

Finally, in the late afternoon, still dressed in her robe, her hair uncombed and deep circles beneath her eyes, she ventured down to the kitchen. She heard muffled voices as she pushed at the swinging door. Selda and Beatrice both hovered over a figure in a chair. Selda was clucking her tongue and mumbling. At the sound of Lindsey's steps both women glanced up, looking as if they'd been caught with their hands in the cookie jar.

"What's..." Lindsey stopped as her gaze fell on the third figure—Jay. His face was a mass of cuts and bruises. She blinked, her gaze taking in a torn shirt sleeve and a hand in the process of being bandaged. "What happened?" she breathed.

No one wanted to speak; they all kept looking at each other. "Well?" Lindsey insisted.

"Jay had a bit of a tussle with Michael," Beatrice said, returning to bandaging his hand.

"Michael?" Had the entire world gone crazy? Lindsey wondered. "What in the world for?"

Jay squirmed. "Personal reasons," he said huskily. "Ouch. Watch it, Selda."

"You're the one who should have watched it," Selda scolded.

"Oh, Jay," Lindsey said, her heart rending at the sight of him. She touched the hand that seemed free of injury then noticed that it, too, had a scrape.

"Well," Jay grunted as Selda again dabbed medicine on his face. "Garrity didn't look so good, either."

"Michael?" Lindsey's heart jumped to her throat. "Is he all right?"

"Guess so," Jay muttered. "He walked away—I wish he hadn't."

Lindsey brewed coffee for everyone then returned to her bedroom, all the while thinking of Michael. How badly had he been hurt? Surely he was all right. He'd walked away, Jay had said. Yet fears tumbled over one another in her mind, and her imagination conjured up pictures of Michael, beaten and bloody, each picture more horrible than the one before.

It was late evening, and the sun was casting a last pale golden glow when she decided she had to drive over to Michael's apartment. She simply had to find out how badly he'd been hurt. And she had to speak to him.

She slipped into slacks and a light sweater and hurriedly brushed her hair. Good grief, she looked dead, she thought, catching her image in the mirror. On the run, she applied blush and lipstick. It helped some.

It was only a few minutes' drive on a late Sunday evening. There was no traffic to contend with. Her mind spun with questions and fears. *What would she say to him—providing he could talk?* Yes, yes, he'll be able to talk, she calmed herself. Jay could talk; he was bruised and scratched, surely Michael would be no worse. But she had to see for herself.

What if he turned away from her, didn't even want to look at her? Why was she doing this? What would she say to him? What she intended to say was muddled in her head, her mind bouncing from one subject to another. All Lindsey knew was that she had to see him. Her heart clutched at a ray of hope—maybe somehow they could find each other again. But even as she thought it, her mind mocked her that she was being irrational. Yet she drove on.

When she pulled into the building parking garage, nearly deserted of cars now, she realized she didn't know how to get up to Michael's apartment. He'd used a key to open the private elevator doors on the two occasions when she'd been with him.

And maybe he wouldn't even be there. . . . Then she saw his car parked beside the elevator. On the other side of the elevator was a compact Cadillac. Lindsey cast it a questioning glance, debating. It could belong to someone visiting Michael. She didn't want to barge in and perhaps cause embarrassment to them all.

Then she determinedly jutted her chin, deciding she had to chance it. She had to see him.

Perhaps there'd be a bell or something, she thought as she headed for the elevator, her eyes scanning the buttons beside the closed doors. There was a button, just below a sign that read, Ring for Entrance.

Lindsey hesitated; then before she could change her mind, she pushed it, hard.

Seconds ticked by. She could leave, Lindsey thought; she should leave. This was foolish, demeaning. With a quiet whoosh the elevator doors opened. Lindsey looked at the small empty elevator then stepped inside. She pushed the penthouse button. Michael had taught her to go after what she wanted. Well—just what did she want? She wasn't sure, but maybe seeing Michael would straighten out all the questions that had been building in her mind since that day she'd hurled the accusations at him.

The elevator doors opened onto his apartment, and slowly Lindsey stepped out. There was no one at first; then someone stepped from the hallway.

But it wasn't Michael. It was the elegant woman who'd come to the office for Michael one day. Gwen, Lindsey remembered her name. Gwen stopped, her smile slipping into uncertainty as she stared at Lindsey.

Lindsey's heart rose to her throat. She never should have come and wanted only to get away with as much grace as possible. Apparently Michael was perfectly fine and had not wasted any time mourning over her as she had over him. Even as her mind willed her not to run and to smile, if stiffly, Lindsey wanted a hole to open up and swallow her.

Gwen's smile was taunting. "Yes? Can I help you?"

Lindsey took a breath. "Obviously not," she said smoothly. Then she lowered her gaze, knowing pain was written there, loathe to let the woman see it. She never should have come, she repeated to herself. "Excuse me." Her voice was far from being firm, and she hated herself for it as she turned to the elevator.

"Lindsey!"

Instinctively Lindsey turned at the call. Michael was striding toward her from the direction of the kitchen. She couldn't bear for him to see her and to look into his eyes. She moved into the elevator.

"Lindsey! Wait!"

The elevator doors began to slide closed. Deliberately Lindsey kept her eyes to the floor, knowing the doors would hide her in a moment.

But they didn't close. Michael's hands were pushing them apart. She looked into his face and sucked in her breath. His hair fell disheveled over his forehead; and his eyes were hard and glittery, determined. "You're not going to leave. You've come this far. We're going to talk."

He took her hand, pulling her back into the apartment, and she didn't resist. She couldn't do anything but stare at him, allowing him to pull her along like a limp rag doll. She saw that one of his eyes was black and blue, with a nasty cut across the eyebrow. There was also a cut on his chin and a welt on his cheek. Lindsey's eyes widened as she realized he wore no shirt, and she searched for other injuries. There were scratches across his chest.

His hand was firm in hers, and his gaze was hard upon her. Then he glanced at Gwen.

"I think I'll leave now, Michael," Gwen said slowly, giving a wry smile of defeat as she reached casually for her purse on the nearby entry table. Then she stepped into the elevator. The doors closed behind her; Lindsey and Michael were alone.

Lindsey's gaze ran over Michael's face, taking in the swelling, the dried blood. Her heart cried out in protest. "Oh, Michael . . ." She lifted a finger to his eye, tentatively touching the bruised skin.

Gazing down at her, he gave a lopsided grin. "How does Fordham look?"

Lindsey shook her head. "Why?" she breathed. "Why did you two do this?"

Holding her hand, Michael led her into the apartment and toward the kitchen. "He wanted to avenge your honor."

The breath caught in the back of her throat at the fact that she was the cause of two people she cared about hurting each other. Two people she cared about—the words echoed in her mind. She still cared for Michael. She still loved him; she always would.

"I give you my word, Lindsey," he said, "I tried to avoid him, but in this instance, he remains a little boy."

Lindsey blinked as her eyes worked to adjust to the brighter light of the kitchen. Michael's torn shirt was tossed on the nearby counter. The sink was filled with water that was tinged pink from blood, and a damp cloth lay nearby, as well as a bowl of ice cubes. Michael reached for the cloth, but Lindsey took it from his hand.

"Where's Elwin?" she asked, wetting the cloth. Her heart squeezed as she looked again at his wounds.

"Out at the beach house . . . ouch!" He winced as Lindsey dabbed at dried blood where the skin had broken below his eye.

"You two should have known better. This . . . this is something for children," she admonished, dabbing a cut at the corner of his mouth.

"I didn't start it, Princess. But I wasn't going to stand there and do nothing while Jay determinedly busted my face in. There was no getting around him." He grabbed her hand, arresting her motion with the cloth. His gaze was hard and questioning on her own. "Why are you here?"

"I . . ." Lindsey wasn't sure what to say, was afraid to speak the truth, afraid of rejection, of putting herself in for heartbreak again. She was as sore in spirit as Michael was in body. She simply couldn't take any more, but his eyes pressed her for an answer.

"Dare I believe you cared to find out if I was okay?" he asked.

Lindsey swallowed, her gaze never leaving his as she nodded. "I was afraid . . . I didn't know. Jay said you were hurt, too."

Slowly Michael kissed her, lightly at first, then more demandingly. Lindsey felt him flinch. "Oh, Michael . . . your lip." She caressed his cut lip with her fingertip, wanting to heal it with her touch. His gaze was warm upon her, and Lindsey felt her spirit flutter with hope.

"Today was our wedding day," Michael said huskily.

Doubt and fear rose again within Lindsey. She looked down at the cloth she still clutched in her hand. She knew she'd been wrong not to listen to him before, yet she didn't know if she'd believe what he told her, even now.

Still holding her hand, Michael pivoted and pulled her along into the living room. "Michael?" But he said nothing, only continued striding across the room to his desk in the corner. He pulled a paper from the desk top and handed it to her. Dropping her hand, he stepped back.

She cast him a puzzled glance then looked down to the paper, slowly unfolding it. She sensed that here was his attempt to explain. Her eyes scanned the paper, her heart threading faster at what she read. It appeared Michael had arranged legally to turn all the Ingraham's stock now held by Directco over to Miss Lindsey Ryland.

Looking up from the paper, she stood there looking at him, her eyes holding questions. Michael raked a hand through his hair.

"I did start buying that stock behind your and Beatrice's back to try and get a hold of Ingraham's," he said. His eyes flinched with regret. "But that was before us, Lindsey. Before we fell in love. And even then I was doing what I thought was best for everyone. And then... when I realized what was happening with us, all that was important to me was you. I still continued with the buy, intending to give the stock to Beatrice as a present on our wedding day. I know how much she wants it to be a family-owned company again." Sighing, he averted his gaze. "And I guess I was trying to find a way to secure our marriage, a way to bind you to me." His gaze returned to hers, and she saw the same doubt, the same fear, and yes, the same hope she herself felt.

"Oh, Michael. I'm sorry I didn't listen to you," she said now. "I...I was afraid..." She paused, hoping he could read the apology and the promise of love in her eyes. "I understand."

But something haunted him. Lindsey saw it in his face. She waited, sensing he had more to say and wanting to help him all she could.

Taking her arms, he drew her closer and looked long into her eyes. "I should have made you listen," he said. "I love you. Do you believe that?"

"Yes," she said softly. "And I love you—so very much."

His eyes clouded. "Then I want you to listen to me," he said firmly.

Lindsey felt her breath stopping as she wondered what he was going to tell her.

"I've done something else you're not going to be too happy about," he said. She looked at him, her shoulders stiffening as if to accept the blow, but knowing she could forgive him anything. "I've paid off Ingraham's debt at the bank. I swore Adam Hendry to secrecy. You were to know nothing about it. It was going to be my wedding present to you."

Lindsey stared at him, stunned, knowing the outlay of cash it was for him.

"Now, don't get angry, Lindsey. I didn't mean to step on your toes. I only wanted to... ah, hell, I'm not sure what I wanted." He raked a hand through his hair, grimacing as he hit an unknown bruise.

"A simple diamond ring or gold necklace would have done," Lindsey said, still somewhat stunned.

Michael let out a loud sigh. "I guess I wanted to bring you to me—bring us together. What's so wrong with it, Lindsey? I don't want to take over, but I want to help, to be a part of it. Oh, maybe I do want to take over," he said in exasperation. "It's hard for me to accept your being so damn good, so capable in an area I want to be the big cheese in. I want to be the leader." His eyes widened. "And yes, you need my help—what's so wrong with that, either?" He paused, looking at her. "You don't need to do it all alone, Lindsey."

Lindsey looked into his eyes, seeing his earnestness, his doubt, his fear, the same as her own. And his love. Then even as she watched the silver flecks in his eyes, she felt their love burning bright, melting away the distrust, the fear.

"There's nothing wrong with it, Michael," she said, answering his question of before. Slowly she smiled. "I love you."

His face softened almost in wonder. "We'll be great together, Princess." His hushed voice caused a tingling joy to burst and flow within her. "You and I, together, can reach the rainbow...and go beyond." Then he kissed her, heedless of his cuts and bruises.

And they were together. The shadows within Lindsey's heart faded, replaced by the bright colors of love.

They stood on the porch of the beach house. Possessively Michael held Lindsey to him, staring out over her head to the ocean, the morning sun a hot ball on the horizon. Inhaling her fresh womanly scent, he tightened his embrace. She wore a thin, flowing gown, and he enjoyed the feel of her as he ran a hand over her back.

He'd been gone two days, two long days, on business in the north, while Lindsey had had to stay to see to matters at Ingraham's. He hadn't liked it, but the feeling of threat had passed away. He was very proud of her, in fact. She was doing fantastically. And he was secure in her love and knew she was in his.

She stirred. "Michael...I have something to tell you."

"Uhmmm." He nuzzled her hair, thinking of other things than talk.

"Now, stop that and listen," she said firmly, raising her head to look at him. "I tried to tell you last night, but—" she blushed "—you wouldn't listen. Now you must listen."

He grinned then made an effort at a straight face. "Yes...I'm listening."

"Michael," she said, her voice softening, "we're going to have a baby."

He blinked, looking at her, wondering if he'd heard right. They'd been married less than four weeks—four weeks that he could count every day of.

"We're..." He couldn't say it. "Already?"

"Yes." Her expression turned anxious. "You're glad, aren't you? It is what you wanted?"

"Yes. Yes!" he repeated. Then the light dawned. "It was while we were touring the Ingraham's stores, wasn't it? Before..." It hit him hard. It was during that glorious time they'd spent in the world of their own making.

Lindsey nodded, a sweet smile playing on her lips.

Michael crushed her to him, so glad, so grateful she was his. He trembled to think of what might have happened if they hadn't found each other again. He'd have lost Lindsey and his own child. Putting a tentative hand to her abdomen, he gazed into her eyes. Was she happy? His eyes asked the silent question.

"I think we'll have a boy," she said with a wide grin then added, "I love you, Michael."

Silhouette Special Edition

COMING NEXT MONTH

AN UNEXPECTED PLEASURE—Lucy Hamilton
Cate and Jesse had been childhood friends, but hadn't seen each other for years. Chance brought them together again, seemingly forever. Then betrayal threatened to tear them apart.

HEART OF THE EAGLE—Lindsay McKenna
To ornithologist Dahlia Kincaid, Jim Tremain was like an eagle—dangerous and powerful. But he wasn't the predator he'd first seemed. Could she risk her heart for such a man?

MOMENTS OF GLORY—Jennifer West
Maggie Rand was a proud, wild, mean-tempered woman. Chance Harris knew better than to become involved. But somewhere in those velvet eyes was his future—and he couldn't turn away.

DREAM LOVER—Paula Hamilton
Her script had a message and there was no way Susan McCarthy would let some Hollywood wheeler-dealer twist it into a comedic vehicle for Bruce Powers's massive ego. But Susan had forgotten that Bruce was every woman's fantasy—including hers.

CATCH THE WIND—Caitlin Cross
It was Terminator's last chance—as well as trainer Allegra Brannigan's. Then Scott Charyn returned home to make peace with his father, and Allegra began to feel that she had another chance—this time at love.

TUCKERVILLE REVIVAL—Monique Holden
Tuckerville was a perfect example of a sleepy little town. But the town was fading, and Mayor Rhetta Tucker knew she had to save it. Then Bates McCabe buzzed into town—with a plan that could save them all.

AVAILABLE NOW:

THE ARISTOCRAT
Catherine Coulter

A SLICE OF HEAVEN
Carol McElhaney

LINDSEY'S RAINBOW
Curtiss Ann Matlock

FOREVER AND A DAY
Pamela Wallace

RETURN TO SUMMER
Barbara Faith

YESTERDAY'S TOMORROW
Maggi Charles

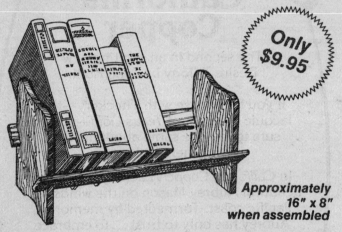

Silhouette Desire

**Available
October 1986**

California Copper

The second in an exciting new Desire Trilogy by Joan Hohl.

If you fell in love with Thackery—the laconic charmer of *Texas Gold*—you're sure to feel the same about his twin brother, Zackery.

In *California Copper*, Zackery meets the beautiful Aubrey Mason on the windswept Pacific coast. Tormented by memories, Aubrey has only to trust... to embrace Zack's flame... and he can ignite the fire in her heart.

The trilogy continues when you meet Kit Aimsley, the twins' half sister, in *Nevada Silver*. Look for *Nevada Silver*—coming soon from Silhouette Books.